Fatal Connections

Also by Debbi Mack

Sam McRae Novels

Identity Crisis

Least Wanted

Riptide

Deep Six

Erica Jensen Novels

Damaged Goods

Other Novels

Invisible Me

The Planck Factor

Short Stories

Five Uneasy Pieces

Fatal Connections

An Erica Jensen Mystery

Debbi Mack

Renegade Press
Savage, MD

Renegade Press
P.O. Box 156
Savage, MD

This is a work of fiction. Any resemblance to actual events or persons, living or dead, is entirely coincidental.

Library of Congress Cataloging-in-Publication Data
Fatal Connections
ISBN: 978-1-7341094-4-3
Library of Congress Control Number: 2021917040

First Publication: November 2021

Dedication

This book is dedicated to my husband, Rick Iacangelo, who continues to put up with my writing habit.

CHAPTER ONE

I'd pay a million dollars for a good night's sleep, if I thought such a thing could be bought. But it wasn't my nightmares that woke me at the ridiculously early hour of 0500 hours on a Saturday, it was my phone. I let it go, and the ringing stopped. A few seconds later, it started up again.

I rolled toward the side table where the phone jangled and aimed my hand in its general direction. As luck would have it, my hand landed right on it, so I grabbed it and by forcing my eyes open, I saw the caller ID. Marian Harcourt. WTF?

So I answered with "Yeah?" which came out more like "Ugh."

"Erica, we're in trouble," she whined. "Please come to the house. Right now."

I suppressed a groan and several colorful phrases. "This can't wait until the sun comes up?"

"We're in danger. And I can't call the police." Her voice, edged with panic, spiked upward when she said "police."

Okay. The Harcourts, a married couple, had hired me to run a background check on a possible hire—a live-in personal assistant. Now she was calling me about an imminent threat, but why me and not the police?

I sighed loudly into the phone. "Why not?" I tried not to snarl the words.

"Nick told us you were a Marine. Help us. Please."

Am a Marine. I suppressed the correction that came to mind. *Just because I'm not actively deployed doesn't mean I've lost my membership card.*

I tried to focus, which could be hard for me even in the best of times. I wasn't sure why she felt the need to call in the Marines and not the police, but the desperation in her voice sounded very real. I had the sense that questioning Marian's state of mind could lead to a discussion I was ill-equipped to handle without more careful thought. Or more precisely, coffee.

I cleared my throat. "I gotta get dressed and stop for coffee." My voice held only a touch of snark, when I added, "Don't worry. I'll make it to-go." Then I hung up.

Madness? Sure. But that's life for a Marine veteran who digs up information as an unlicensed private eye.

CHAPTER TWO

I arrived at the house at about 0600 hours, a simple brick rambler with a trim lawn in front. Hanging back in the car, I wondered what might be going down.

Clients usually had needs I could understand and meet with a minimum amount of face time. My one IRL meeting with the Harcourts had been at a local coffee shop, and after that, our contact was either by phone or email. I'd never seen the Harcourts' house. Its humble appearance surprised me.

Ron and Marian Harcourt were a power couple, sort of. They were Instagram stars or "influencers," which is kind of odd because I'd never heard of them before this. Apparently, it had all started with a blog. They had both quit their jobs to travel the world, sometimes bringing their two children along and other times leaving them with their nanny.

Things took off rather quickly because they attracted sponsors from the hotels, restaurants, and resort facilities where they stayed. The couple had just signed a book contract about their experiences going from rags to riches by using the internet.

And they had probably amassed a small fortune by not spending much of their money on their house.

I wondered about this so-called emergency. The neighborhood was as quiet as a morgue. I was still wondering why Marian would call me but not the police.

I was actually in the process of wrapping up my background check on their candidate for a personal assistant. Before I started the job, Nick told me that the Harcourts had a publicist and a business manager. I wondered why they needed yet another assistant, but who was I to judge? And money is money.

So I took the gig. Even though I was adding final touches to the written report, I had the distinct sense that I had missed something.

I tucked my handgun—a Sig Sauer P320—into my waistband, careful to hide the gun's bulge under my jacket, and left my Fiesta parked on the street. I doubted that many people were out this early on a Saturday morning, but with my luck, the neighborhood could be rife with morning joggers or other early risers. Scanning the grounds, I eased toward the front door. Anticipation made me a little itchy.

It was just past mid-March. Too soon for the warmer part of spring. I gave the door three raps and clutched my jacket against the chill air as I waited. Time passed. Then I rang the doorbell. Still no answer.

I pressed my ear to the door and thought I heard an indistinct murmuring inside. The only other sound was that of distant traffic from the main road.

This time I knocked and rang the bell, feeling a little foolish. Still no response, so after a couple of minutes, I dug out my cell phone and called Marian. Straight to voicemail. I could feel a knot forming deep in my belly. This wasn't right.

Reluctantly, I tried the door knob. Unlocked. *Fuck*. My fingers sprang off the knob, as if it were molten metal. An unlocked door likely meant trouble, unless the Harcourts had intentionally left it unlocked, which I doubted.

I returned to my car and retrieved my leather driving gloves, plus one of the spare napkins I'd collected over the course of many take-out meals.

Back at the door, gloves on, I wiped the only evidence of my ever having been there off the knob and its door. And, as a resident of a place called Paranoia, I gripped the door knob with the napkin, turned it, and entered. Inside, it felt as airless as King Tut's tomb.

The heat was understandable given the weather, but the air felt stuffy, as if the house had been sealed. Of course, it was nowhere near as stifling as the heat in the desert locations in Afghanistan where I'd served as a Marine. Even so, the temperature and its suffocating effect did not evoke pleasant memories.

The place was too quiet, apart from what sounded like a television burbling from within. *Where the hell are the Harcourts?* My hand, on autopilot, moved to my Sig.

Hand over the pistol grip, I moved further inside, all senses on high alert. I was halfway past the living room, aimed toward the kitchen when I stopped. Should I continue? Was I in some sort of danger here? I had my gun, but frankly, I try to avoid using it for legal reasons: I'm in court-ordered coounseling for a misdemeanor offense. And I don't usually do the kind of business that requires me to meet clients armed for protection.

After a few more seconds of wrestling with my thoughts, I made my way further into the house, ignoring the feeling of being suffocated by the overheated air pressing in around me.

My eyes swept the living room, the kitchen, and the dining room. Then there was the hallway leading to the bedrooms and bathrooms. As I inched toward them with tortoise-like speed, a few random thoughts popped up. Maybe it was a prank call that brought me here. Maybe the Harcourts were on vacation. And maybe I had imagined that earlier phone call. Yeah, right. Three bedrooms, two baths. I checked them all. Nothing but the drone of the TV. Where was that coming from?

The only place left was the basement. After stumbling across a closet or two, I found the basement door. Upon opening it, the TV's volume blared. I paused before going down the steps, but not nearly long enough to prepare myself for what awaited me.

CHAPTER THREE

I sat in my car and contemplated the horror I had just seen inside the house. Whereas the upstairs was neat as a pin, the basement had been torn apart. As for the Harcourts, they had been treated similarly. The result was two dead bodies and an ungodly mess. The sort of scene that brought back nightmares from my previous life.

Outside, the wind blew in gusts, and yellow crime scene tape stretched, flapping, around the entire property. I shut my eyes but couldn't unsee the Harcourts' bruised and bloody bodies, throats cut. Nor could I shut out the memory of Marian Harcourt's voice on the phone.

It looked like a burglary, like the perp had torn through the basement seeking something. But burglars usually don't kill people or use them as punching bags.

As for the bodies, having the heat on in the well-insulated basement would no doubt play hell with the medical examiner's findings. Had I not been awakened just a short time before, I could imagine how quickly the Harcourts' remains would have started to deteriorate. Let's hear it for energy-saving houses. Not only will your utility bills be lower, but you'll biodegrade faster if someone breaks in and whacks your ass.

Three raps on my window startled me. I opened my eyes to see a uniformed officer standing beside my driver's side door. From the way she held her hand up, I assumed my look was less than friendly. She said a few words that I could make out well enough through the window. Words like "detective" and "statement." She pointed toward the house and made what I assumed to be a request or an order to get out of my car. OK.

The officer, a young woman, maybe in her mid 20s, with just enough creases around the eyes and mouth to suggest she had more experience than your garden-variety millennial, seemed relieved. "Detective Gordan would like to ask you a few questions." I nodded in agreement and she added, "Follow me, please."

Together, we ducked under the tape and approached a man wearing a wrinkled gray suit, surrounded by a clutch of crime techs. Made me glad I had taken the precaution of stowing my gun in the back storage area of my car, sans bullets, which I placed in the glove compartment. The detective stopped talking to the techs long enough to tip me off that he was watching us.

"Thank you, Officer McNab," he said. "And thank you for waiting, Ms . . . ."

"Jensen," I said. "Erica Jensen."

The man in the wrinkly suit thrust a hand toward me. "I'm Detective Thomas Gordan. This won't take long."

So you're a detective and a fortuneteller? That's what I wanted to say but didn't.

A woman, mid to late 30s, in a stylishly cut suit, came out of the house and joined us. Detective Gordon of the Wrinkled Suit gestured toward Ms. Stylish. "My partner, Detective Meredith Sully." Sully nodded. I did likewise.

"What brought you to the Harcourts' house today?" Gordan asked.

"They were my clients. Ms. Harcourt called me a couple hours ago and asked me to come by." I phrased the statement with a barely detectable question mark at the end.

Gordon gave me a hard look. "What time did Ms. Harcourt call you?"

"Uh, it was almost five. Right around five ay-em." *Only an hour before I'd arrived. Oh five hundred.* Military time was drummed into my brain. Switching to the "normal" system was just another adjustment I hadn't quite made to civilian life.

Gordan, unphased by my unspoken thoughts, returned to scribbling notes. "What business are you in?"

I fished a business card identifying me as a "freelance researcher" from my shoulder bag and handed it to him. He gave it a glance. Sully peered at the card from where she stood. One corner of her mouth turned up.

"What sort of research were you doing?" Gordan asked.

"Background checks," I said with what I hoped was a breezy air. Which was absolutely true. Just not the whole story.

Gordan gave me the cop's standard x-ray stare. I was spared the same look from Sully. Other than the suits, these guys were pulling a twins act. Gordan opened his mouth slowly as if his jaw hurt. "Can you think of anyone who might have done this?" The way he said "this" emphasized the total depravity of the perp's actions.

I shook my head. "No one in particular, but the victims were . . . what? Internet famous? And there are all sorts of sickos out there."

"So you understand our problem," Detective Sully said in her low alto voice.

Movements on the periphery caught my eye. The street fronting the house had turned into a circus of cars and vans, police and civilian. And now, the media was moving in. Several robed or half-dressed people loitered outside the crime tape, holding phones and of course taking videos. At that point, the detectives brought our little exchange to a halt. Not that I could have helped them much. Before we parted, both detectives handed me their cards.

"We may need you to come in to the station later," Gordan said. "We can reach you here then?" He held up my card.

"Sure thing," I said, sounding more chipper than I felt.

I pushed past the throng of onlookers and headed straight for my car. When I got inside, I started it up and made tracks, but not too fast. I found another place to park far from the crime scene. I figured I owed Nick, a friend who was also my sponsor, a heads up, since he'd referred the Harcourts to me.

CHAPTER FOUR

Nick answered on the third ring. He sounded almost as tired as I did.

"I'm sorry if I woke you," I said.

"No problem." His voice was muffled, as if he'd wiped his mouth while talking. "Actually, I was up until 3:00 this morning trying to meet a deadline. Then, I didn't really fall asleep, but just fell into bed and zoned out."

"I have bad news." I wasted no time getting to the point. "The Harcourts have been murdered."

"What? Good Lord . . . ."

I steeled myself to go on. "I discovered the bodies. They weren't just killed. They were beaten and stabbed several times and their throats were cut." I didn't bother to describe the blood spattered all over the place, which I hoped to forget.

Nick said nothing. I could imagine what he was thinking. I tried to swallow, but my mouth was really dry. And the memory of the horrid sight and smell in the basement was still fresh.

"I just thought you should know before the cops and the press come knocking," I said. "You realize they'll check your article about the couple for clues."

Nick cleared his throat. "Plus whatever they said off the record. Not that there was much."

"They may want your sources."

There was a snort at the other end. "Erica, the article was a puff piece. I did it for the money." Nick's voice had a hint of disgust.

I paused in an effort to choose my words. "Can you think of any reason why the Harcourts might have felt in danger?"

"If they were in danger, they never mentioned it."

"Do you know why they wanted to hire a personal assistant then?"

"They didn't tell me. I just assumed they were too busy being internet big-shots to do their own dishes."

"Could there have been another reason?" I asked.

When Nick didn't respond, I added, "Did you get any sense at all that they were hiding something?"

"Well . . . ." That one word told me plenty. "I sensed some tension between them. If I'd been doing a proper job, I would have dug further into it. You don't suppose . . . ?"

"Many things can make people tense, but most of them don't lead to murder."

"But I should have seen it."

What the hell? Silence filled the line. I let it continue.

With an audible sigh, Nick added, "At some level, I could tell these people had bigger problems than they were admitting to me. If I had been doing an investigative piece, maybe this could have been avoided."

"Don't," I said. I knew that feeling too well. "That wasn't your job. Whatever happened was because of their choices, so you don't need to blame yourself."

Another long pause. "You're right, of course." He managed to get the words out, but he spoke without conviction. "But . . . ."

"Is there anything I can do?" As a fellow recovering opioid addict, Nick helped keep me on the straight and narrow, no matter how trying the various group meetings got. He was my sounding board and a life raft in a sea of trouble.

"Maybe," he said.

CHAPTER FIVE

Nick said he wanted to write about the murders, but he wanted to do a genuinely investigative piece this time. I did what I could to make sure he stayed off any chemical aids, and he returned the favor. At this point, I had a mere handful of close friends, and Nick was the closest I had come to finding a kindred spirit outside the Corps.

According to Nick, the Harcourts' publicist, Marge Calhoun, was the font of all the intel that she felt was fit to print. Getting past her shield and beneath the shiny surfaces of the couple and their two grown children (one boy, one girl—without the average statistical one-half kid) was a task that went beyond the purpose of Nick's article, which was allegedly to go for your dreams or to inspire, I guess. Now, that in itself, I found hilarious. In a culture that values good looks over depth, I find our obsession with celebrity a bit much. Plus this search for the perfect lifestyle? Seriously? Like everyone can just pick up and traipse around the world without a care. Sure. Before I rang off with Nick, he gave me the contact info for Marge Calhoun. I wondered whether she would answer a phone call or email me a press release.

Back at my apartment, which also served as a home office, a copy of the *Washington Post* was waiting on my doormat. *Like no other millennials within a hundred miles.* I wondered about that, but what can I say? I like newspapers. I rubbed my eyes and settled in with my laptop, my coffee mug within easy reach. It was looking like a six-cup day. I usually try to limit myself to no more than five cups, but a six-cup day could easily expand to seven or more.

I mentally reviewed the timing again. Marian Harcourt had called me at about 5:00 AM. I reached the house a little after 6:00 AM. That didn't give the killer (or killers) a lot of time to act. Could the Harcourts have been dead before I got the phone call? That thought got stuck in my head. I needed some time to figure this out. If that wasn't Marian Harcourt on the phone, the caller was good enough at doing voice imitations to start a new side hustle teaching voice acting skills. Create a new blog, a YouTube channel, an Instagram account.

My work for the Harcourts had led me to search various social media, since that's pretty much where they lived. I had focused on their potential employee's background. No red flags. Further digging turned up no criminal record. Not even a speeding ticket.

The job candidate's name was Blair Fenton. I wondered then and I still wonder whether he was from a prominent family in Silver Spring, which has a Fenton Street and more than a few connections to the historic Blair family. Or maybe it was just a weird coincidence. I scanned my report, looking for holes. Seemed solid, but . . . I knew better than to assume I had done a perfect job.

And then there was Marge Calhoun, PR pro. The Harcourts had hired me directly, so Marge might not even know that I exist. I needed to call her. I punched in the number and got voicemail. I pictured her spinning a story to the cops. Or reporters.

I began writing an email and then stopped. I shook my head as if the contents of my brain had settled and I needed to stir them up. Then I used a search engine to find her address. No warnings. I'm coming to see you, Ms. Calhoun.

CHAPTER SIX

Marge Calhoun worked out of a home office in North Bethesda. Technically, South Rockville, but anyone could live in Rockville. Living in Bethesda meant you weren't one of the hoi polloi. The location may not have been as ritzy as Chevy Chase, but the two places did share a high school, which made it close enough.

When I first saw her house, I was impressed. The style blended right in with the Chevy Chase ethos. It was a brick rambler set on a wide swath of lawn adorned with shrubs and flowers that would have been the envy of many Better Homes and Gardens readers. A series of stone slabs had been placed so as to help visitors up the incline toward the entrance. I made my way to the front door and rang the doorbell.

It wasn't long before a woman who was probably in her late 40s opened the door. She had bottle-blonde hair cut short and coifed. I thought she was going to tell me to buzz off, until she smiled, raised an index finger, pointed toward her tiny ear piece, and held up a cell phone. I put on my "friendly Erica" expression and refrained from interrupting her call.

"Look. Someone's here. I've got to go." Calhoun disconnected the call. "Sorry about that. You're Erica, right?"

I squinted. "Have we met?"

Calhoun shook her head. "I make it a point to know who my clients deal with. I got your name from Nick. He speaks highly of you, but his description doesn't do you justice."

How nicey-nice of him. "May I . . . ?" I nodded toward the house.

Calhoun's pinkish complexion turned a shade deeper. "Yes, please come in." She waved the invitation.

She was so polite and matter-of-fact, I wondered if the police had told her yet. I figured they would contact the kids and any other close family first. How long would that take? Especially with all the paparazzi hanging around outside the house.

As we moved deeper into her home, I instinctively checked my surroundings. Living room to the right, small bathroom on the left tucked beneath the stairs, kitchen straight ahead down a short hallway. The kitchen was airy and bright, and it looked newly renovated. Sparkling and as up-to-date as in a model home. It opened into a dining room on the right, home office to the left. I followed Calhoun as she went into her office.

"Can I interest you in a cup of coffee?"

Silly question. "That would be great."

After learning that I take mine black, she waved an arm toward the office. "Have a seat. Be with you in a sec."

I walked past her and sank gratefully into a comfy leather guest chair. This room was obviously where Calhoun spent most of her time. The walls were lined with what I assumed were client photos. Naturally, the Harcourts featured prominently. But not so prominently as to take center stage. The photos front and center seemed to be focused more on Calhoun who stood smiling with various Oprah-level celebs. A bookcase covered one wall. I considered checking the books for dust but decided not to.

Calhoun came into the room holding two steaming mugs. "How can I help you?" she asked, while passing one of them to me.

I took a sip. Perfect. "Have you heard about the Harcourts?"

Calhoun licked her lips and set her mouth in a solemn line. "Yes. Just horrible."

"Any thoughts about who might have done this?"

She gazed in my general direction, avoiding direct eye contact. "People like the Harcourts can have plenty of enemies."

"Of course," I said. "But how many of them would do what this one did?"

I had the advantage of knowing exactly what that was, since I was the one who had stumbled across the mutilated corpses. If the police hadn't already told Calhoun, I wasn't going to be the one to provide the gory details.

Calhoun gazed at her lap and then at me, or more precisely, at a point on my shoulder. "Some people say that, given the right circumstances, anyone is capable of doing the most horrific things."

Sure. But usually the cops like to have a motive to hang their cases on. What could have prompted such violence against this particular couple and the ransacking of their basement, unless they were involved with some seriously unsavory types? Say, loan sharks. Or drug dealers.

I didn't dare toss those thoughts into the conversation. As a PR professional, Calhoun probably wouldn't give me a direct answer, even if I asked what color the sky was. I tried a different tack. "Why did the Harcourts want to hire a personal assistant?"

Calhoun's eyes widened just long enough for me to notice. Then back to her business-as-usual look. "My clients are always pressed for time," she said. "Everything they do takes away from doing other, better, more satisfying things. And having children doesn't make it easier—"

I cut her off. "But they're grown children now."

"You're not a mother. Even after your children have grown up, you never stop being a mother."

What about fathers? And how much do grown children really eat into one's time? Her answer seemed evasive. I had the distinct impression my role in this was new to her. "Were they ever threatened?" I asked.

Her face suddenly assumed an expression I couldn't read. "Why do you ask?"

I said nothing for a moment, but if I had spoken, I would have barked, "That's not an answer."

Before I could say anything, she added, "The police have already contacted me, and I have answered their questions. Perhaps it's best if we leave the job of finding the killers to them."

CHAPTER SEVEN

I considered Calhoun's deflection before responding. "I'm not trying to do their job. I do background checks. As far as I could tell, their candidate for hire seemed clean. But you never know." And wouldn't it suck if I had missed a problem? Or made an inquiry that stirred up a hornet's nest?

Calhoun nodded. "I see." But her tone suggested she didn't. She rose with her coffee mug in hand. "I'd love to chat more, but I need to wrap this up."

OK. People get tortured and killed, but life goes on. After taking one last swig of coffee, I stood up and was summarily hustled out the door. Now what was that about? A random thought made me stop short. Were the Harcourts hiring a replacement for their publicist? Again, they never told me what the exact nature of their new hire's duties would be, other than being a personal assistant. Perhaps they'd meant the term more broadly than I'd imagined. But that was a mere possibility, at this point.

I tried not to make too much of Calhoun's seeming detachment. People deal with grief in all sorts of ways. Some throw themselves into their work and rely on activity plus an extra-large dose of denial to survive the emotional turmoil. I should know about that.

I returned to my car and drove to a nearby coffee shop. I have a routine that I follow when I research a problem. It helps to sit down and brainstorm possible sources of information, including people I might want to talk to. It gets me started. Right now, apart from every user of social media, my sources included Calhoun, the Harcourts' kids, and a business manager. After making a short list of their names on a legal pad, I created a flowchart with each person represented by a geometric shape, with names and relationships identified in text and lines connecting one shape to another. I sat back and admired my handiwork. Very pretty, and very neat. I suspected that the picture would end up a lot messier if I kept at it.

Then I called Nick. After we exchanged greetings, I asked, "Did the Harcourts' business manager know they were hiring a personal assistant?"

"I assume he did, but I couldn't swear to it."

I nodded as if he could see me. "I've never dealt with him. The Harcourts hired me directly, claiming they got my name from you."

"Which they did." Nick paused. "Why the questions?"

I tried to choose my words carefully this time. "I just met their publicist," I offered. "She wasn't exactly eager to talk to me." I filled Nick in on what we had discussed and on Calhoun's guarded reactions. He digested my intel in silence. "If you want to dig into this further," I said. "I'm willing to help."

Nick grunted. "Erica, I don't want to abuse our friendship. Besides, I'm supposed to be doing the investigative work."

"I'm not suggesting I take over your job," I hurried to reassure him. "I'm just . . . here for you. If you need the help."

"Thank you. Just don't devote too much time . . . ." His voice trailed off.

"Well, I'll do what I can. I like getting paid as much as the next guy." I was rewarded with a small laugh.

CHAPTER EIGHT

After our call ended, I started work on my hodge-podge of cases. Among them were an overdue debt, a man who'd skipped bail on a serious domestic abuse charge, and the missing heir to a tiny fiefdom. My research is usually pedestrian, but at least these cases offered some variety.

That done, I took another look at my flowchart for the Harcourt murders. According to Nick, the couple's son, Jaden, and their daughter, Amy, still lived in the area. Amy Harcourt was in her final year of undergraduate studies at the University of Maryland in College Park. School was still in session and she lived on campus, so I assumed she spent her weekends there. Going to her parents' house was obviously no longer an option.

At around noon, I got a phone call. "Ms. Jensen? It's Detective Gordan."

"Hi. What's up?" I kept my tone casual, but I thought: *What the hell does Mr. Wrinkled Suit want now?*

I heard the scuffing sound of a hand covering the receiver and a muffled sneeze. Then clearly, "We need you to come in and make a formal statement."

"Gesundheit," I replied. "I already told you everything I know."

"We need that in writing. On the record." It didn't sound like a request. "And thank you," he added, belatedly.

What could I say? Pain in the ass that it was, I wanted the police to find the killer. "When would you like me come in?" I asked, trying to sound helpful instead of resigned.

"We can send a car around for you anytime today," he offered.

I paused at the idea of depending on the police for transportation. "If I promise to show up, could I just drive myself?" Detective Gordan seemed amenable to this. In fact, he didn't sound like he cared one way or another. We arranged a time for me to swing by his division right after lunch.

When I arrived at the two-story brick building that housed the Montgomery County Police Department's local division, a uniformed officer ushered me through a maze of offices and cubicles into a small room with a table—a government-issue rectangle with legs that were bolted to the floor—and three equally plain chairs. A small, triangular camera peeked out from an upper corner of the room.

The uniform stood in the doorway as I entered. "Have a seat," he said. "Would you like coffee? Soda?"

I forced a smile. "No thanks." *I do not intend to stay very long.*

The uniform nodded. "The detectives will be with you shortly." With that, he shut the door, leaving me alone with the camera. I resisted the urge to give it the finger. On the bright side, the officer hadn't handcuffed to me to the table.

I expected to be kept waiting a while, so when Detective Gordan appeared within about ten minutes, I'll confess I was mildly surprised. I was also surprised not to see Sully. Yet.

"Thanks for coming in." Detective Gordan nodded at me as he approached the table and took a seat opposite me. "We just have a few more questions."

I spread my hands. *Here I am!* "Ask away."

Gordan's face turned from neutral to grinning. "How well do you know Nick Baxter?"

My mind churned with a sudden flood of thoughts. I maintained a stoic expression, but it was a struggle. Detective Sully made her entrance just then. This time, she looked slightly disheveled but Mr. Wrinkled Suit looked dapper. That was an interesting twist. And Detective Gordan had just asked me the last question I ever expected to hear from him.

CHAPTER NINE

Before answering, I took half a second to gauge the situation. I couldn't afford too long a pause or they'd assume I was holding back. They had called me in to give a written statement. I assumed our little talk would lead up to that. But since I don't like to assume, I stalled for time.

"Well enough to know he's a good guy. Do you want me to write that down?"

Detective Sully stood clutching a thick file. She shook her head, slowly, as if to loosen her neck muscles. Tucking the file under one arm, she used her other hand to pull out a chair—it scraped the floor with a sound like fingernails on a blackboard—and she slowly sat down. She then picked up the file with both hands and held it in front of her like a flag offered to the bereaved at a military funeral . . . and dropped it onto the table. Thunk!

"Did you know that he has a record?" she asked.

Did it make the Billboard Top 100? Or go Platinum? Or viral? I thought better of saying any of that out loud. After I reined in my sarcasm as far as it would be reined, I said, "For some odd reason, I've never felt the need to do a background check."

Sully smiled in a way that projected an *ooh, girl—things I could tell you* vibe. "You might be interested to know—"

"I'm not." I was tiring of this game fast. "Do you want me to make a written statement or not?"

"Yes, actually, we do." Detective Gordan's voice was low and even. Apparently, now he was . . . what? The good cop? He added, "First, we'd like to ask you a few more questions and videotape your answers for the record. Would that be okay with you?"

"Sure," I said, then proceeded to answer the same damn questions they'd asked at the crime scene. Maybe a few more, but nothing that provided any earthshaking insights.

Gordon ended the recording session. "Thank you. Now, we'd like you to write it down. Please write exactly what happened this morning when you found the bodies."

Was it my imagination or did he emphasize the last four words? I glanced at Sully. Her lips held the hint of a smile, but her eyes hardened.

"Fine." Let's get this over with. "Got something to write on? A pen?"

Sully shoved a legal pad and pen my way. I dragged them toward me. Then, wrote exactly what I had told them already. I tried to keep it short and thought of shortening it further. Maybe to one sentence with really small words—words with no more than four letters. They watched me write. Your tax dollars at work. I slid the statement across the table. "There. Signed and dated." They stared at me.

I suppressed a nervous laugh. "You guys must really be bored, but I'm glad to have entertained you." I stopped there.

"You also have . . . ." Sully's voice trailed off. "You've had your previous brushes with the law."

Hold on, I thought. Surely, they didn't think I killed my clients.

"Am I under arrest?" I asked. I was fast losing patience. My lizard brain silently screamed at the two detectives. If someone didn't explain what the fuck they really wanted, I'd rip the table off the floor and throw it at them. Maybe sock Ms. Stylish in the jaw for good measure. Sully was appraising me, but Gordan's expression didn't change.

"No," she said.

"Then I can go?" I shot to my feet so fast, I toppled my chair backward. It hit the wall and bounced back, grazing the backs of my knees.

Gordan waved his hand dismissively. "Sure." He tossed the word out. I wondered if he ever blinked.

CHAPTER TEN

Well, that was a crap way to spend the last hour or so. Nice to know I had served my country in order to get treated like this. I wanted to say, "I fought for you people and now my body is wreckage, even though I'm barely in my thirties. Good to know you only see me as a madwoman who would kill her own clients." I cracked the car windows. Chilly air blew in and stung my face. It felt good and reminded me that I was alive.

It also snapped me out of my funk and got me thinking more rationally. Maybe I had overreacted with the cops. Perhaps I should have thought twice before rejecting Sully's offer of Nick's background information. Unfortunately, the post-traumatic stress I suffer is very real and has diminished what little patience and what few social skills I had to start with. Being in court-ordered therapy after an unfortunate incident made it even more important that I try to be cooperative. Especially since I had done nothing wrong. But never mind my awesome tendency to fuck things up. Why did they ask me about Nick?

It was still early enough in the afternoon for there to be plenty of good parking spots in my building's garage. I drive an old Fiesta. Old, as in, made before I was born.

I backed the car in, grabbed my stuff, and tromped up to my second-floor efficiency—a word that applies equally to my furnishings. I tossed my things onto the small workstation positioned behind the sofa, walked over to the tiny kitchen, and dumped the cold coffee so I could make a fresh pot. As it dripped, I turned on my laptop.

After checking email and doing a quick browse for updated headlines, I decided to call Nick. The coffee had sputtered its last few drops into the carafe. I found a mug and filled it up as I explained my morning's semi-grilling.

"At the risk of invading your privacy, should I be concerned that they asked about you?" I said.

"What possible motive would I have?" Nick said.

"That didn't seem to stop them from wondering about me, the one who found the bodies and reported it to the police." I paused. "Not that I don't understand. There are weirdos who commit crimes, then tell the police. Whatever their mental state is, it doesn't apply to me."

But Nick hadn't answered my question. Forging ahead, I put the question to him again, with different words. "Have you ever been arrested?"

The brief pause before he answered made my heart skip a beat. "Well, technically, yes. I took part in a protest against the government's failure to pass adequate gun control laws. I was part of a group of concerned journalists who organized the event after the shooting in Annapolis."

"And they arrested you for that?" I couldn't suppress my disbelief. Not only because I joined the Marines to defend our right to do that very thing, but I couldn't see any way it would suggest a motive to commit murder.

"They told us we didn't have a valid permit," he said. "It's really not a big deal," he added. "They ended up dropping the charges."

"Yeah, well, the detectives were having great fun using your quote-unquote arrest to mess with my head while they questioned me," I said. "Is there anything else from your past that would put you on their radar in terms of motive? Anything at all?"

"Absolutely not." He spoke it without hesitation and with such conviction, I wanted to believe him.

CHAPTER ELEVEN

Nick and I ended our call on that somewhat less than satisfying note. Not that I imagined for even one second that he'd committed some horrendous crime, but why were the police questioning me about Nick? And what was that crack from Sully concerning my previous "brushes with the law" all about?

I tried to push these thoughts into the back of my mind, but I knew I couldn't rest easy until Nick and I were eliminated from the pool of suspects. In my case, that should be easy. Apart from our first meeting, my only contacts with the Harcourts had been by phone or email. And what possible motive could I have?

My larger concern was with Nick. He'd been to their house several times to interview them. He had almost certainly left fingerprints. But wouldn't the police need to show more than just his mere presence in the house to establish a real case against him? Any forensic evidence would have to link him to the crime, wouldn't it? Plus I couldn't think of a single motive.

But Sully's malicious expression when she spoke of Nick's record lingered like a bad smell. I suppressed the urge to return to the homicide division and punch her lights out in favor of a brief fantasy of spitting right into one of her judgy eyes.

I devoted an hour or so to digging up assets on a deadbeat debtor. Something attachable. There was precious little so far, but I had promised to keep looking. As for the missing heir, he stood to gain a 10-year-old car, a modest house, and a three-figure bank account. Not exactly a windfall, but it was better than nothing.

The really pressing case was the domestic abuse bail skipper. Apparently, the man was accused of beating his live-in girlfriend so badly that she ended up spending more than two weeks in the hospital. The judge would only let him out on a six-figure bail, which he'd managed God knows how. Now, he was in the wind and the bondsman, Mitch Delgado, was freaking out.

"Erica, I'm serious as a fucking heart attack." Mitch's voice was rough, as if he'd gargled sand and broken glass. He paused for some violent coughing. I pictured one of his lungs collapsing from the effort. "If you can't bring in Troy Fairchild, I'll be in deep shit."

Calls from Mitch Delgado of Delgado Bail Bonds threatened to become a daily ritual because Troy Fairchild chose to evade justice or, at any rate, a court appearance. Mitch was a vet. Vietnam. Different war, different country, same bullshit. He had health problems, just like the rest of us. And, like me, after returning from duty, he'd chosen to set up a business that was almost guaranteed to lead to even more bullshit.

My first and second passes at online searching for the suspect had come up empty. I thought about the possibilities. Maybe he had an alias. Even so, would that be enough to completely wipe a person's existence under their real name off the map?

I worked halfheartedly on my cases, while visions of the horror in the Harcourts' basement and the coldness in Sully's eyes kept coming back to me.

Worn out by my restless brain and the early wake-up call, I couldn't sit still, but I didn't feel up to a walk outdoors either. So I got up and paced in a circle around the apartment. Moving got my blood flowing. No matter how tired or discouraged I am, the simple act of walking gets my brain in gear. Midway through my fourth or fifth circuit around the apartment, I decided to talk to the Harcourts' business manager. The only address I could find for him was his office, which was closed according to his voice mail message. Well, it was Saturday.

I decided to let that matter lie for the moment in favor of handling cases for my living clients. I had assumed the easiest would be a search for assets for another creditor client. After a bit of digging, all I had managed to unearth was an auto registration (the car was a 20-year-old Buick) and a bank account with fifteen bucks in it. Okay, maybe that one wouldn't be the easiest. I also managed to find the debtor's last known address in a somewhat sketchy Takoma Park neighborhood. Not a comfort but at least a lead. I set that aside for the moment and focused on the skip. It was the most serious of my three latest cases, because the man who had skipped bail was accused of domestic abuse, and his bail bondsman was on the hook for a healthy chunk of change.

For anyone who thinks everything you need is on the internet, allow me to disabuse you of that notion. Half the information out there is either too old to be reliable or just flat-out wrong. Not to mention that the information available today can be gone tomorrow.

When it comes to finding someone on the run from the law, nothing really beats the power of legwork, interviews, and surveillance. The bail bondsman, in this case, had the name and address of the relative who'd posted the bond. Time to initiate some face time with said relative.

The skip's uncle had coughed up the cash. He could probably shed some light on the skip's friends and other relatives who might be willing to help a man who portrayed himself as unfairly accused. While I seriously doubted the skip would seek refuge from a source as obvious as the uncle himself, I couldn't rule it out. Along with being too poor to bail himself out, my suspect could also be really stupid.

The uncle lived in University Park. Another nice neighborhood. Next thing you know, I'll be snooping for leads in Potomac.

There was a reason University Park had the name it did. It was right near the University of Maryland. However, the university itself was within the city limits of College Park. Since the university started out as an agricultural college, the University Park area seemed like a tacked on addition made after the school's promotion in status.

The Harcourts' daughter, Amy, lived on campus in College Park. I needed to meet face-to-face with both kids. While I was in the area, I figured I might as well stop by her dorm after visiting the uncle. But before I tackled any of those tasks, I figured I owed myself some serious sack time.

CHAPTER TWELVE

After a good night's sleep uninterrupted by emergency calls, I got right to work. Sundays are the worst. Nothing going on, nothing much on TV, and I get fidgety, so I find it's best to stay busy. Armed with only my file, a clipboard, and a paperback, any of which might come in handy, I headed toward University Park.

My first stop was the uncle's house. Rechecking my file, I noted that his name was Melvin Stubbs. Always good to know who the hell you're talking to before attempting an interview.

The screen door was locked, so I rang the bell and waited on the stoop of the squat, brick rambler. A small square of landscaping fronted the house. The weather had warmed slightly, temps reaching into the 50s. Background noise in this neighborhood was mostly the sound of barking dogs and distant traffic.

The relative quiet was disturbed by the metallic rattle of a door chain from inside. Whoever scoped me out through the peephole had decided I was either trustworthy or threatening on sight alone. The door cracked open and a slice of weathered, gray face came into view, and I could see the chain.

"Good day, sir," I said in my most stranger-friendly voice. "Are you Melvin Stubbs?"

One gray eye in the weathered face bore into me. "Depends. Who's asking?"

I forced a smile. "Sir, I represent Delgado Bail Bonds. I understand that a man named Melvin Stubbs paid the bondsman to cover his nephew Troy Fairchild's bail. Are you Mr. Melvin Stubbs?" I smiled wider.

The steely look in the gray eye softened into something more like quicksilver. A heavy sigh blew through the crack. "Yeah," he said, as if he'd just been sentenced to death. "That's me."

"You might not know this, but your nephew recently failed to appear in court. It would be extremely helpful to my client to figure out where he might go under the circumstances."

The eye looked me up and down. "Hang on," he said. He shut the door, and I heard the chain lock rattle again, and then he opened the door wide.

"That little bastard," he muttered. "I told him, clean up your act or don't bother to come to me again. Shit." The man snapped out of his brooding and focused on me. "Come on in. I can probably come up with a few places he might go. And I can assure you that here is not one of them."

My hour with Stubbs ended up being one of the most productive of the day. He invited me into his living room and even offered me a cup of coffee. I decided to risk it. As Stubbs shuffled off to the kitchen, I scanned the surroundings. There might be a clue hiding in plain sight.

The furniture was not what I would associate with a bachelor . . . more like what you would find in a grandparents' home. A long sofa covered in a brownish floral pattern with a dust ruffle brushing the floor dominated the room. A not-very-well-matched red-and-navy-plaid easy chair sat opposite the sofa with a round wooden coffee table between them. The mantle over the fireplace held a few framed photos. The air smelled faintly of cigarette smoke.

I was about to take a closer look at the photos when I heard the rattle of dishes on a tray. Stubbs reappeared with a vintage serving platter holding two steaming mugs. After a few minutes of warm-up chitchat and a bit of coffee, I learned more than a little about my quarry. Troy had dropped out of school, lost his last job, and spent most of his time in a seedy bar somewhere between here and Baltimore. In short, he'd done nearly everything he could to disappoint Melvin.

"I've done the best I could to help him out," Stubbs groused. "But then he goes and does another damn stupid thing."

I clucked my tongue to convey that I disapproved of such antics, which seemed to please him.

"I'd hold an intervention," Stubbs continued, throwing his hands up. "But it would take the National Guard to force him to sit through it."

"And where did you say he was fired from?" I asked, in a bid to wrest back control of the conversation.

"Office supply store. Not far from here." He held up a hand. "Hang on."

Stubbs hoisted himself to his feet and tottered down the hall. The silence was broken only by the sounds that came from deeper in the house . . . the sound of doors opening and objects being shifted around. I went back to the fireplace mantle to take a closer look at the photos.

One revealed a much younger Stubbs with a woman roughly his own age. Not a wedding picture, but the two were formally dressed and they were beaming. Ready for a night on the town. Based on what they wore and a quick calculation, this might have been taken in the 70s. I wondered vaguely whether they were headed for a wedding or a disco.

Another photo looked like it had been taken on a vacation. The couple were wearing casual clothes, and the setting was outdoors. The photo appeared to be about twenty years old, judging by Stubbs' appearance and the woman's, too. There was also a young man in the picture, maybe mid to late teens, with shaggy, dark, tousled hair of a color that in no way matched Stubbs's light brown or the woman's blonde hair. The couple were smiling. The young man was not.

I realized the background noises had stopped and instinctively glanced toward the hallway. Stubbs stood there watching me with a sheaf of papers and a small notebook in hand. Actually, he seemed to be staring right at me, but I'm not sure he actually saw me. When he noticed that I was looking at him, he blinked and managed a wan smile.

"My wife, Greta," he said. His voice was thick with loss, regret, love, pain . . . . For a moment, he couldn't speak. Neither could I, for that matter. Stubbs recovered. "She passed two years ago," he added. He shook his head and waved me toward the sofa. "Anyway, I found a few things that might help you."

Before we got into that, I pointed at the vacation photo. "Is that Troy in the picture?"

Stubbs nodded. "Yep." He sat down and set the papers and notebook on the coffee table.

"Where was it taken?"

"Los Angeles." His voice turned wistful. "She'd always wanted to see Hollywood. Unfortunately, it wasn't the best place to take Troy on a vacation."

CHAPTER THIRTEEN

Over the next fifteen minutes, I got a short history on Troy Fairchild. His parents were both losers. His dad spent half his time in jail, the rest eking out a living as a petty criminal. His mother was usually drunk before Troy woke up. His parents having been less than attentive, the duties of raising a well-mannered child had often fallen to his aunt and uncle.

When Uncle Melvin noticed the boy's tendency toward risky behavior as he approached his teens, he tried to guide Troy down a better path. But the older he got, the further Troy withdrew from the adults around him. Melvin's hopes that the trip to LA would bring them closer were dashed when Troy made a midnight visit to the beach and stumbled across a bunch of kids drinking. Apparently, they were quite friendly and willing to share.

"And that's how the drinking began," Stubbs finished. "He's only violent when he drinks."

I nodded. "Yeah, I know the type." A little too well.

Stubbs straightened the papers and shoved them my way. "Receipts," he explained. "For the stuff he bothered paying for.

Maybe someone at one of these places knew him." His voice ticked upward at the end, turning his statement into a subtle question. Then he opened the notebook to show me the entries. Names, addresses, and amounts.

"Right around the time he dropped out of school, I found this hidden in his room," Stubbs said. "Now, that was fifteen years ago. I have no idea if he's still in touch with these people." Stubbs closed the notebook and handed it to me. I took it.

"Gotta start somewhere," I said.

As I drove toward the nearest Staples to make copies of the receipts and notebook entries, my thoughts drifted back to Nick and the Harcourts. Stubbs' account of his somewhat fractious relationship with Troy had triggered a thought that I had buried earlier. *What about the kids?* By now, the police must have informed them. And surely they must have questioned them.

These were kids who had been raised to a certain extent in the public spotlight, their photos posted online during summer trips, weekend outings, and in candid shots at home. They were not actors, musicians, or any other kind of entertainer. They had been raised on free trips, always on the go, always on the internet, and subject to all its joys and indignities. That couldn't have been easy.

There was also the matter of the nanny who served as a part-time parent. Possibly more than part time. Who was the nanny and what was her (or his) relationship with the deceased parents?

CHAPTER FOURTEEN

Amy Harcourt lived on campus. I knew the name of the dorm, but not much else. So I checked in with Nick and got a few more details. Her major was English and one of her favorite places to hang out was the McKeldin Library. I also got her cell phone number, but I would use that only if I couldn't contact her otherwise. I hate giving up the element of surprise. I also got the name of the most recent nanny—Astrid Gunderson. Nick had interviewed her, but because of the article's slant, he had steered clear of the most sensitive issues.

I always wondered what a person would do with a degree in English. Perhaps Amy wanted to be an English teacher. That alone made her a worthy person in my view. Really good teachers were scarce, and these days, they're paid small money to put up with big problems. With my curiosity piqued, I figured I would ask Amy how she planned to use her degree, assuming there was a plan.

I could only hope that Amy was staying in her dorm instead of with a relative or friend. But since I was in the area anyhow, I figured a visit was worth a try. Free street parking in College

Park is tough to come by, even on a Sunday. I squeezed the
Fiesta into a small, curbside space that two other drivers had
barely allowed me. After another glance at my flowchart and
notes, I grabbed the book I brought and headed for the dorm.

After a short walk across campus, I spotted Amy's dorm and
was struck by its resemblance to a middle-class apartment
building. I had been expecting something a bit more, I don't
know, ivy-covered? As I approached the dorm, I was surprised
to see actual bay windows.

I walked into a shadowy canyon between two buildings and
continued toward the sunlight that warmed the entrances. I
turned left, climbed a short set of stairs, and tried the door.
Locked. Naturally. A sign near an intercom informed me that all
visitors required escorts. I scanned the area. A few students
wandered through it.

Among the intermittent stream of students who trickled by
me, one or two entered the other building. I considered simply
following a student into Amy's dorm but dismissed that idea
because it was likely to raise questions about why I was there.
It's a dangerous world nowadays, even on a semi-sheltered
college campus. So I pressed the intercom button. A young
woman's voice crackled a greeting.

I smiled as hard as I could—because when you smile, it
makes you sound all happy—and announced myself as an
acquaintance of Amy Harcourt's parents. Which was true. I
knew them. Once.

"I'm here to see Amy," I added, which seemed obvious. I
hesitated to say more, because God only knew how privy Amy's
cohorts were to her exact situation.

There was a long pause before the intercom crackled to life
again. "I'll see if she's in her room," the tinny, but cheery, voice
responded.

A longer silence followed. People of all ages walked up and down the sidewalks. A group of young people had gathered across the street. The vibe I got suggested that the gathering was impromptu. Their expressions varied from intensely serious to joyful. I heard enough laughter to confirm that it wasn't a fight about to break out. And why would I even think that? For all I knew, they could be discussing a test or working on a group project, planning a night out, or planning a revolution.

A bicycle or two whizzed by. I was about to give the intercom another go, when the tinny voice returned. "Are you a friend of the family?"

I suspected Amy was feeding lines to the owner of the voice. "I worked for them," I said very briefly. *And I found their bleeding bodies!* Which I left unsaid. A few seconds later, the door opened.

The young woman who peered out looked barely old enough to be in college—her features had an almost babyish quality, and her light brown hair and hazel eyes accentuated her youthful appearance. She was a couple of inches shorter than me and was wearing an oversized hoodie that nearly swallowed her petite frame, making her look beyond shy. I started to explain why I was there and was shocked when she blurted out "Did you really know my parents?"

She didn't sound angry, but I'll admit I was mildly surprised at her bluntness. And she was clearly being cautious. Who could blame her?

In fact, it finally hit me that it was only yesterday morning that her parents had been murdered. My anxiety over police suspicions and badly timed phone calls had overridden any thoughts of waiting a few days, enough of an interval to satisfy common sense and decency.

"Yes, I did know them," I said. "I assume the police have spoken to you?"

She nodded. Her eyebrows drew together as if she were doing division in her head.

"I'm so sorry for your loss," I said. *God, I'm terrible at this stuff.* I plunged on, feeling like I was jumping into the deepest part of the ocean. "For personal reasons, it's really important for me to understand more about what happened to your parents."

"You aren't with the press then, are you."

She said it like a statement, but I knew it was actually a question.

"No," I replied, handing her a business card. "But I do have an interest in finding out who murdered them."

She flinched. *Goddammit.* I wanted to punch myself for my lack of manners.

"I've . . . I've told the police all I know," she said. Her gaze pivoted toward a point beyond me, as if seeking a teleprompter.

"Amy." Saying her name earned me brief eye contact. "I could really use your help. Because I want to make sure they find the right person."

CHAPTER FIFTEEN

After explaining how I knew her parents, Amy seemed to lower her guard. At least, she didn't run back inside and slam the door in my face.

"Would you mind if I ask you a few questions?" I said, doing my best to sound sympathetic.

She looked thoughtful, or maybe that was just her normal expression. She nodded and said "Sure."

Awesome. "Let's find a place to talk," I suggested.

That place turned out to be the coffee shop in McKeldin Library, not far from the dorm. The place was packed, which caused me to wonder if we'd be sitting on the floor for our discussion. But Amy managed to snag a table in the rear of the coffee shop while I ordered our drinks. I was surprised when she appeared next to me.

"What about the table?" I asked. My back, tortured by years of wearing ill-fitting, heavy military gear, would not be pleased about having to sit cross-legged on a hard floor.

Amy dredged up a smile. "Don't worry. I left a book and my hoodie."

I nodded but kept the table in my peripheral view. "We'll keep an eye on it, okay?"

Then it hit me. I had known Amy less than an hour and had no desire to harm her. But there was no way she could know that. Or what I might do to her drink. Her parents had been well-known on the internet. That alone probably attracted more than a few crazies. If I thought too hard about living in a society where one had to worry about such things, I would end up being more than a little depressed.

After we got our order, we moved to the table. While we waited, the empty chairs around it drew more than a few interested looks, but Amy's book and hoodie thankfully warded off any interlopers.

Coffee in hand, we settled in for a chat. I told Amy more about why I was interested in finding out who might have killed her parents. Her eyes grew wide as I described the odd circumstances that led me to her parents' house at the crack of dawn the previous morning.

"Did anyone ever threaten violence against your parents?" I asked. "I realize you've already gone over this with the police, but I'd like to learn the facts for myself and make an independent judgment." One that doesn't involve any pressure from a higher-up to close the case.

Amy chewed her lower lip a bit, and then she spat out "Mom and Dad had their haters. That's just part of being on the internet. A few of them said some pretty mean things." Her voice caught and she paused. Grief distorted her face for a moment before she recovered. "But none of them were outright violent. At least, not that I know of."

"How about you?" I asked. "What's your social media life like?"

Her somber expression morphed lightning fast into the frowning expression of a person who has just learned that they failed a test. She stared at the table for what seemed like an eternity and then turned to me with an almost pleading look in her eyes.

"I tried. Taking the trips, wearing the clothes, posing for the photographer." She framed her face with her hands in a mock "A Star is Born" pose, à la Judy Garland in the old version. "Having fun, right? Not really." Amy sighed heavily. "Nothing I chose to wear, listen to, watch, do—none of it fit the program quite right. None of it was part of the . . ." she paused and wrinkled her nose before uttering the word "brand."

I nodded and tried to imagine living under such a microscope. Sounded like hell to me. "I take it you've pretty much called that stuff quits?"

For the first time, she smiled like she really meant it. "Absolutely. In fact, I have totally avoided social media for years."

Frankly, I couldn't blame her, but I had to ask, "So, no fear of missing out?" I hoped I didn't sound too sarcastic.

"Ha," she said in a soft voice. "Missing out on what?"

Excellent question.

CHAPTER SIXTEEN

Given that Amy had removed herself from her parents' social media circus, I wondered how much intel I could actually get from her. Of course, one never knows which random scrap of information might end up being useful. So I continued.

"In that case," I said. "I don't suppose you know much about their recent online activities. Or even their offline activities."

"Can't help you much there. Once I started college, I had no involvement at all with their business." Not a terribly helpful answer, but one with enough of a defensive edge to set off a silent alarm. *Careful*, I thought.

"Do you know why they wanted to hire a personal assistant?" I asked, hoping I wasn't pressing my luck.

Her mouth contorted into a knowing smirk, but her eyes radiated incredulity.

"Really?" Amy said. "Another one?"

I smelled blood. "How many have there been?"

She shook her head. "I've lost count. Some have been with them for years. Others couldn't put up with the . . . ." Her voice trailed off.

I considered what she was saying, not at all sure whether I should ask what she stopped short of telling me. "You make it sound like they had—"

"An entourage?" Amy cut me off. She laughed without mirth. "I'd call it a fleet, considering the number of assistants two people thought they needed."

So much for my impression of mouse-like shyness. This girl was opinionated. And not at all shy about expressing herself.

And since we were on the subject, I asked, "How closely did you work with their various assistants?" I scrambled for the exact question that I needed here. "How well did you get to know them?" I added, burying the question of how much their childhood had been like having a job.

Amy frowned. A moment passed. "I don't know about Jaden. My brother. But I didn't get very involved with them. Lupe was cool. She was our cleaning lady. And, of course, I got to know Sasha, and Ingrid, and Astrid."

Astrid Gunderson was the nanny Nick had interviewed. "And what did they do?" I asked, as if I didn't know or couldn't guess.

"They were in charge of the house. Looked after my brother and me when we were too young to live on our own while my parents did their thing."

All three were nannies then. I nodded and made a mental note.

"So, they were cool?" I asked.

"I had no problem with them. Jaden, though. Well, you'd have to talk to him about that."

Jaden was getting more interesting by the minute. So were the nannies.

"My parents have every right to do what they do, but that doesn't mean I want to join the family business," she said, her expression open. She looked straight at me. "I think what bothers me most are what people assume about me based on my parents' . . . occupation."

Was it my imagination or did she struggle to conjure up that last word? I was getting into some potentially sensitive areas here, so I needed to word my questions with the greatest of care.

"What assumptions are those?" I could easily imagine, but I didn't want to make any assumptions of my own.

"People who don't know me figure my life is perfect. That I can go anywhere and do anything, so I'm living the dream." Her face contorted briefly in an expression of combined ferocity and puzzlement but relaxed seconds later. "That makes it hard to actually reveal my true self to other people. It also makes it hard to figure out what I really want. I do know that I don't want to be an internet influencer. I don't like being scrutinized like a specimen under a microscope. But I am trying to figure out my purpose in life."

I nodded and let that sink in. "You did some traveling with your parents when you weren't in school, correct? Did you enjoy that?"

She nodded, but her expression radiated uncertainty. "I went to some really cool places, and I realize I was privileged to be able to do that. But after a while . . . people develop all these expectations . . . ." Her voice trailed off and, for the first time, the strain of her parents' death revealed itself. Amy blinked rapidly to hold back welling tears.

"Don't get me wrong." She choked up, but forced herself to speak. "Saying all this makes me sound ungrateful. It's hard to explain. I don't have the words."

God, I felt like a heel.

"How about your brother?" I said. "Are you guys close?" I had a million other things I wanted to know about their relationship, but peppering her with questions about her brother seemed more intrusive than necessary.

Amy reigned in her sorrow and became nearly stoic. "I think growing up together as the kids of famous-but-not-really people brought us together. But when Jaden turned 15, everything changed. While I was trying to adapt—to be more like the image my parents projected—he totally went out of his way to show everyone he wasn't part of it." She let out a sigh. "Unfortunately, we rarely talk now. I haven't heard a word from him about . . . this. And I'm trying to figure out what to do. How to handle this. It's just overwhelming."

Sensitive subject? I think I've poked that sore spot quite enough.

Switching gears again, I asked, "I'm sorry if this is difficult, but would you mind if we go over a few more details about who worked for your parents? Now and in the past." She seemed uncertain how to respond, until I added, "Focusing on the ones who left under less-than-ideal circumstances, if you know what I mean."

Amy then gave me a laundry list of assistants (mostly from the past and some barely remembered), including cooks, cleaning ladies, a personal trainer, a hairdresser, and two organizers her parents had hired and who either had been let go or quit. She also gave me the name of the Harcourts' first publicist plus the three nannies, two of whom had quit for "personal reasons" and one who'd been fired for reasons Amy could only guess.

My efforts may not have solved anything, but they certainly yielded more possible sources and entries on my flowchart.

CHAPTER SEVENTEEN

Before I finished up with Amy, she named a few more possible contacts, including a Mr. and Ms. Kincaid—James and Marie—a couple with whom the family socialized when they were at home. James and Marie lived down the street from the Harcourts. Amy also had an Aunt Joan on her mother's side, who had moved to New York City after graduating from high school. Her father's parents lived in Boca Raton, and her maternal grandfather had passed away two years ago, but his wife lived in a senior community in Towson. The flowchart would soon overflow at this rate.

In a (lame) attempt to keep the conversation light, I asked Amy about her studies. After telling me what I already knew about her major in English, she said she hoped to go into teaching. *The poor kid.*

I spent the rest of Sunday online, confirming the addresses for the Kincaids, and the aunt's residence on the Upper West Side of Manhattan. Nice digs, I'm sure. As for the grandparents, I opted for running by the Towson facility before making any sojourns to Florida. And, in case the front desk of the senior community gave me any problems, I would bring my clipboard and tell them I came to check out the fire exits or whatever. Or maybe I would sneak in a side door.

The following day, I contacted Ryan Douglas, the Harcourts' business manager. He was also a financial planner who had offices in Bethesda, at a high-dollar address on Wisconsin Avenue. His office suite probably cost the equivalent of a third-world country's economy.

Given the address and the circumstances, I decided to make an appointment to see Douglas rather than try to sweet talk or muscle my way past his secretary. The former was probably beyond my capabilities, while the latter would only lead to more trouble. Fortunately, the secretary was kind enough to squeeze me in right after lunch.

At 1255 hours (or five minutes to one, in civilian), I parked my car in the basement garage of the ten-story building. Before leaving the car, I devoured the remains of a donut I'd picked up on the way, then grinned at myself in the rear-view mirror, scanning for unsightly bits of pastry wedged between my teeth. Having passed inspection, I locked up and headed for a small bank of elevators, one of which took me to the top floor.

The elevator opened directly into the waiting room. I stepped into a sanctum filled with elegant furnishings. Sofas and overstuffed chairs in cozy groupings, each group arranged to create the illusion of intimacy. On one side, a floor-to-ceiling window afforded a panoramic view of commercial Bethesda. Beyond the plethora of living room furniture, there was a massive reception desk. A barely visible sliver of head poking above its surface suggested that there was a person back there.

I walked through the maze of conversation pits toward the desk. The head behind the desk popped up to reveal a young woman with an inquisitive expression.

"I'm Erica Jensen. I have a one o'clock appointment with Mr Douglas."

"Yes, of course." She perked up, her voice was welcoming if automated. "He has a rather full schedule, but he can see you shortly." She made a grand gesture toward the furniture showroom. "Have a seat. Would you like something to drink?"

"Coffee. Black, please." And the faster, the better.

After fifteen minutes, I was still sitting on a divan with cushions smooth as calf skin. I had grown bored after five minutes of reading Douglas's collection of crappy magazines. I stowed my cell phone because, frankly, being online or otherwise fiddling with tech stuff for work wears me out as it is. Say what you will about millennials. Not all of us are internet addicts. Thank you. I focused on my breathing, which was supposed to help calm me. Sometimes it did. Not this time. After another five minutes, I checked again with the receptionist.

"I'm sorry about the wait," she said, treating me to an orthodontist's dream of a smile. "He shouldn't be long."

And I shouldn't be addicted to opioids. But that's the way it is. "Okay," I said, doing my best to keep from snarling.

"More coffee?" she offered. Silly question.

Another twenty minutes crept by. I used the time to mentally run through my various options for next steps on this and other matters, scribbling possibilities into my small notebook. I also berated myself for not at least asking Amy if she had any pull with this guy. If I hadn't been so concerned about Nick, I would have written off the time and beat it out of there.

Miss Perky was almost on the verge of taking her third order for coffee when Douglas finally appeared. His clothes were as color-coordinated as his office furniture. He was a few inches taller than me, and his dark hair, cut short but still slightly wavy, was threaded with iron gray. The price for his dark blue silk suit would likely have paid several months of my rent.

"I'm sorry about the wait, Ms. Jenson." His gave me a brief, but warm handshake. "Got stuck on an endless conference call." He scrunched his nose in a weirdly prissy way. "Do come in." He led the way into a spacious corner office, featuring a blocky, modern-looking desk with a round table surrounded by cushy chairs off to one side. He continued to talk as we moved toward his desk. His voice was soothing, like smooth jazz. "I'm truly sorry about the wait. The whole morning's been nonstop calls and interruptions. Would you like more coffee?" he asked, in his flowing baritone.

"No, thank you." If I drank any more coffee, I would float right out of the office.

He waved his hand toward one of the guest chairs and sat behind his desk. "How can I help you?"

Let's just get to the point. "I assume the police have contacted you about the Harcourts?"

Douglas lowered his head and looked at me under furrowed brows and over steepled fingers. "Yes." He shook his head. "Terrible news."

"They were my clients, as well. Can you think of any reason why this would happen to them?"

Douglas gave me a steely look. "I've already spoken with the police, and I can't think of any good reason for this."

Or you don't want to tell me a thing. Or get involved. Instead of bashing down that barricade, I chose to edge in sideways. "Did you know that the Harcourts were hiring a personal assistant?"

Douglas nodded, but his eyes never left me. "They kept me informed on all financial matters."

Yet another non-answer. I should start a collection. "So you did know they were hiring someone?"

Douglas grunted what might have been assent.

"Is that a yes?" *I will get a straight answer out of you, if I have to reach down your throat and yank it out.*

He smiled without humor. "Yes, I knew."

I paused to consider my words before committing them to another question. *How can I word this in the most persuasive, least obnoxious way?*

"It seems they hired lots of help. Did they mention why they needed to hire an assistant?"

Douglas pressed his lips between his teeth and then blew out a breath.

"Look, the police know this, but . . . what's the harm if I tell you?" He stared at a spot on the wall, then shifted his gaze to me. "They didn't use the word 'assistant.' They told me they were hiring a bodyguard."

CHAPTER EIGHTEEN

Well, this was news.

"The Harcourts felt threatened?" I asked, although obviously they must have.

"I asked them about that." He dipped his head in a brief nod. "They claimed it was to maintain a sense of security. It was getting to the point where total strangers would accost them with a million questions. Walk right up to them and grill them on this or that."

"I see." The price of fame—internet or otherwise.

"But," he added, "they never mentioned a specific threat."

"And I assume you knew they hired me?" I turned the statement into a question, with the hope that it would avoid yet another evasive response.

"Of course," he said.

"I'm also assuming their kids inherit their assets?" Douglas seemed to warm up to statements phrased as questions.

"You'd have to ask their lawyer about that." I thought I saw a look of relief on his face. A financial planner with no clue about his clients' will? I held off on expressing my doubts.

I also sincerely doubted the Harcourts' attorney would give me the time of day. "Who is that?" I asked anyway.

"Aaron Gallagher of Gallagher and Bernson. I have a card." He grabbed the handle of the middle desk drawer to pull it open and produced a business card with a flourish.

The card was dark blue, high-quality stock, with silver lettering. I tucked it into my shoulder bag. I took a few more minutes to extract a bit more intel from Douglas, but I packed it in when I sensed I was digging a dry well. I stood up and so did he. "Thank you for your time," I said, shaking his hand again.

"It was nice to meet you," he said, smile fixed in place.

"Same here."

Always nice to end on a polite exchange of lies. I wondered if that was the only one he'd told me.

After I left the splendor of Douglas's office suite, my stomach grumbled with discontent at the measly half donut I had for lunch. I vaguely recalled a cute little deli located just off Wisconsin Avenue with a reputation for great sandwiches. After two days filled with dead bodies, police interrogations, and non-answers to my questions, I deserved a small reward.

Within minutes, I was seated at one of the deli's bistro-style tables, chowing down on a turkey club, crunchy with bacon and slathered with a spicy, slightly mustardy, spread—a sandwich to die for. After filling the void in my stomach with most of the sandwich, I retrieved my phone and placed a call to Nick. When he answered, I clued him in on the bits and pieces I had managed to discover.

"A bodyguard?" Nick sounded less surprised than thoughtful. "I hope the police know about this."

"Douglas said he mentioned it to the police." At least, that's what he claimed. "Speaking of which, have they been in touch with you?" I asked.

"Yeah. I'm meeting with them later today."

"That's good." And it was. If Sully's subtle suggestions about Nick's record were in any way seriously damning, wouldn't they have arrested him?

Nick coughed up a nervous laugh. "Should I bring a lawyer?"

That was a really good question, one I wished I could answer.

CHAPTER NINETEEN

After wrapping up my call with Nick, I finished my sandwich and pulled out my writing pad and pen to record what I'd learned from Douglas. I scribbled a few notes on my diagram of the players, trying to imagine connections, motives, possible secrets . . . anything that could lead to the next profitable clue.

As worried as I was about Nick, thoughts about the weird timing of the Harcourts' murder gnawed at the edges of my subconscious. The medical examiner could only guesstimate the time of their death, something like 1 to 3 hours before I found the bodies. Which made for a rather curious window of time between Marian's phone call and my arrival at the house. It was conceivable (if unlikely) that someone had beaten and butchered the Harcourts after Marian called me. But that could be a mighty small window of time compared to the one before the phone call.

What better way to escape detection than to make it look like someone else did the deed? Someone like, say, an opioid-addicted Marine with PTSD and a resulting bad attitude? But surely no one connected with the Harcourts knew about my problems. I know Nick would not have told them. Despite the comfortable temperature in the deli, I shivered. Surely, the police would not seriously consider me a suspect. Wouldn't they need a little bit more than bad timing? I had to believe that they did. Otherwise, I would end up being a paranoid wreck.

Finished with lunch, I returned to my car and, if only to preserve my sanity, set aside the Harcourt matter in favor of pursuing Troy Fairchild, Bail Skipper. A quick shuffle through the mishmash of receipts turned up little of interest. Many of them were old, and I doubted that anyone at CVS would remember Troy because he bought a toothbrush there. However, there was one exception. A recent receipt for a place called The Void. I did a quick search on my phone, using precious minutes of data to discover that the place was a titty bar.

I thought about paying a visit to The Void, wondering exactly what sort of hours they kept. Surely they'd cater to the lunchtime crowd. After all, lust operates around the clock. I started the car and aimed north, away from Bethesda and across the proverbial tracks.

My trip took me to a mixed office/light industrial neighborhood in Baltimore County. Moving from the posh trappings of lower Montgomery County to the seeming miles of low-slung brick buildings that stretched across this particular piece of real estate felt a bit surreal.

As I pulled into the cracked macadam lot surrounding The Void, my first thought was that the place was well-named. Essentially, the building was a concrete box. I assumed that it might originally have been white but was now dulled by layers of road grit. Or someone had come up with a new paint color—dingy.

A sprinkling of vehicles dotted the lot around the building. I backed into a spot, left the car, and quickly scanned the area.

Two vehicles, a maroon Buick, maybe ten years old, and a rust-orange pickup truck, quite well used, were parked in the rear of the lot. I assumed anyone parked in back would probably be an employee. But then again, maybe not. On a hunch, I moved toward the back, on the lookout for possible threats.

A sudden gust of wind kicked up and I hugged myself for warmth. The breeze sent a hodge-podge of debris flying across my path. Paper cups, cigarette packages, and take-out bags danced to the arrhythmic thump of bass emanating from the concrete box. Like being on the set of the world's crappiest music video.

Once I had made my way to the rear of the parking lot, I snapped photos of each vehicle and its license plate. As I stowed the phone and moved toward the front door, the faint sound of a distant siren pierced the dull thumping coming from the building. I could see my shadow moving across the wall as I walked. Another shadow appeared behind mine, moving in fast and silent.

I let the shadow catch up, planted my right foot to pivot, and delivered a roundhouse kick to the owner's groin. Unfortunately, I failed to connect clean. So while that move brought the man down in a kind of semi-controlled squat, it only bought me a half-second before he lunged at me like a puma.

He caught both my hands in a steely grip, to keep me from raking his eyes. I was focused on snapping his knee when someone must've come up behind me. The next thing I knew, it was lights out.

CHAPTER TWENTY

A timeless period passed where my consciousness was in a big black hole. The darkness reddened. *Light*, I thought. *My eyelids are closed.* A slight bounce and side-to-side movement beneath me. *I'm on my back.* Another shudder. *I'm in a moving vehicle.* A wave of pain burst in the back of my skull. I thought about opening my eyes—and also considered keeping them closed for a very long time. Maybe a few years. A rattling sound on my left made me curious enough to risk a peek toward the noise. A uniformed guy around my age sat on a small bench, fiddling with the contents of what looked like a drug kit. So I was in an ambulance. The question was, how did I get here?

I tried to gather my thoughts, but they refused to cooperate, floating through my mind like dandelion seeds on the wind. I considered asking my uniformed friend what he knew about me, but the thought of uttering a full sentence was exhausting. Then I remembered the parking lot. Troy Fairchild. My notes. My phone. My car. My eyes snapped open.

"Hey," Uniform Guy said, his voice low and soothing. "How do you feel?"

I grunted. "Like I was hit on the head and left in a parking lot."

Uniform Guy nodded. "Someone called it in as a passed out drunk." He gave me a sharp look. "I don't smell booze on your breath."

"It's a bit early for me." Even now, I tried to mine some humor from my bizarre situation. When it comes to alcohol, it's always too early. I quit drinking after coming back from my last tour and being groped in a bar by some handsy dipshit. I was trashed and didn't think twice before giving him a broken nose.

"Did you find a purse?" I asked, putting every effort toward attempting a coherent conversation, because I was too curious not to ask.

"This it?" he said. He raised his hand with my shoulder bag in it.

"Oh, thank God," I said. "Do me a favor. See if my phone's in there." He rummaged through the contents and nodded a "yes." With that, I relaxed on the stretcher, shut my eyes, and feigned unconsciousness, until it actually came again.

By the time I awoke, they had checked me in and moved me to a hospital bed. I blinked and did a quick visual survey of the room. The pale blue walls had turned grayish as the day's fading light filtered in through half-drawn Venetian blinds.

"Erica?" A woman's voice—a familiar one that I didn't want to hear. So I pretended not to. I let my eyes close again. A stretch of time passed, and I used it to suss out what had happened. I had gone to The Void to find out what I could about Troy Fairchild, only to—what?—be mugged? I still had all my stuff, so no. Walk into an ambush? Why? Or was it simply a random attack? Bad luck? All this thinking simply made the headache I already had much worse.

When a nurse came in to check my vitals, I forced my eyes open. I knew it was only a matter of time before I would have to deal with yet another headache. My mother.

CHAPTER TWENTY-ONE

The nurse assured me that I'd suffered only a mild concussion, but not quite mild enough to keep them from wanting to hold me for 24 hours. My mother must have given the go-ahead on that while I was out cold.

I silently berated myself for not replacing her name in my emergency contacts with Nick's or anyone else's. A few years had passed since we had even been in the same room. As always, Mother was dressed as if she were about to board the QE2 and have tea with the captain. I noted with mild astonishment that she had changed her hairstyle. She wore it a touch longer and closer to this century.

"What about after she's released?" my mother pressed the nurse. "Shouldn't she stay with someone?"

"The doctor will be with you in a few minutes," the nurse told my mother. "She'll give you more specific instructions."

"Hi," I said. The two of them turned toward me, and I waved. "Patient here. Alert and awake." *Ignore my mother*, I wanted to add. I knew what she was aiming for. Staying with my parents. So not an option.

My mother put on her patented tragic expression. "I'm just trying to help," she said, her tone bordering on outright weeping.

"I should go. The doctor will be here soon," the nurse said hurriedly as she rushed out of the room.

My mother scowled. Her voice went from Hallmark Movie Mom to drill sergeant. "Erica Lee. I swear to God, you're going to be the death of me. Can't you at least settle down and get a normal job? Work in an office? Get a decent haircut?"

I tried not to grit my teeth. My mother's voice all by itself was enough to mess with my head.

"I tried that, Mother. Remember how well that worked out?" It hadn't, of course. "Or don't you remember?" I matched her drill sergeant rant with all the sarcasm I could muster.

My mother shook her head. "I realize this is a difficult situation for you, Erica. For all of us. But this is your health we're talking about."

"Exactly. My health. My decisions." My head throbbed again, so I took a deep breath. And then another. "You forget that I've been through worse. And besides, it's not like I don't have friends." Not many, but at least a few.

Her stern look softened a bit. I almost felt sorry for her, but given her penchant for emotionally manipulating me, that was asking a lot.

"I gave up my mani-pedi for this," she moaned. I swear she sounded like her best friend had died. We might not have talked in a while, but I could still read my mother like a book.

There were three short raps on the door, and a woman in a white coat stepped into the room. The doctor was petite and small-boned, with dark hair cropped short, a milk chocolate complexion, and a purposeful look on her face. She glanced at her clipboard as she came toward me.

"Ms. Jensen. Erica?" She looked up from her clipboard and said, "I'm Dr. Sharma. How are you feeling?"

"Not bad, considering," I lied. The headache I had when I came in was gone, but my mother was giving me a new one.

"Could you do me a big favor?"

Dr. Sharma cocked her head. "Perhaps, depending . . . ."

I nodded toward my mother. "Get that woman the hell out of this room," I said, managing not to scream.

With a bit of persuasion from Dr. Sharma (and help from hospital security), Mommy Dearest left the room. Without the aggravation caused by her mere presence, I started to feel better right away.

The doctor did a basic examination. Asking what year it was, testing my reflexes, checking my orientation in all spheres, the usual head injury drill. I'm pretty sure I passed.

"We were a bit concerned given the reasons for your military discharge," Dr. Sharma confided. "But you seem to be doing well enough that an overnight stay should be sufficient."

"I'm feeling a lot better. Really." Given how bad I'd felt earlier, that wasn't saying much.

The doctor grinned. Her teeth were blinding white, but her brown eyes were soft. "Very good. I'll be by tomorrow morning." Before she turned to leave the room, her smile faded into the neutral expression of a professional.

Alone at last. Just then, it occurred to me that the room was a single. Mother had probably seen to that. I didn't bother to think anything more about it. I was too busy wondering how Nick had fared in his talk with the police.

CHAPTER TWENTY-TWO

After I recovered enough to consider Nick's situation, I checked
with a nurse to make sure my gear was stowed, so to speak. The
smiling Hispanic woman assured me they had locked my
valuables in a cabinet tucked beneath the small bedside table.
She demonstrated this by producing a small key and using it to
open the cabinet door. She pulled out my shoulder bag and
lifted it for me to see, still smiling.

"Could you hand that to me, please?" I asked.

The nurse complied. She also handed me the key and then
went on her way.

The first thing I did was dig out my phone. And of course it
was dead. But I could use the bedside phone. When I picked up
the receiver, Nick's phone number failed to come to mind. Try
as I might, I couldn't recall it. Damn! My smartphone was
making me dumb. So any intel from Nick's meeting with the
cops would have to come out later.

The next day, I awaited word from the doctor regarding my
official discharge from the hospital, a stay I could ill afford. I

was hoping (but not quite sure) that it would be covered by insurance.

In the interim, I received a visit from a man I didn't recognize. I guessed his age to be pushing 40. He wore "day off" casual clothes, but his manner was all business. After knocking and entering, he approached my bed. The moment he stepped in the door, I could feel his gray-green eyes assessing me.

Before I could ask who he was, he said, "Ms. Jensen, my name is Parker Adams. I saw what happened to you, so I know why you ended up here."

The details of the attack on me were a blur when I first regained consciousness, but with each passing hour of being awake, they sharpened into focus.

"Did you see the person who did this?"

Adams nodded. He moved as fluidly as a cat toward a nearby chair. He settled onto the edge of the seat and, elbows propped on knees, leaned forward, tensed as though he might spring to his feet any moment.

"I know the guy who did it," he said. "I can't go into why. But I can tell you that you chose a bad place to take photos of license plates."

I thought about that for a few seconds. "You a private eye?"

Adams just looked at me.

"Are you?" I asked.

"Could be."

We could do this all day. "Just don't tell me I was conked on the head because some dude was afraid his wife or girlfriend would find out he went to that club."

He smiled, but the smile disappeared as quickly as it came. "With all due respect, ma'am, I wouldn't have come here if my knowledge of The Void were about such frivolous matters."

"So what's this all about?" Whatever the guy had come to tell me, it was already making my head hurt. Adams looked at me with the unfocused, yet penetrating, manner of someone who's seen combat. You may have heard of the thousand-yard stare.

"There are . . . things so terrible, it's hard to imagine. Humans are capable of such atrocities and violations of other people's rights."

He paused. So far, I hadn't heard anything new. I was on the verge of telling him to get to the damn point when he resumed his soliloquy.

"I know a few things." Adams seemed to be looking right through me, and he remained silent for a time. Then his eyes snapped back into focus. "I checked your military record, so I know that you're a Marine and I know about your medical discharge. I know that you handle . . . research," he said with a very slight smile. "Under normal circumstances, we wouldn't be having this conversation, but given what you do, it seemed like a good idea to give you a heads up that you should probably stay clear of The Void."

"What's going on in there?" I asked.

"I can't go into specifics," he said. "I'm sorry."

I tried to think through the possibilities, but my mind was still a bit foggy. "Do you mean, like, organized crime? And how do you know so much about me?"

Adams continued to scrutinize me. "As to the first, maybe. As to the second, I have sources."

He shrugged. "I wanted to let you know what happened. I tend bar there, part time. And I keep my eyes and ears open, fortunately for you.

"I got a little suspicious when two people of interest decided to have an impromptu meeting in the parking lot. I was stuck making a drink but followed them out as soon as I could. By that time, they had disappeared, but I saw you snapping pics. I figured the two guys had taken off. But as I headed back inside, I heard the scuffle and turned back—to see them attacking you."

I managed a weak smile. "Timing is everything, huh?"

"They were in the midst of learning that your phone was password-protected when I broke up the party. But I came here today to make sure that we don't trip over each other. Besides, you don't want to get caught up in this."

I wondered what "this" was, but I knew better than to ask. "So you called for an ambulance, like any good citizen would," I said.

The quirky grin returned. "Right."

I didn't quite know what to say. "Could you have stopped them?" came to mind, but I decided against it. "Thank you," I said, wondering what I was thanking him for.

CHAPTER TWENTY-THREE

Adams swung a foot up on one knee with the grace of a dancer. A move so sinuous I thought he might then wrap his leg behind his neck.

"That's my story," he said. "What's yours?"

"Looking for a guy who skipped bail—Troy Fairchild. Ever heard of him?"

Adams shook his head. "Must be small time. I'm assuming he's not involved in anything I'd know about."

Delgado had given me a photo of Troy. It was in my file which, to the best of my knowledge, was still in my car.

"Could you do me a favor?" I asked. "When I get out of here, can I keep in touch with you? And if you could take a look at Troy's mug shot to see if you recognize him, I'd appreciate it."

Mr. Yoga Stretch gave me a decisive nod. "Sure." He put both feet on the floor and stood up, moving like he was made of elastic. As he rose, he retrieved a card holder from his pants pocket. And plucking a business card from his stash, he handed it to me. Printed on it in simple black type was his name and a phone number, nothing more. "Call me anytime."

After being cleared to leave the hospital, I called a taxi to take me back to my car. During the ride, I thought about Nick. But my head still throbbed, and the thought of describing where I'd been, what had happened to me, and why was overwhelming. Of course, I still needed to charge my phone. I could have asked the taxi driver to charge my phone, but it didn't seem right to deal with all this in the back of a stranger's car. Especially since I still didn't know how Nick's interview with the homicide detectives had gone.

I kept thinking about my meeting with the flexible Mr. Adams. Although he had told me "his story," he hadn't told me much. If he were a private investigator, that would explain his interest in me. Because his business card revealed only his name and phone number, he could easily run off cards like that and be whatever he wanted to be. Including a private eye. Was his name really Parker Adams? My head was still pounding, and I tried to quiet my mind as we made our way to my car.

To say I was somewhat relieved to find my Fiesta still parked where I left it with no visible signs of damage is a major understatement. I paid the driver, making sure to add a good tip, because he looked a little nervous as we drove through a neighborhood that could kindly be described as plain (not so kindly as "industrial wasteland"). Before he left, I asked the driver to wait until I started my car. From his response, you'd have thought I had asked him to clean a cesspool. I offered him an extra twenty.

"Fifty bucks," he said.

"Never mind."

As I got out, he gave me a look of combined disbelief and disgust at my stingy behavior before driving off. *Have a nice day*, I thought. *And fuck you.*

As it had when I left it, my car looked isolated and vulnerable with few others nearby. I speed-walked across the decaying lot, senses on high alert, eyes searching for any sign of trouble.

I got into my car and immediately checked the doors. Locked. Were the windows shut tight? They were. The margin of safety was too thin, so I hurried to get out of there. Adams had told me just enough to clue me in that this place was not cool, but not nearly enough to understand exactly how uncool. I might be a trained killer, but why take chances?

My relief as I drove away was palpable. I don't mind telling you that I took one or two good, deep breaths to steady myself. However, that feeling of relief evaporated instantly when I remembered I still needed to find Troy Fairchild, the reason I'd gone to that shithole to begin with. I needed to ferret out some new leads, because even if Adams was willing to help me, I couldn't rely entirely on his good graces.

I also had to charge my phone. As soon as freaking possible. So I pulled over to the curb in front of a warehouse big enough to house several football fields, extracted the phone from my shoulder bag, and connected it to the charger on the dash. Thus reassured that I could connect with the rest of the world, I continued out of the crap neighborhood.

Once I found my way into a halfway decent area (at least on the surface), I pulled up to the curb and parked beside a small playground. By this time, my phone was charged enough to work, so I called Nick. While waiting for him to answer, I watched the prekindergarten-age kids clamber over jungle gyms, slides, and swings, all specially designed to protect them from harm. I wondered how many of the adults on the playground were pedophiles.

Nick's phone rang three times, then went to voice mail. *Damn.* In the hope that it just wasn't a good time for Nick to take a phone call, I sent him a text: *RU OK?*

As I waited for a reply, I watched the children play. I thought about turning the radio on, but opted instead for their laughter and squeals of delight. Ten minutes passed. Then fifteen. Nothing. Mentally shouting down all the dire speculations about Nick being arrested, I fired up the car, switched on the radio, and drove away.

CHAPTER TWENTY-FOUR

In my rush to escape the charming atmosphere of The Void, I had made a hasty exit from that neighborhood and drove into one that was unfamiliar. I pulled over again to consult Waze on my phone. I enlarged and shrank the image this way and that, and after sufficient squinting, managed to find a back way to I-95. I knew I was in Baltimore County, so I'd go south on the interstate. Now, if I only knew what day it was. That answer was on my phone, too. Oddly, the radio beat the phone to it, when the DJ announced that it was Two-fer Tuesday.

I cracked open my windows again. I needed the air. I tried to plan my next steps while weaving my way through the back streets. If it was Tuesday, 72 hours had passed since I discovered the Harcourts. Was the autopsy report done? What had forensics found? For all I knew, they might have caught a suspect while I was cooped up in the hospital. And why was Nick unreachable?

Which reminded me. I needed to make sure to identify Nick as an emergency contact on my phone. That was the last time I wanted to wake up anywhere to the sound of my mother's voice.

As I sped down I-95, my cell phone dinged an incoming message. I glanced at the phone and saw that it was a text message from Nick. With nothing but guardrail to my left, I resisted the urge to swerve across three lanes of traffic to pull over and read it. I don't text and drive. It's illegal, and it's crazy anyway. So I took my time making my way toward the right lane and into a visitor center lot where I could stop and read the message. Just knowing that Nick responded inspired me to do the rational thing.

Once I had backed the car into an out-of-the-way spot, I grabbed the phone. Nick had texted: *I'm fine. Slept really late. Talk later?* I had so many questions—some with potentially complicated answers. In short, this was important enough to merit a real conversation, instead of a frantic exchange of terse, digital phrases. So I texted back: *K.* And did my best to avoid anticipating the worst.

As I headed toward home, I mentally shuffled through all the variables that had emerged from my inquiries. My talk with Amy had produced a wealth of information, maybe even an overabundance. Which did nothing to get rid of that pounding inside my skull.

Dr. Sharma had prescribed rest, but that wasn't in the cards. As far as pain went, my options were limited to over-the-counter or registering for medicinal cannabis. I had been putting off that last one, even though it was legal in Maryland. I wished the feds would follow suit. And I had too much to do, too much at stake to simply take two weeks off. Besides, lying around bores me silly. Work is my best therapy, as long as I pace myself.

Once I got home, it might make sense for me to sit down and list the names Amy had given me, organizing them as I went and performing a bit of triage on the results.

In the meantime, I zoomed down I-95, listening to an old tune by Simple Minds. In the interest of not getting a speeding ticket, something I couldn't afford in any sense of that word, I kept to the right lane. Cars passed me, some of them like I was standing still. *Morons.*

But I let go of that thought a nanosecond later, choosing instead to focus on the music and the feel of cool air on my face. I tried to set aside all thoughts of the Harcourts' murder, Nick's talk with the police, Troy Fairchild, the elastic Mr. Adams, my various aches and pains, and instead, speculate about what might be in store for me.

CHAPTER TWENTY-FIVE

I arrived at my apartment to the welcome sight of my newspaper, tossed up against the door. I opened the door, lined up the shot, then kicked it inside as though it were a misshaped soccer ball. Damn thing flew nearly halfway across the one-room studio, and in a straight line. *New career option?* I grinned at the thought. *Yeah, right.*

My first order of business was to eat something. The hospital food was surprisingly good, what I'd had of it. And it's not as if they had starved me. I just felt the need for some good old comfort food, something to keep me going.

Since I didn't have a handy master chef to whip up an award-winning omelet or anything that might involve using a recipe, I settled on heating up a big bowl of clam chowder in the microwave. While the soup was heating, I heard a faint scratching at the window that made me jump. When I looked, all I saw was a black squirrel. I went limp with relief and felt a little ridiculous. That recent blow to the head had done nothing to help relieve my PTSD. And I knew that squirrel.

"Hey, Rocky," I said. "Want a peanut?"

Rocky's bright, inquisitive eyes seemed to acquire additional sparkle, and he sat more upright as I reached inside a cabinet for the jar of unsalted peanuts. I twisted off the lid and opened the window. A chilly breeze blew in, but I doubted that any waste of energy due to my animal feeding ritual would make a dent in climate change. I quickly poured out a small pile of peanuts for Rocky, and he made no pretense of not wanting them. Even before I withdrew my hand and had closed the sliding screen and window, Rocky pounced as if he hadn't eaten in weeks and scarfed down half the pile of nuts in record time.

"It's not that bad out there, is it pal?" I muttered.

Rocky paused as if he'd heard me. He cocked his head my way, then turned back to the peanuts. Except that he began stuffing them in his cheeks.

"Okay," I said. "Good move." I laughed despite the weirdness of giving life advice to a squirrel.

I knew I should probably take it easy, but that so went against my nature. Instead, I did a few yoga stretches and ten minutes of meditation. That would have to do for now.

Then I turned my attention to who might have murdered the Harcourts. I now had a long list of possibilities. But first, I would have to do some triage and narrow down the list in terms of likelihood or importance as best I could with what little I knew.

In many cases, all I had was a first name and a position. Not overwhelmingly helpful. But I had noted a few things Amy mentioned. For instance, of the two cleaning ladies, Marta and Lupe, she recalled that Lupe's last name was Steinberg. Amy noted that Lupe's first name and occasional use of Spanish were an intriguing contrast to her Jewish surname. Apparently, Lupe reciprocated Amy's interest in her and had been something of an adult friend to her.

The three nannies also stood out, in that some of Amy's most vivid recollections were about them. She easily remembered the names: Astrid Gunderson, Ingrid Swenson, and Sasha Krikorian. As Amy recalled, Ingrid was the quiet one, Sasha was the strict one, and Astrid was the coolest one—and their last one.

CHAPTER TWENTY-SIX

Of all the hired help, those four—Lupe, Sasha, Ingrid, and Astrid—had for various reasons been the most memorable. At least for Amy. And that was enough to move them to the head of the list for now.

I set the rest aside for the moment, with every intention of returning to them if I wanted to. This (unpaid) investigation was starting to feel like too much to handle. Don't quit before you've tried, Marine. And don't forget—there is no try.

So I started with a basic internet search on their names, looking for social media accounts or other signs of an online presence. Of the four, only Lupe, the friendly cleaning lady, and Astrid, their last nanny, had social media accounts. Both were on LinkedIn. Not one sign of a Facebook or Twitter account. But that was understandable. Maybe working for the Harcourts had dampened any desire they might have had to participate on any social media sites.

Astrid's LinkedIn profile showed her location as Reston, Virginia. Lupe Steinberg was in Gaithersburg, Maryland, a much closer, less annoying drive. Which one to contact first was an easy call, but I still needed an address.

I used the most economical databases I could to do a slightly more targeted search that would also reveal last known addresses. I focused my search on the Baltimore-Washington Metro Area, which includes Maryland, D.C., and Virginia. At some point, it might even include West Virginia and southern Pennsylvania, but we weren't there yet.

I found addresses plus cell phone numbers for only two of the four. Someone's full name could lead you to all sorts of information these days. As to accuracy, that was still to be determined.

With little hope of actually meeting either of the remaining two, I broadened the search to include the entire United States. Ingrid lived in Pittsburgh, and Sasha must have moved, because she lived in California, and at the time of her hire, the world was a lot less virtual.

As I revised the notes on my flowchart, my cell phone sprang to life with Bikini Kill's "Rebel Girl," my ringtone of choice for the month. To my relief, the caller ID revealed that it was Nick.

I grabbed the phone. "Hey, Nick. How'd it go?" *Just tell me the cops are off our backs.*

There was a short silence before I heard Nick say, "Not too bad."

His failure to elaborate irked me, but I suppressed the urge to snap at him. "So what did they ask you?"

After a small eternity, he said, "Just, you know, about my relationship with the Harcourts. Where I was at the time of the murder. Things like that."

As we spoke, I periodically chewed my lower lip. Something was off. Nick wasn't telling me everything, which didn't help to calm my sense of increasing anxiety.

"What else? Because I know there's more," I said, suppressing the urge to shout. "What aren't you telling me, Nick?"

He swallowed loudly enough to be heard at my end. "Mind if I come over to talk about this?"

Are you for real? I pondered either yelling no or disconnecting. But that would just be childish and stupid. I slowly inhaled a lungful of air and then blew it out in a rush.

"Before I agree to that, can you at least give me a hint?"

"Fair enough," he said. "Even though I'm not a prime suspect, I get the feeling I'm not quite off the hook yet. But I get a worse feeling that they might be more interested in you."

CHAPTER TWENTY-SEVEN

I decided to hold my questions for Nick until he arrived. Frankly, I found the situation to be stress-inducing beyond words. What motive would I possibly have for committing such a brutal act? On my own clients? Was all of this because of the timing of that goddamn phone call?

I got up and paced like a caged lion from the tiny kitchen area to the tiny sleeping area and back. There must be an explanation because I knew I was innocent, and I intended to prove it—beyond any doubt. I forced myself to stop and simply stare out the window. I needed some proof soon, before I wore a trench into the floor.

When Nick arrived, my first words were, "Just what the fuck is going on, dude?" He didn't even flinch. He knew me well enough to expect my greeting would be something less than gracious.

We stood in silence for a few seconds, way too long at any rate. Nick finally cracked a slight grin. "May I come in?"

Exasperated and embarrassed by my initial outburst, my cheeks warmed despite my attempt to hide my feelings. "Of course," I said, tossing my hand in the general direction of "inside."

Once we had settled in with two mugs of coffee, Nick said, "I think there are a couple things that have raised the detectives' interest. One is Marian Harcourt's phone call and the other is the time of death."

"Yeah, no shit," I said.

Nick seemed to consider his next words. "The other thing that struck me, other than the way they kept asking questions about you, was the type of questions they asked. How much detail did you give them about your actions that morning?"

I tried to think back. "Pretty much the bare bones."

"Did you walk up to the house, then go back to the car to get gloves?"

"Well, yeah. The door was open. I was worried. Turned out I was right to be."

"Did you tell the cops about that?"

What had I said exactly? Had I mentioned the gloves?

"You think someone saw me," I said.

Nick nodded. "They didn't say it outright, but I got that impression."

I shook my head. "Do you know how easy it would be for a decent lawyer to cast doubt on a witness like that? People usually fail to recall little details or remember them wrong because they don't pay close attention."

"Perhaps it was a neighbor," Nick mused. "Someone who might have noticed you because you weren't normally in that neighborhood."

"Or had ever been there before," I said. "And I'm still dying to hear what the cops think my motive was."

The look on Nick's face was one of mild shock. Okay, maybe my word choice wasn't that great. His gaze drifted past me and he said, "Seriously, Erica?"

I must have given him a look of desperation, because he quickly added, "I'm not being judgy here. Look at it from their point of view. Given your history, given all the circumstances, would it be right for them as investigators to simply rule you out now?"

CHAPTER TWENTY-EIGHT

Nick must have asked me if I was going to be okay at least twenty times before he left. I assured him each time that I had no intention of overdosing or blowing my brains out over the situation. As aggravating (and potentially perilous) as it was for me, it only redoubled my resolve to find the actual perpetrator or at least prove that I did nothing but report a crime.

Rather than stewing over what seemed like rather threadbare evidence against me, I turned my attention back to my lists of names from the Harcourt retinue. Perhaps one of them could tell me about the neighbors.

I checked the time. It was nearly half-past three. I could try for some face-to-face-time with either Astrid in Reston or Lupe in Gaithersburg. From a traffic perspective, both locations sucked. They are popular bedroom communities and, given the D.C. area's employers, schedules, and commuting patterns, rush hour can start as early as three in the afternoon and end well after sundown.

Approaching potential witnesses and suspects cold is my preference, but in this case, there were a couple of reasons to call ahead: the first was to make sure they still lived at the address and the second was frigging gridlock. Along with the Gaithersburg address, I had a phone number for Lupe Steinberg. I scribbled a few points on a writing pad that I wanted to cover in case she felt like talking.

The woman who answered the phone sounded like a Sunday school teacher. Or at least the way I imagined one would sound. The undercurrent of optimism in her voice wasn't really saccharine nor was it blissful ignorance. How I picked this up from the first two words she spoke—"Steinberg residence"—I have no clue. Maybe it was something in the pitch of her voice or the cadence.

"May I please speak with Lupe?"

"Who shall I say is calling, please?" Cheerful, but formal. A hint of starch crept into her delivery.

Since the cops were apparently obsessed with me, it seemed wise to take the lie-free approach. "My name is Erica Jensen. I used to work for the Harcourts and I need to speak to someone who's worked for them before."

"I see." She dialed down her upbeat tone just a notch, but it hadn't vanished. "May I ask why?"

I paused before answering. "It's a bit complicated. I was hoping to meet with her." I also had the distinct feeling that I might already be talking to her, but she wasn't quite ready to admit that.

A brief silence. I wondered if the line had died. "Is this concerning their . . . ?" Her voice trailed off, as if uttering the word "murder" would destroy her happy world.

"Before I answer that, may I ask who I'm talking to?" *You want formal, lady? You got it.*

"I'm Lupe's sister, Amara." Her cheerful voice held a hint of concern.

"Then I can understand your being protective of her," I said. "I assume the police have questioned her?"

"No," she said. "We read about it in the paper."

Fantastic. I don't watch many cop shows, but when I do, they always have that big whiteboard, with all the witnesses and suspects rendered in photos or drawings, lines connecting each to the other. I wondered if all police departments really did keep such a flowchart and if it was anywhere near as crammed with lines and images as mine.

"I'll be honest." The words slipped out even though I hate them because every time I hear them, it trips my bullshit meter. "I'm right in the thick of things. These people were my clients. And I'm the one who discovered them. If I managed to track you down, but the police haven't . . . well, they should have contacted you. Someone needs to make sure that the police don't rush to judgment. I was hoping that Lupe had noticed something that could shed light on the matter."

The line resonated with a sympathetic "hmm." "Okay, but I need to check with her first. Be back in a moment." I heard a faint click as she put the receiver down.

While Amara went to check with Lupe, I thought about Lupe's circumstances—and her sister's. This raised enough questions that I spent the entire wait time furiously scribbling them in my little notebook.

CHAPTER TWENTY-NINE

When Amara finally brought Lupe to the phone, she seemed amenable to meeting me halfway. The optimistic lilt in Lupe's voice matched Amara's. Perhaps it was a genetic trait.

"There's a cute little place I've heard about, just off Georgia Avenue in Silver Spring," she said. The name she gave me rang a bell. "I'd love to give it a try. We could meet for coffee at, say, eleven?"

"Works for me," I said. "You sure you don't mind making the drive? The parking around there can be . . . ." I left out all the pertinent expletives.

"No worries. I've been meaning to go there anyway to check out the old neighborhood."

The following morning at ten to eleven, I entered Perk Central, glad that I had added 30 minutes to my ETA, most of which was consumed in finding a place to park. After Lupe and I had finished our conversation, I realized the coffee shop's name was the one from *Friends*.

I saw no sign of Joey, Chandler, or Ross. Nor did I see Rachel, Monica, or . . . what was her name, the goofy one?

Phoebe! The six pals were not scrunched together on a couch in some kind of alternate-reality version of New York where twenty-somethings have enough time and money to hang out and trade jokes with each other endlessly.

However, the decor suggested that the owner might have purchased the show's set from the studio. Was this supposed to create the illusion that we were equally cool and funny?

Along with the (apparently) obligatory sofa-dominated conversation pit, small round table-and-chair sets dotted the seating area. About half were taken by people on laptops or tablets. Or scrolling through their phones. I noticed one woman reading an actual hardcover book. I suppressed the urge to run over to her and congratulate her and throw my arms around her or do anything equally weird in favor of placing an order for a cappuccino and staking out a spot with a clear view of the front door.

At 11:00 AM, on the dot, a petite woman wearing yoga pants and a loose-fitting, long-sleeved T-shirt entered and looked around. *Lupe Steinberg?* From a distance, she appeared to be in her mid to late 40s, blonde hair tucked up into a loose top-knot. Okay then. Name: mixed ethnicities. Appearance: all WASP.

I raised my hand like a kid in school. *Yes, hello. Present.* That caught her eye. She smiled and approached the table. As she got closer, I stood up. We did a standard "you must be" name exchange and extended our hands to shake. Lupe's handshake had a comforting firmness and a certainty to match her optimism.

We quickly exchanged introductions. So, yes, this was Lupe. And now that she was closer, I upped my estimate on her age a bit. The worry lines about the eyes, the parenthetical creases around her lips were a touch beyond faint. Plus the blond hair was run through with nearly imperceptible strands of gray.

After Lupe bought her own coffee plus a muffin the size of a small melon, we sat together. She offered to split the muffin and pushed the plate my way. I thanked her and tore a small chunk off the side. Lupe picked up a plastic knife and sawed the thing in half, then set the dish right between us.

"I really appreciate your coming here to meet me," I said. Despite having mentally practiced meeting this woman, I still struggled for just the right words to ask her about Amy Harcourt and her dead parents.

She flashed a bright smile at me. "No problem. I really did have plans to visit this area." Lupe waved an arm, raising a merry jingle from the silver bangles she was wearing. Then her expression turned serious. "I was just crushed to hear about the Harcourts."

"When did you last work for them?"

She squinted, thoughtful. "My goodness. It's been nine or ten years since I sold my cleaning service." A woman-owned business. Cool. I hoped to be able to retire from one of those—someday.

"How long did you work for the Harcourts?

"About two years." She squinted. "Two years and three months."

"What were they like?" I asked.

"Very nice."

I waited for her to offer more, but the only thing she offered was another smile. No teeth this time.

I swallowed hard to keep from laughing before I asked, "Could you expand on that just a bit?"

Lupe straightened in her seat. Had my question taken her by surprise? Or was it merely that, like me, she suffered a bad back?

"I only meant that they were very nice to have as clients," she said. "Very reasonable. Generous, even," she added, rattling her bracelets some more.

I cringed inwardly at her response. Were Lupe's impressions going to be unvarnished or candy-coated? Was Lupe holding back out of fear of speaking ill of the dead?

"Did you get to know them on a more casual basis?" Something between a mere business arrangement and out-and-out BFFs. "I mean, as more than just clients." Which I'm assuming is perfectly fine. Certainly not forbidden by law or the Cleaning Ladies' Code of Ethics.

She nodded and seemed to steel herself. "When I was going through my divorce, they were kind enough to have me over for dinner now and then." This time her smile was wistful, eyes glistening. "It was a tough time, and they were there for me."

This was a side of the Harcourts I hadn't heard about yet. "Did you ever get the sense that the Harcourts had any serious enemies?"

She leaned toward me so suddenly, I had to check my impulse to stiff-arm her back. "That's what I don't understand. Now, I'm not going to claim that they were saints, but some of my other clientele could be—I'm sorry—damn snooty. Apart from their online lifestyle, Ron and Marian lived like most other people. And, like I said, they were thoughtful. Why would anyone want to kill them?"

Sure. They lived a simple life in an ordinary house in the suburbs. And hired enough assistants to satisfy a legion of rock bands and A-List celebrity actors. I also wanted to ask her how most people lived.

CHAPTER THIRTY

"You say they lived like most other people," I said. "In what ways were they like most other people?"

Her lips formed a rosette. "Oh, I couldn't tell you specifically. My impressions came from those little things you pick up when you pick up after people." She laughed at her own verbal cleverness. "Things they do around the house. Their habits." She gave me a sly smile. "Now and then, they'd invite a few neighbors over. Have drinks or whatever."

"Big parties?"

She shook her head. "Oh, no. Quite the opposite. There'd be four of them, at most."

Okay. Let's make the math clear. "Do you mean four other people or only four people?"

"Only four. Like, you know, another couple?"

That was interesting. Maybe. And, then again, maybe they had known only one other couple.

"What were these get-togethers like? Did you ever see them?"

"Oh, no," she said, her expression suggesting such a thing was unthinkable. "In fact, it was only now and then that Ron and Marian were too tired to clean up afterward. That's the only reason I knew about them at all."

"Sounds like they entertained a lot."

"Oh, I don't know. I got the sense that they just liked to have people over. Maybe to feel more connected with the people who lived near them." Jingle-jangle, clatter-clatter went the bracelets.

Yeah. Maybe. Approaching from another angle, I asked, "Did you have much contact with the children?"

"I got to know them fairly well while I was going through that rough patch," she said. "Amy, in particular, liked to talk. She was at a tricky age." Lupe did a tinkly *comme ci, comme ça* wave with her hand. "That anxious phase that hits girls right before middle school."

I paused again to get just the right words. Since she had obviously liked the Harcourts, I needed to be careful not to say anything that would alienate her. I finally settled on, "How would you describe her relationship with her parents?"

She hesitated for just a moment, suggesting that she, too, was thinking about how to respond. "They pretty much got along. Amy acted independent, mature. More like an older teenager than a child on the verge of adolescence. Even so, she still had the changing body, mind, and questions of a middle-schooler."

I sensed a problem beneath the rhetoric—that Amy had tried to act more mature than she actually was but might have felt out of her depth because of a lack of parental guidance.

Lupe paused again, before adding, "You asked about the parties. There is someone who might know more about who attended them."

I gave her my patented interested look, but I didn't have to fake it this time.

"I remember they had a cook at that time by the name of Frank Minetti. He handled everything related to food for the family." She paused with a small start. "I might even be able to find his email for you."

I jotted down his name as Lupe checked her phone. After a few seconds of scrolling, she rattled off his name, email address, and phone number. Duly noted.

Lupe stared for a moment at her phone, which now displayed the time. In general, her body language indicated I should wrap things up.

"Just a couple more questions," I assured her. "Who was the nanny at the time you worked for the Harcourts?"

Lupe looked like she had just taken a big bite of a lemon, but that expression disappeared quickly. "The first one was Sasha." She shook her head. "I'll admit we weren't the best of pals, but my job didn't require that. And neither did hers." She shrugged and her expression scrunched up again. "She was kind of a tight-ass."

Sasha Krikorian. The strict one, according to Amy. "Who was the next one? What was she like?"

Lupe squinted. "Something Swedish? She came on not long before I left. Inga or something."

Seemed safe to assume she meant Ingrid Swenson. "I don't suppose you have anyone's contact information?"

"Naw."

"What can you tell me about Jaden?"

Lupe's mouth dropped open and her eyes had that "don't get me started" look. "Now, that one was a whole 'nother story. He was in middle school, but he was well on his way toward full-on teen rebellion."

"Any idea where he is?"

"No. Like I said, we didn't really keep in touch after I closed the business." Lupe looked sad.

"How about close relatives? Did everyone get along?"

Lupe jerked upright, as if surprised. "I suppose. I never heard them argue."

I was trying to think of what I might have missed, when it hit me like a slap in the face. "When you worked for the Harcourts, did you ever get the sense they were concerned about their safety?"

Lupe pulled a prune face. "Not at all. Like I said, they were lovely people."

I considered asking her about the Harcourts' relationship, but decided not to waste our time with a continued litany of the couple's virtues.

CHAPTER THIRTY-ONE

While I drove back to my apartment, I tried not to obsess over the bits and pieces of information about the Harcourts I had picked up. Not having my flowchart while driving down the road made it harder to fit things together. And the pounding in my head? I thought it had tucked tail and run, but it was back now with a vengeance.

On top of which, after I parked in my building's basement garage, I managed to knock over my shoulder bag. And since, like an idiot, I hadn't zipped it, the contents spilled all over the floor of the car. I gritted my teeth. *Not really in the mood for this.* After corralling most of what had spilled, I saw my little notebook in the farthest corner. Frustrated, I lunged for it. That was a huge mistake. My back twinged so painfully, it was all I could do not to shriek like a banshee. I managed to reach the notebook though.

"Goddamn it." I gripped the book and slowly pushed myself back in small increments. Each movement sent a small jolt up my spine and straight to my brain. Then, over the course of a few minutes that felt like hours, I gathered up all my crap, stuck it in my shoulder bag, and zipped it shut. For once, I bypassed the stairs and took the elevator up two whole floors.

Back in my apartment, after stretching for almost fifteen minutes, I lay on the floor, contemplating my stash of Oxy. I considered crawling to the bathroom where the pills were hidden among the rolls of TP stored below the sink. But I dismissed the thought in favor of lying there for the rest of my life.

"On your feet," I muttered.

I held my breath as I raised my upper body, inhaled as I felt the twinge in my lower back. But the pain was less intense this time, so I powered through it.

Back at my workstation, in an effort to focus on a non-Harcourt matter, I turned toward my paying clients. A deeper search into the deadbeat debtor's assets revealed possible connections to offshore accounts. The creditor had provided one account number in an almost offhand way, suggesting that it might be important. I managed to connect the numbers with an account in Cyprus and was on the way to unearthing more.

I also shuffled through Troy Fairchild's paper trail again. This time, I noted the locations printed on each receipt. Then, I checked an online map to find the ones I didn't know and organized them by area. Most of them were depressingly close to The Void. Oddly, there were a few from the food court in Columbia Mall.

On a positive note, I got an email from a potential new client who'd been referred by an old client. All my clients come by referral. A man who was, as he described it, a "small business owner" sought to hire me to conduct surveillance on an employee claiming disability.

I took a moment to consider the potential scenarios one could tease out of the terse message. Trying to think really sucks when you have stabbing pains in your back and hammering pain inside your head. I replied that I would be willing to discuss his request by phone and inquired about the best day and time to do that. I wondered if the employer even carried workers' comp insurance.

On a hunch, I checked the dates on Troy Fairchild's Columbia Mall receipts. They were all within a two-week period. That was a clue. So for two weeks, Troy Fairchild hung out at Columbia Mall. Or worked there. I checked the dates again. All in January. Two months ago. He apparently hadn't been Christmas shopping.

How could I use this information? You don't Google "Troy Fairchild" and "Columbia Mall" to get the answers. But there were no public records connecting Fairchild to the area. Would it be worth the time to go there and ask people about him? I had my doubts about the food court employees remembering much about one customer, but you never know.

And then I remembered something. The license plate photos. They should have been the first thing I checked. That knock on the head had obviously messed with me.

So I checked my phone. The photos from The Void were still there. Another thing I should have checked right away. What with the pounding in my head and a stabbing pain in my back, it was hard to concentrate. I figured whatever came next would keep, and I decided to give myself a small treat.

It was midafternoon. The store shouldn't be crowded and I was ready for anything chocolate. The more calories, the better. The promise of some good chocolate motivated me to get moving in spite of exhaustion and pain, so I did a slow shuffle out the door and took the elevator down to the garage.

I eased my car partway through the exit, but then I paused to look around. By now, I was quite familiar with certain vehicles that normally parked here because this street had several regulars. Every now and then, I'll get a bad vibe from a non-regular. This was one of those times.

I kept the suspect car, an old brown Dodge sedan, in view as I turned onto the street. No movement. Maybe I was paranoid. Maybe not. When I reached the corner, I made the turn so slowly, I expected to hear honking or a few choice words. Nobody honked or swore, but I had just enough time to see the plain brown sedan pull away from the curb.

CHAPTER THIRTY-TWO

Could it be coincidence? I glanced between the road ahead and the rear-view mirror. Just as I thought I might have overreacted, the Dodge sedan turned at the corner behind me, but it slowed to keep a distance. That was going to cost them.

I kept straight down the road, slowing just enough to tease them into following a bit closer. Tentatively, over the course of about a mile or so, they crept up, keeping a one- or two-car space between us the entire time. Up ahead, a light was green, but stale—I hadn't seen it turn green, so I had no clue when it might turn red.

The timing was crucial here. I kept a sharp eye on the light and the other cars. When the light turned yellow, I jumped into the center lane. The way was clear, so I floored it.

The brown Dodge darted over to the center but couldn't make the light without running it. The driver chose not to. My little Fiesta isn't a muscle car, but it doesn't lack power. If it were a dog, it would be a scrappy Chihuahua. So, with help from the light, I left their plain-brown-wrapper asses in the dust. Unfortunately, I wasn't able to catch the plate number. But I'd picked out a distinguishing feature. A very noticeable dent above the door on the driver's side. The kind produced either by a bat slammed in anger or by seriously close contact with a massive vehicle. Still I had to wonder. *Had the car really been following me? Or had I just jumped to that conclusion?*

I tried hard not to think about the whole incident. I did the shopping and returned home, but my brain continued to puzzle over the matter as I unpacked my shopping bag. I had the fixings for a simple dinner—stir-fried chicken and broccoli. Nothing to it. A bit of cooking would keep me occupied. It could actually be soothing, aside from any nutritional health benefits. Plus I had a pint of the most chocolate ice cream I could find: chocolate with chocolate chunks.

Before I managed to get out the wok I planned to use for the stir fry, the ice cream said, "Eat me," like a character from *Alice in Wonderland.* Why not? Life's too short, etc., so I put the pint in the microwave at the lowest setting to soften it, and then used my spoon to dig in—relishing the sweet, creamy contents straight from the carton. As I shoveled out huge chunks of ice cream, I flipped idly through the parts of the newspaper I hadn't read. That's when I saw the announcement.

A public memorial service had been arranged for the Harcourts. It was to take place at a church not far from where they had lived. In lieu of flowers or sympathy cards, the family had asked that donations be made in memory of the couple to an animal welfare organization whose name seemed vaguely familiar.

And it was scheduled for tomorrow. Should I go or was that too presumptuous? Ever since interrogating people in a war zone, the few instincts I had to begin with regarding proper etiquette or behavior in social situations were numbed. Not that I would be obvious about grilling anybody. I would just talk to people, like I would at any gathering. Which is exactly how I interrogated people when I was in a war zone. So . . . confusing? It was worse when I first got back from the sandbox.

They were clients. And I found them dead. Therefore, going to their funeral would not be an odd thing to do, right? Because don't killers often show up in situations like this? If that were true, I would fully expect to see Detectives Gordon and Sully in attendance. And if they saw me—well, our reasons for being there were the same. But only one of us was potentially on the hook.

CHAPTER THIRTY-THREE

In the final analysis, any fears running through my mind about running into the cops at the memorial service were shouted down by my intense curiosity over who else would show up there. And besides, Morgan and Sully might infer my guilt under either approach—going or not going. Given my life lately, I consigned myself to the notion that this might be a no-win scenario.

I dug through my closet for anything low key and appropriate that I could wear to the service. My problem is I don't give a damn about clothing. That makes it hard to judge what's right for any situation that doesn't involve a uniform.

I did own one decent suit, bought on special and worn all of once for a fancy-pants rich client who ended up firing me anyway. Never liked the thing and swore I'd never wear it again. I kept meaning to give it away, but now that I looked at it, the jacket could be paired with a set of dark slacks. Add a suitably drab top and I'd be dressed for the occasion and hopefully go unnoticed.

I finished up the day by working on various cases. This included writing a short report on the offshore accounts I had found for the Case of the Deadbeat Debtor. That sounded like the name of a show my grandparents would watch.

I also thought about calling Adams to let him know what I'd found in Troy Fairchild's receipts. He said he had never heard of Troy, but apart from Adams' agenda, I wondered why Troy was hanging out at The Void. If there was any connection between Troy's reasons and Adams' affairs, it might be worth sharing what I knew. Hopefully, he'd share back.

Adams answered on the second ring. "Uh-huh," he grunted, when I revealed why I had called.

"I don't know what kind of thing you're working on," I said. "But since my man on the run chose to hang out at The Void, I'm wondering whether our cases connect."

"I doubt it."

"How can you be sure?" I asked.

He paused for a very long five seconds. "Sorry. Need to know only."

"But I do need to know."

"No, you don't." I couldn't see Adams, but I could visualize the smirk on his face. And that pretty much settled that.

The following day, I again debated the wisdom of going to the service. I wasn't sure what to expect of the turnout, but I assumed it wouldn't be small. Too many people to make it worthwhile? Then again, I could fall back on my experience in assessing crowd situations. And hope my Spidey sense was sharp enough to zero in on the one bad actor among a hundred complete strangers.

Before I dressed, I did some asanas to increase my flexibility and calm myself. My back continued to complain. Again, I struggled not to think about my hidden Oxy. I tried to breathe deeply and exhale slowly. In and out. Patience.

I also tried my damnedest not to think about that Adams dude. The way he'd said those words "Need to know only." Those weren't the words of a private investigator. Possibly those of a cop. Maybe a Marine. Or maybe . . . something else.

I arrived at the church, which looked like an upscale hotel with a steeple. Lots of glass and angular beams. I aimed to be just late enough to slip in unnoticed. Of course, the lot was jammed, so I spent even more time looking for a place to park. And then there was the walk, which couldn't have been much more than a mile or ten.

Given the amount of media attention on the day I found the Harcourts' bodies, I was surprised that I didn't see at least one or two news vans somewhere around. Maybe they were waiting for the reception.

The door opened noiselessly as I entered the church, and no one was around to notice my arrival. The spacious foyer had glass walls through which sunlight splashed across the tile floor. A woman spoke with a faint but audible voice from somewhere within.

I didn't have to go far to find the source. Crossing the foyer with the stealth of a cat, I stood by one of two sets of padded double doors. The voice continued to filter outward. I cracked the door and took a peek at the seating area for the congregation. Large enough for at least 500 people. And it was nearly at capacity.

The woman spoke from behind the pulpit. A breathtaking stained-glass window rose behind her. Above that was a wide picture window of clear glass. Obviously, there was no way I could identify and investigate 500 people. But I figured it might be most efficient to determine who was sitting up front, as well as who was sitting in the back row. And I wondered if there was any way at all that I could possibly get photos of all those people without calling attention to myself.

CHAPTER THIRTY-FOUR

I looked around the room for a way to photograph the front
and rear of the church's seating area. Way up front and off to
the side, a discreet door with a small curtained window
presented a possible viewpoint. Assuming, of course, I could
manage to find my way to that location.

I looked around for other options, but short of parading
down the aisle, cellphone aloft and snapping, or dangling from
the roof to take photos from behind the big picture window, I
didn't have many ways to photograph people surreptitiously that
would result in anything more than close-ups of arms,
shoulders, legs, and torsos.

So I slipped inside. Fortunately, the door was recessed
enough to allow me to position myself just behind the last row.
The speaker had changed. Now, a man sporting a buzz cut and
what looked like a naval commander's uniform was doling out
what sounded like the usual platitudes. They were pillars of the
community. Church volunteers. Nobel Prize winners. I wasn't
really paying attention. While some of the congregation seemed
unmoved, others were openly weeping.

This might not be the best view, but it might be all I can get. My phone was already set to vibrate, with the flash off. Seizing the moment, I entered the sanctuary, took two snaps of the last three rows on each side, ducked back out, and moved into a hallway. If anyone noticed, they didn't have time to stop me. As I searched for the room behind the windowed door, I checked the photos. Not bad, considering I had had zero time to aim the camera and focus.

I set off in the direction that seemed likely to lead to the desired vantage point. But I suspected there'd be yet another door to open before I reached it. I checked each possibility as I went and found one labeled with a name and the word "pastor" beneath it. It seemed likely a pastor would want the kind of direct access to the pulpit that windowed door would provide. Worth a look. By then, my hand went toward the door knob as if each were magnetized.

The faint sounds of the service continued to drift through the air, muted by padded doors and distance but still barely audible. I tried the knob. Yes, the door was locked. I guess Christian goodness is only so reliable, even in church. So I fiddled with the bump key and entered the inner sanctum, my ears straining for the continuing drone of the mourners.

It was an office, pretty much like any other, although it struck me as exceptionally plain. The furnishings were all natural wood and muted colors. Almost unnaturally plain, given the sleek, modern look of the rest of the church.

I didn't see the door with the window, but I did see another door. So, I crossed over to it, opened it, and entered a smaller room. A large closet, really. Those robes they wear were hanging all askew from hangers that dangled from a thin, cylindrical clothing rack. They were set apart from a full complement of silk suits for all occasions mixed with high-end casual wear but much more neatly arranged. I had never been in a pastor's office before, but I couldn't imagine that very many of them would have a closet like this one.

Either the offerings were really good or the minister, pastor, or whatever he was ended up with a big chunk of what remained after they built this modern marvel of church architecture. Or somebody was moonlighting. Big time.

CHAPTER THIRTY-FIVE

For a moment, I just stood and looked at the array of clothing. Until a sudden flood of thoughts distracted me from my purpose. For some reason, I felt panicky. As if the walls of the small room were closing in. I inhaled deeply and let it out, feeling my belly extend like a balloon, then collapse. After a few more deep breaths, a calm settled over me. Until I remembered where I was and why I was there.

Just then, I spotted the object of my search: a small door with a curtained window. The muffled sound of a eulogy came from the other side. I had no idea how much time had passed, so I hurried over to the door. Just enough of a crack in the curtain to get a glimpse of the speaker who appeared to be the minister. Or pastor. Along with a halfway decent view of the first few rows of pews.

I took my time snapping photos. I couldn't help but notice that the Harcourts' publicist and business manager were sitting right up front, but I couldn't see Amy.

I checked the photos over carefully, with the hope that they might come in handy later for identification purposes.

Meanwhile, my mind was consumed with questions: If the Harcourts' own daughter chose not to attend this memorial service, then who had arranged it? And why would she not attend?

Part of me wanted to poke around a bit more in this guy's office, but people were singing, chanting, or whatever in the auditorium behind the windowed door. They might be wrapping up. Another part of me worried that I might have another panic attack. Nonetheless, I couldn't resist making one last sweep of this inner sanctum of fine menswear. The seconds felt like minutes as I dug through the clothing to check a small set of shelves embedded in a corner. Checking pockets was out of the question without at least a few hours to do it.

As I scanned a four-level shelf with cubbyholes that held roughly 50 pairs of shoes, a white triangle appeared. Turned out to be a plain white business card wedged between the wall and the shoe storage shelf. I extracted it and snapped a quick pic. The card was nearly as plain as the office. Beneath a graphic of a gray koala with a white ruff, the words "Embrace the Wild" were printed in black lettering. Before I left the room, I tucked the intriguing card back where I had found it.

I shut the door on the plethora of clothing and crossed the ostentatiously plain room. Then I stole a look out the door and made my exit. I returned the way I had come until I reached the intersecting hallway that led to the church's foyer. By now, attendees were drifting out of the sanctuary, some heading for the door while others milled around and chatted in small groups.

I held back at the intersection, taking a few sneak peeks around the corner and occasionally glancing behind me to cover my rear. I didn't notice either of the detectives in the crowd, but it would have been easy to miss two people in a crowd of 500 or more. So I stood there long enough to realize that I looked ridiculous and that what I was doing was ridiculous. I should have just gone into the service and sat down with the mourners. If the detectives were there and saw me now, I would have some tricky explaining to do about where I was sitting and why they didn't see me. Of course, if I had behaved like a regular mourner, I would never have gotten my photos. Or found that interesting office with the very interesting closet.

Rounding the corner, I proceeded toward what remained of the crowd. Marge Calhoun was speaking to a younger woman who was taking notes. Marge's perky demeanor was there, but it was appropriately muted. Ryan Douglas emerged from the sanctuary surrounded by a clot of chattering people. No sign of the detectives.

CHAPTER THIRTY-SIX

I walked straight toward Calhoun, who had moved on to chat up a middle-aged woman wearing spike heels and a little black dress that was two sizes too small. I stopped when I reached them, as if I had been invited to join their conversation.

Calhoun didn't stop talking to the cougar to look at me, so I coughed discreetly. That didn't get her attention, so I brazenly jumped right in the minute she stopped for a breath. "Hi, Marge."

Calhoun turned to me, her expression blank for a fraction of a second. But recognition came quickly and with it, Calhoun's practiced smile.

"Yes, hi. I'm sorry. What was your name?"

"Erica Jensen."

"Are you with the press?" She bared her teeth like a fricking shark.

I tried to suppress a look of disbelief. "They were my clients," I told her. Again. "The Harcourts," I added, as if that wasn't obvious.

Calhoun's eyes snapped wide open. "Oh yes, of course." The wide open smile turned into a sheepish grin. "The researcher." Calhoun shook her head. "I'm sorry, but the last few days I've been crazy busy."

Tell me about it. "I understand," I said.

As we spoke, I looked out over the gathering. Still no sign of Amy. Or the detectives. Unless the cops were conducting surveillance from enough distance to monitor the comings and goings without being seen. I explained to Calhoun how I had learned about the memorial service and came by to pay my respects.

"How are the kids doing?" I tossed the question out nonchalantly but was anxious to hear her answer.

Calhoun's expression morphed into one of concern. "I've tried to reach Amy and Jaden." She shook her head and spread her hands. "Several times. I left at least two messages with each of them, but no one called back."

In my peripheral vision, I saw Douglas give a friendly shoulder-clap-see-ya-soon to one of the guests and then stroll toward the front door. I considered intercepting him but stopped myself when I saw the pastor—minister or whatever he was—emerge from the sanctuary.

"I should go thank Reverend Leland for the lovely service," Calhoun murmured. A terse nod to me. She started to angle her body as if to turn away. "Good to see you—"

"Did he take it on himself to set up this service?" I almost shouted the question but managed to keep my voice at a civilized volume.

She looked surprised. "No, I did."

That was interesting, but I couldn't think of a follow-up that wouldn't send us down a long, twisting conversational path. So I resorted to a lie. "Well, I agree. It was beautiful." I also intended to join her in thanking the Reverend.

Reverend Leland was tall and lean, maybe in his early 50s. He had short dark hair and a folksy "aw shucks" manner. He gestured broadly as he spoke to a woman who was maybe in her 40s. As we approached, his words drifted our way.

"Thank you so much for helping me, Hannah." His baritone was thick, almost gooey, with gratitude. I think he saw Calhoun and me coming and decided to wrap it up with Hannah.

"I'm just so glad I could help." Hannah's reply was nearly as sickly sweet as the Reverend's. She looked at him with doe eyes.

Reverend Leland lowered his voice a bit and leaned toward Hannah. "I'll let you run along. I know you have a lot to handle, what with the reception . . . ." The Reverend's voice trailed off as he nodded and smiled.

Hannah beamed in return. I almost expected her to bow before she hurried out.

"Reverend Leland." Calhoun spoke as she extended a hand for him to shake.

The Reverend grasped the hand and gave it a hearty pump or two, held it maybe two seconds too long before letting it go. "My sincerest condolences on the loss of your clients, Ms. Calhoun."

Calhoun gestured toward me with her now-free hand. "I'd like you to meet Erica Jensen. She did some work for the Harcourts."

Reverend Leland gave me a look that made me feel like I was standing in a spotlight. He seemed to give off an almost radioactive energy.

"A pleasure to meet you, ma'am," he said, shaking my hand and letting me take it back at just the right moment, while he still had that toothy grin. Then his expression turned on a dime to solemn. "We are all feeling the loss of this lovely couple." He sounded so sincere. I wondered if he sold cars on the side. It was also the second time I had heard someone extol the great virtues of the Harcourts.

"Judging by the attendance . . . ." I said and smiled. I had no idea how to finish that sentence, but I let my voice trail off so Reverend Leland could infer the right words.

"Yes, ma'am." He nodded so slowly it was more like a bow. "They were a very popular couple. And not just for their travel stories."

He rambled on for a bit about how they had helped so much in organizing the upcoming Easter event. I nodded and "um-hmm-ed."

While we were talking, I surreptitiously scanned the immediate area. The place had almost entirely cleared out and there was still no sign of the detectives. The front door opened as the last few people left. Through the opening, I thought I caught a glimpse of Douglas chatting with someone. But the door closed before I could be sure.

CHAPTER THIRTY-SEVEN

Reverend Leland accompanied Calhoun and me across the church foyer to the front door. He hung back as we proceeded outside.

"My sincerest condolences, ladies." In other words, bye.

"Would you happen to have a card?" I asked before the door closed.

I caught a ripple in his expression. *Mild curiosity? Annoyance?* "Sure," he said. He produced a standard-issue business card holder from somewhere on his person and withdrew a plain business card. Almost as plain as his office.

"Thank you," I said. By this time, Calhoun looked like she was ready to make a run for it. "How long did you know the Harcourts? I mean, how many years have they been involved with the church?"

Leland shrugged. "Three, four years maybe."

"I'm sorry if I seem nosy, but . . . ." I stopped and looked at Calhoun. "Please don't feel you need to wait for me. This probably wouldn't interest you."

Calhoun looked stunned, but she recovered with apparent ease. "Well, perhaps I can help."

That was about the last thing I expected her to say. But if she wanted to hang around, fine by me.

"What sorts of things did they volunteer to do?"

"I could count on them to organize our annual Easter event every year," he said.

"Oh, okay. So that would involve . . . I'm just guessing here . . . an Easter egg hunt, refreshments, entertainment?"

"Right, right." He nodded with each word.

"And the refreshments . . . would they be catered?"

"No, of course not," the Reverend said. "Our members make the refreshments."

"And the entertainment?"

"All volunteer." The Reverend gave his watch a not-so-discreet glance.

"I'm so sorry," I gushed, my voice catching. *I'm going to make myself sick if I keep this up.* "It's just that one minute, they were clients, and the next . . . I find them . . . ." I flashed back to the moment I'd found the Harcourts and put every bit of my horror into the words. "It was a shock."

Reverend Leland extended a hand and gripped my shoulder. "Have faith. And stay strong." And then he shut the door. By the time the Reverend had called "cut" on our little scene, Calhoun had hurried off. But not quite fast enough for me to miss seeing her in the passenger seat of a car cruising toward the exit. With Ryan Douglas at the wheel.

I silently cursed my late arrival. Had I parked closer in, I could have followed them. And speaking of following, I noticed a plain brown sedan parked right across the street—with a dent above the driver's-side door, just like the one I thought was following me yesterday.

I took a closer look at the car, which was parked in the shade of a tall, dense hedge of arborvitae. I could just barely make out the silhouette of someone behind the wheel.

"Fuck this," I muttered. Maybe fifty feet separated us, but coming straight at the vehicle wouldn't be the smartest thing to do. I desperately wanted to know who was behind the wheel, but I also knew I could not approach the car without being obvious. It was possible that the driver was a stalker, someone I'd pissed off, unknowingly or otherwise.

I strolled across the street without stopping. My gaze swept past the driver's side window but failed to make out enough detail to describe the car's occupant. From what little I could see, I gathered that the driver was a male with short hair. The rear of the brown sedan came into view, and I noted its tag number. The alphanumeric identifier played on auto-repeat in my head.

Once I had the plate number, I power-walked toward the Fiesta, which now seemed to be parked a hundred miles away. Unfortunately, my would-be stalker had other ideas. The roar of his car engine told me he wasn't planning to stick around. I sprinted toward my car, adrenaline surging through me. By the time I slid behind the wheel, the brown car had disappeared, its engine noise fading into the murmur of distant traffic.

CHAPTER THIRTY-EIGHT

I made sure to write down the tag number before heading back home. Noting the license plate number reminded me that I had two others to check out. So I searched for identifying information for all three. Turned out the two cars behind The Void were owned by the same person—Mabel Forbes. The brown sedan's license plate number was the real oddball. I couldn't even find a listing.

I took a moment to sit still and close my eyes. The need to ignore reality felt overwhelming. My life was becoming increasingly surreal. To think that a week ago, I was a Marine with PTSD and an opioid addiction who was trying to make a living as an unlicensed private eye. Now, I'm still the same thing, but with a couple of dead clients, the cops suspecting me of murder, and a mystery man in a brown sedan who may or may not have some interest in me.

As to the mystery man's license plate, I thought at first that he might have altered the tag number. Then it occurred to me that he might have forged the thing. I imagined that someone could actually do that. After all, people are using 3D printing to do all sorts of things that were previously unimaginable.

As for Mabel Forbes, I could picture her being the owner of the joint. Or maybe married to the owner. I checked her address. The street had one of those goofy names that Columbia, Maryland, is mocked for. Columbia? I recalled the receipts from Columbia Mall belonging to Troy Fairchild. Could my bail skipper be hiding out with his strip club–owning girlfriend? And what was she into that involved the limber Mr. Adams?

I did another quick search in the state business records. After a bit of poking around, I confirmed that Mabel Forbes essentially owned The Void. Technically, under an LLC. But she was named as the principal. I searched Google maps and zoomed in on Mabel Forbes's house using Street View. The neighborhood looked like a typical Columbia residential neighborhood on any given weekday. Color-coordinated, nonconformist conformity, and empty of cars and people.

Now I could play this a few ways. I could go to the house on a pretense of some sort, gain access, and look for clues. Or I could do a bit of surveillance before I took that step. Troy Fairchild had evaded capture long enough to suggest he wouldn't be so dumb as to create a trail to his hiding place by setting up any accounts or do anything other than eating an occasional meal at Columbia Mall. But I had to at least perform a due diligence background check for any possible connections. After a good 15 or 20 minutes of this, I felt like I had run the databases dry. It was time to go old-school.

I had done enough work with the Marines to have developed something of a toolkit and some standard operating procedures. I had a wardrobe of low-cost costumes consisting of a clipboard, a lanyard with a card holder into which I can slip either my military ID or a fake (if I want to remain anonymous), a lab coat, a worker's uniform, and the chutzpah to make them all work for me. My good friend Terry Morris (or, as his oldest friends know him, Two-Bit Terry) had provided this bounty. How he did it, I didn't know or care.

And I figured on making an evening of it. So I would go prepared with a water bottle and a receptacle for when it came out the other end. Trust me when I say you don't want to know the details.

I finished up with my other work as quickly as I could. Columbia is only about twenty miles from where I live in Wheaton, but I hoped to reach Rt. 29 before the worst of the evening rush. I might have considered I-95 at one time, but commuter traffic had reached the point where you were screwed no matter which way you went. With my tools stashed in the car, all I had to do was grab my phone, shoulder bag, and case file. Before leaving, I fed Rocky his ration of peanuts.

CHAPTER THIRTY-NINE

Half an hour later, I was cruising past Mabel Forbes's house, which had a forest green front door that didn't quite jibe with the sky-blue color of the siding. I wondered if she took shit from the homeowners association over that somewhat incongruous mismatch.

The house sat atop a small hill and had a driveway that led to a one-car garage. Both driveway and garage sat low enough to suggest they led to the basement. No vehicles were parked in front of the house. In fact, the entire street was empty. But it was only 3:30. Maybe, as people returned home from work, I'd have better luck blending into the neighborhood.

I did stop once, pretending to check an old ADC map book of Howard County. This gave me time to do at least a pro forma reconnaissance on what might be Troy Fairchild's safe house. Who uses an old map book? A few people, probably. Besides, try hiding your face behind a cell phone.

The house was a recent model. Two stories, the lower level brick-fronted, the upper floor covered with the sky-blue siding. A set of steps crossed a steep slope of lawn, providing access to the non-matching door. I caught a glimpse of a low basement window gleaming from the rear corner of the building. As to access from the backyard, I wouldn't know for sure without taking a closer look.

Taking care to park a good distance from the place, I donned the lanyard with my veteran ID card tucked into a plastic holder clipped onto it. If anyone asked, I could say I was doing a door-to-door survey for a small nonprofit. A really small one.

I grabbed the clipboard and moved toward the house, trying to look purposeful. I hadn't yet decided what my nonprofit did. Save the whales? No. Save the crabs? Yes. That was closer to home.

As I neared the slightly nonconformist green door, a woman appeared from behind the rise of the yard and looked up at me. She might have been in her mid 40s. And she was dressed like a Brooks Brothers model in a tasteful black pencil skirt and a matching jacket over a light blue silk blouse. Apart from the fact that her hairstyle was a tidy helmet of monochromatic auburn hair of a slightly too-red shade, she actually matched the house better than the door did.

"Hi," I chirped, putting on a friendly smile as I went back down the steps, sporting my clipboard with an air of authority. She eyed me with thinly veiled curiosity in return. "Are you Mabel Forbes?" I asked. I noted the closed garage door and wondered if she'd been hiding behind the house.

The woman shook her head. "Oh, no. She moved out."

"You must be the new owner then." I said, raising the clipboard. "I'm doing a resident survey, so I need to talk to the owner."

"No, I'm not." Ms. Brooks Brothers paused, looking strangely perplexed, as if not quite sure what to say to me. "The house is on the market. I'm just looking after it."

"Oh, you must be a real estate agent then."

She stiffened slightly. "I work with an agency."

"I sure hope you can help me out. Because if Ms. Forbes still owns the property, I need to get some information from her. I assume you have a way of contacting her?"

Ms. Brooks Brothers glanced from my face to my midsection where my ID hung. I had positioned it just low enough that the clipboard could be used as a handy shield.

"Look," she said. "I really don't know. To be honest, I came by for a friend in the office."

That sounded reasonable. She didn't use any of the standard "obvious liar" tells—averting her eyes, fidgeting, crossing her arms, stepping back, and so on—so what she said was probably true. Or she was a great liar.

"Hey, I'm just a volunteer." I tried saying that in a real casual, empathetic tone. "But this is about a serious issue. If you're saying the house has been on the market a while, I won't go around telling everyone. But it would help me a great deal to know when Mabel Forbes moved."

She nodded once. "It's been at least six months," she said. "Probably longer."

I scribbled on a piece of scrap paper that I keep attached to my clipboard, along with the official-looking form beneath it, because I can't write everything on the form, can I?

"I take it six months is a long time for a property to be on the market."

Ms. Brooks Brothers looked resigned. "I said probably longer. Much longer."

"Why do you say that?"

She shrugged. "Just a feeling I get. Jokes around the office. That kind of thing."

"And Ms. Forbes current address?"

She shook her head. "Can't help you there. I only know that she was very old."

"How old?" I asked.

"I don't know." The agent shrugged. "Easily in her 70s, maybe 80s. Old enough to be tired of taking care of a house."

I wanted to ask a lot more questions, but I was fast approaching the kinds of questions that would sound weird in a neighborhood survey. "Is someone else handling the sale for her? Perhaps I could get more information from them."

She gave me a sharp look. It gave me the distinct impression that I had asked one question too many.

"I honestly can't tell you." She continued to look from my face to the spot where she assumed my badge was and suddenly she turned suspicious. "What kind of ID is that?"

She looked so wound up, I thought she might make a grab for the badge. Time to go.

"Don't worry about it," I said. "I'll take it from here." I held my identification badge up for a fraction of a second and then dropped it. "Military issue."

That was my exit line.

CHAPTER FORTY

After speaking with Ms. Brooks Brothers, it seemed like a good idea to get in the car and leave. As I walked toward my car, I heard a garage door rattle its way up. On my way to my Fiesta, I stopped short and did a 180-degree turn as I heard the garage door rise. The rattling sound was followed by the slam of a car door.

Before Ms. Brooks Brothers hit the road, I hoped to catch a glimpse of her license. I could hide and take a photo, but where? The relatively barren suburban landscape didn't provide much cover, but I spied a nearby hedge that might do the trick.

My ears pricked up at the sound of a car backing up. As I crossed the road to the hedge and hid behind it, I heard the garage door rattle its descent. The car nearly shot out onto the street and motored by so fast I was barely able to see the tag or many other details. I did snap a few photos of the beat-up Hyundai Ms. Brooks Brothers drove. I guess she hadn't yet made Realtor of the Year.

And I hoped at least one of those shots had caught her license plate. I took a quick peek at my camera roll and was disappointed to find that none of them had caught more than a blurred one.

Now that Ms. Brooks Brothers was out of the way, I returned to the house for a look around the perimeter. I wondered if the house had a security system. Even an unoccupied house could have one. I snapped a photo of the house front. Google Earth images tend to run anywhere from one to three years old. If the house was for sale, where was the sign indicating same?

When I approached the front door, I saw a small lockbox. I circled around the house. The backyard gently sloped to a small buffer of trees. The house had two doors in the back: a downstairs sliding door to the lower level and a set of French doors that opened onto a raised deck. I also looked for windows and other potential points of entry. As I noted these things, I remembered that Ms. Brooks Brothers never told me her name nor did she mention that of the realty company she worked for. The fact that there was no "For Sale" sign out front bothered me a little. But only a little. There could be several reasons for that. Perhaps a contract on the place had fallen through, and they forgot to put the sign back up. Maybe they took it down because they didn't want the locals to see how long the house had been up for sale. Or maybe Ms. Brooks Brothers was actually Mabel Forbes and she had just pulled a fast one on me.

The more I considered these factors, the more convinced I became that this house would make an ideal hideout for Troy Fairchild. If that were so, I wondered if and how Ms. Brooks Brothers played a part.

After thoroughly casing the place and noting its vulnerabilities, I surveyed the grounds. Basically, the house was part of a line built atop a low ridge, the fronts facing the steeper side. The small clump of relatively young trees at the rear wouldn't provide great cover during the day, but at night it might. The rest of the backyard was a long stretch of grass.

The hum of an occasional passing vehicle floated my way as I thought about the situation. Eventually, the traffic picked up. Workers returning home. Good, I thought. Many of the houses here had a one-car garage, but I was pretty sure that most of the residents owned more than one car. So if I wanted to do a night surveillance, my car stood a decent chance of not being the only one parked on the street. While I was considering this, my phone rang. Delgado Bail Bonds. Mitch, of course. Probably nervous. After taking a deep breath, I took the call. "Yes."

"Erica." My name sounded like it had been coughed up like a hairball. "Are you anywhere close to finding Troy Fairchild?"

"I'm working on a lead right now." My voice was imbued with optimism and bursting with energy I only half felt.

Mitch Delgado's wheezing and coughing came over the line as loud, asthmatic explosions, followed by a wet, rattling noise that came from deep down in his lungs.

"I'm getting too old for this shit," he growled.

"Hang in there." My words felt lame, but I didn't have to fake my sincerity.

"I'm losing my touch." Mitch hacked out the words. "You know how many bail skippers I've had lately? Too fucking many."

The medical bills were obviously killing him. Along with whatever the fuck it was that made him cough. Probably cancer. Probably Agent Fucking Orange.

Don't even get me started about the VA hospital. Hey, I understand. They're understaffed and underfunded, so it's probably really hard for them to give a fuck about an endless number of head cases. So, once again, it comes down to politics and money. And everyone loves us, but no one wants to pay for us.

"Look," I said. "I really do think I'm onto something. Just give me a week. Probably less." I felt pretty confident, but I couldn't be sure. So I gave a conservative estimate that might give him some hope.

"The sooner, the better," he said. "Or I'm done. Busted."

CHAPTER FORTY-ONE

By the time we hung up, my resolve to help Mitch had doubled. He was one of my first clients. And a good friend of Two-Bit Terry's. But that's another story altogether.

I made my way back to my car, thinking I should make myself scarce before the neighbors started to return en masse. At this time of day, only a few cars and vans came through. If Troy were living here secretly, chances were good he was either in the house right now or, if he wasn't, he must be coming and going in the evening or late at night. So far, I had seen no sign of Troy or any other occupant. No shadows in any of the windows. Whether Troy was in the house or not, I needed to move fast.

I thought about using the French doors. They would probably open if I used my bump key, but I wondered how many nosy neighbors would see me fiddling around the back of the house. With my clipboard, I should probably go with the front door. Especially if the house was on the market. If anyone asked, I could pose as a property inspector as easily as I could a residential surveyor.

While I was at my car, I strapped on a utility belt with pouches in which I had stowed my gear, making sure it included wrist restraints and a few extra tools. I had rigged the clipboard to hang from the belt to keep my hands free once I entered the house. For the moment, I carried it, along with the bump key, my stun baton tucked into the belt's holster. Between Marine training and my toys, I should be good to go.

After properly equipping myself, I made for the front door. The faint hum of traffic from the closest main road had risen to a low rumble, punctuated by the occasional louder rumble of heavy trucks. The sun hadn't set to the point where the temperature would go down, but I shivered as if it had already cooled off.

Getting into the house was very easy. The bump key got me inside just like that. I looked around for an alarm keypad and didn't find one. Could there be an alarm that could only be cancelled by voice? And how could a person tell? There was probably a way. I just didn't know what it was. And I wasn't about to let that stop me.

I hooked my clipboard onto my belt, stowed the key in a pocket, and drew the stun baton from its holster, gripping it with both hands. *Sweep and clear.* I moved through the house, starting with the foyer. I moved in a clockwise pattern, from living room to dining room to kitchen and back to the foyer. I didn't see Troy Fairchild, but I did see evidence of occupancy. Take-out containers in the trash. A few dirty dishes in the sink with food that had dried and hardened. Not exactly primed for a viewing by prospective buyers, but if I ever saw Ms. Brooks Brothers again, I would definitely mention it.

Still no sound of movement and my shoes don't squeak. Basement or upstairs? The last time I went into a basement . . . . My mind flashed back to the horrible scene. For a moment, I felt like it was actually happening again. This triggered yet another memory—from Afghanistan. While serving as backup with special ops forces during a routine reconnaissance of one of the compounds, we discovered the hard way that a Taliban zealot was living among the residents as a mole. A firefight ensued, and one of my fellow Female Empowerment Team members was mortally wounded that day. The memory stopped me short. I closed my eyes, then snapped them open. I took a long, deep breath. In. Out.

And I opened the basement door. I went down the stairs as quietly as I could, peering about as I went. The basement was unfinished and empty. A quick survey of the area revealed no one and nothing of interest. The area did not look lived in. I returned to the first floor and moved onward to the next level.

As I made my way down the hall and cleared each room, I found very little until I got to the last room. A few articles of clothing were heaped on a chair. That and an unmade bed were the only furniture in the room. Now it was just a matter of waiting.

CHAPTER FORTY-TWO

While I waited for Troy or possibly some other squatter to
return home, I positioned myself in a corner chair in the living
room from which I could observe as much as possible of the
first floor and be somewhat inconspicuous. The sun was low
enough in the sky to reduce the room's colors to a near-
monotone gray. I kept my eyes and ears open, but my mind was
busy thinking about my other cases.

I didn't have my notes with me, so I tried to picture my
flowchart for the Harcourt murders. It was getting too
complicated to hold it all in my head. Just then, my phone
buzzed. I pulled it out of my pocket and checked the ID. Not a
number I recognized, but the name seemed familiar. Gallagher
Bern. Hmm. Back into my pocket went the phone. Then, I
heard the clicking of a key in the front door. I got up quickly
and crouched behind the chair, stun baton at the ready.

From my vantage point, I could see a man enter. Tough to
make out his features in the shadows, but the build matched that
of the young man captured in the photos Troy's uncle had

shown me. From the foyer, the man must have moved directly to the kitchen because I heard the fridge door open and close.

By the time I got to my feet and crept toward the noise, the man was seated in the dining room, tucking into yet another take-out meal. I couldn't quite make out his face, but the resemblance to Troy was strong. I sighed. Well, if it wasn't Troy, this was going to be awkward. I aimed my stun baton at the man, hit a button, and used it as a flashlight. My stun baton is both stun defense and flashlight. Cool, huh?

Caught in the beam, the man dropped his fork and turned toward me. Blinded by the glare, he blinked and tried to shield his eyes with his hands.

"Hi, Troy," I said, closing in on him fast.

I had to hand it to him. Troy had panther-like reflexes. As I approached, one of his hands blindly grasped a take-out carton, which came at me like one of Stephen Strasburg's fastballs. I ducked. The carton grazed me and sauce sprayed my face and hit an eye. Stung like a bitch. With one eye squinting, I watched Troy run past me and bolt from the room. I took off after him.

He was quick, but a burst of adrenaline made me quicker. Not enough to catch him, but I did gain ground. With a fighting chance of nabbing him, everything seemed to slow as my feet pounded in pursuit.

I was still blinking sauce out of my eye as Troy reached the door. I lunged at him, extended my arms, and aimed the stun baton, just close enough to zap him. He went down, twitching.

CHAPTER FORTY-THREE

I was in the midst of cuffing Troy, when he rolled over and shoved me back. One cuff dangled from his arm. I stumbled but somehow managed to stay upright. Troy's eyes looked wild. *Oh, for God's sake.* This was the downside of working solo on this shit.

As Troy wobbled his way into a crouch, I ran out the door and down the stairs, where I waited beside a short retaining wall supporting the sloping lawn. Eventually, Troy stumbled down the front steps, still a bit woozy from the stun gun, the dangling cuff now a potential weapon. I didn't wait for him to come to me. Instead, I made like a heat-seeking missile and went straight for him.

This time I used the stun gun to catch him in the groin. His eyes widened as he gasped for air. I smashed a foot down at what I hoped would be just the right angle to hobble him a bit. He cried out in pain right after I felt, rather than heard, a crisp snap where the ankle met the foot. *Whoops!* So maybe I hobbled him more than a little.

That and the stun gun managed to subdue Troy enough that I could slap the cuffs on him and get him into my car. After taking Troy to the police station to be processed and giving Mitch the good news, I wondered about the phone call I received while waiting for Troy. The name was starting to seem more familiar. As I drove home, I tried to remember when the name on the caller ID had come up during the last few days. Not to mention who brought it up.

The paperwork and other formalities that came with turning Troy over to the police took long enough that I ended up dining on stale potato chips from an ancient vending machine. Exhausted, I tabled all thoughts about my cases until I arrived somewhere where I could review my notes. Then, I thought about contacting Amy again. It would be really nice to know why she wasn't at her own parents' memorial service, but it might be better not to ask her outright.

Even though I was exhausted, I somehow managed to recharge on the way home. The walk up to my apartment was more like a long slow hike. Tackling Troy had done a number on my back. It complained and my head echoed in agreement as the pounding inside my skull resumed. Had I suffered more than a mild concussion from that attack at The Void? And was it connected to the panic attack I had later at the church?

Once inside my apartment, I tossed everything in the general direction of the sofa and headed straight for the bathroom. I heard a few things fall to the floor behind me, but I also heard the call of the last of my stash of Oxy.

I half-collapsed onto the floor and dug out the pill bottle. Twisting off the cap, I stared at the few remaining pills and nearly succumbed. But then I thought about Nick and Susan, the leader of my therapy group. Even Two-Bit Terry. They would be so disappointed. *I can't do it.*

I turned toward the toilet and held the bottle over the open bowl. Then time seemed to stop. I have no idea if it was ten seconds or ten minutes that I stood there like that, as if posing for a portrait. Portrait of a Marine/drug addict. Semper fi.

You got this. My hand turned slowly as if it was remote-controlled by another brain. Then I tilted the bottle enough to make the pills start sliding toward the opening. I squeezed my eyes tight shut and tried not to hear the splash as the pills dropped into the toilet one by one. *Plop, plop, plop, plop, plop, plop, plop, plop, plop.* Done.

I slumped against the cabinet. *Click, click, click.* Three pills stubbornly clattered back to the bottom of the bottle. I briefly considered dumping them, but I screwed the cap back on and breathed deeply, like a diver resurfacing. And once again, my temptation was stowed away with the rolls of TP under the sink.

After the usual restless night's sleep, I somehow felt sufficiently recovered to review what I knew about the Harcourt murders at this point and decide what to do next. I wondered where the cops were on the case. By now, you'd think they would have arrested me if they really had the grounds. But I'm sure the timing of that phone call from Marian Harcourt must weigh heavily on their minds. I know it did on mine. There had to be an explanation, but what was it?

A few possibilities came to mind. Either Marian Harcourt really did call me for protection, knowing the killer was close, maybe right next to her. Perhaps somebody forced her to call me. If it was not Marian on the phone, someone had done an amazing impression of her voice.

Any of those scenarios could have been the prelude to setting me up. The first possibility allowed for a scenario in which setting me up was opportunistic. The other two strongly suggested the frame was deliberate and I was the target. And if I was targeted specifically, was it because they knew the Harcourts had hired me or because they were aware of my less-than-squeaky-clean background?

CHAPTER FORTY-FOUR

I dismissed the idea that this could be all about me. That seemed ludicrous on its face. But it did suggest the murderer might have been close enough to the Harcourts to know they had hired me. Maybe the person who saw me entering the house that morning was the killer.

I tried to shift away from that kind of circular thinking and instead focus on the content of my notes. Could the killer and/or witness have been among those who attended the little get-togethers with the Harcourts? Perhaps Frank Minetti would know more.

When I called Minetti's number, a woman with a mellow contralto voice answered. After I determined that I was speaking with Minetti's wife and that he was at work, I started in with what was becoming my standard spiel about the Harcourts, which was cut short when Minetti's wife said, "Oh, my! Wasn't that awful?"

I waited a second before I said, "It was. I found them."

Her response was a muted gasp. Then silence.

"The police have spoken to you, then?" I asked.

"Not to me," she said. "But they did speak to Frank."

"Do you think he would mind talking to me about it?"

"I don't think so, but may I ask why?"

I was never quite sure if I was choosing the right words. It's not like I wanted to say outright, "Oh, well, since I found their bodies and a few other problems, the cops suspect me."

What I said was, "I'll be straight with you. The Harcourts hired me to vet a potential hire: a bodyguard. Apparently, I didn't do my job fast enough. It's almost like they died on my watch. If I don't do anything to find their killer, that doesn't help my reputation much." That did the trick. She gave me his number.

Minetti owned a restaurant, La Bella Figura, located in Maple Lawn, one of those "new urban" pseudo-cities in the middle of nowhere. I caught him between lunch and dinner rushes, so he was fine with leaving the kitchen to his two capable assistants.

Minetti, who appeared to be in his late 40s, was about my height, but he seemed taller. His hair was an unruly mop of dark curls and he sported a dark, bushy mustache. The whole classical Mediterranean package, with the exception of his eyes, which were a startling light blue.

Minetti ushered me back to an office that could've been a converted closet, cramped further by an aging wooden desk and gunmetal gray file cabinet. He waved me into a guest chair wedged into the last significant square footage of floor space. I crossed the space in front of his desk in just a couple of steps and took a seat.

"It's unthinkable what happened to that poor couple," Minetti said, plopping into his desk chair, which groaned in sympathy. "They were good people." I nodded. I was starting to wish I had gotten to know them better.

Minetti didn't wait for me to pick up the conversational ball. "My wife told me about you. She explained your situation."

Inwardly, I relaxed a bit. *Glad to get that part out of the way.*

"I understand you used to cook for them," I said.

Minetti nodded. A vigorous nod that made his head bounce as if attached by a spring. "Yeah, before Dad passed two years ago and left me this." He spread his hands to encompass his culinary business domain.

"So, your decision to stop working for them . . . ." I waited for him to finish the sentence.

"Not so much a decision I made as one made for me," he said. "I worked for Ron and Marian for several years, part- and full-time, at different points. But I did have bigger plans. My goal was to start my own catering business. Taking over here has been a real education."

I murmured sympathetically. "I understand you catered for Ron and Marian's little get-togethers." He seemed slightly confused, so I added, "When the Harcourts met with other couples."

Minetti nodded in the affirmative.

"Right. Now and then, they liked to host more intimate gatherings. I think they wanted to get an honest read on their own neighbors."

Now it was my turn to look puzzled, but I maintained a neutral expression. Did the Harcourts not trust their own neighbors? Or did Minetti just mean they wanted to get to know them better?

"What were these get-togethers like?" I assumed they were pleasant, catered affairs, but you never know.

"Friendly, but business-like." My expression must have surprised him. "Those get-togethers with other couples were often connected with some kind of issue they were working on."

"What kind of issues?" I felt my phone vibrate in my pocket and ignored it.

He shrugged. "Could've been any number of things. They were into a lot of causes."

Causes? "Are we talking about controversial causes?"

Minetti paused for a bit and then gave me a wry grin. "Kind of depended on the context. But I guess it's safe to say all of them had some kind of controversy. Otherwise, they wouldn't be issues."

Well, that was helpful. Not.

As if he sensed my dissatisfaction, Minetti added, "The Harcourts were involved in such a wide variety of issues that it's hard to be more specific. For instance, I remember they hosted a meeting about the use of plastics at restaurants and hotels. They were big into ecotourism. That kind thing. But they were also involved in the small stuff, like whether an intersection needed a stop sign. Community stuff."

Minetti leaned toward me, as if anxious to be heard. "So, if there's a motive to be found in any of that, I guess the question is, which of these issues would generate the kind of vicious act the killer committed?"

"Assuming their deaths were related to any of those things." I wasn't ready to assume anything, but Minetti's comments gave me new food for thought. "Given the issues, I'm surprised they met only with a few other couples."

Minetti's eyes widened. "Hardly," he said. "They would occasionally hold meetings at their church. Maybe 50 or 60 people would attend. Sometimes more."

This got me wondering. Were the couple trying to switch careers? Or were these activities part of their brand somehow?

"What about their smaller meetings in their home? Do you know what they discussed?"

Minetti leaned forward again, as if eager to share. "I never really paid close attention, but my impression was that along with the issues, they were just trying to feel more connected with their own neighbors."

CHAPTER FORTY-FIVE

"Just a few more questions," I said to Minetti. "When the police spoke to you about the Harcourts' murders, did they cover any topics that I didn't?"

Minetti frowned, looking thoughtful. "I don't think so. Other than establishing where I was and what I was doing around the time of their . . . deaths."

"Which was?"

Minetti's frown deepened, as if he thought I would accuse him. "I was asleep. This was last weekend, right? I was definitely asleep. We stay open late on weekends, so Fridays and Saturdays, I'm usually here until at least midnight, sometimes later. Last weekend, I ended up working until well past two."

I nodded. "I assume you stopped working for the Harcourts after you took over here?"

He nodded. "As their personal cook, yeah. But I catered their events now and then."

"What was the largest event you catered for them?" I was really starting to wonder.

"A fundraiser. Maybe five, six hundred people. It was quite the—"

The crash of breaking dishes in the kitchen interrupted him and jolted me. With a nervous glance at the door, Minetti said, "You'll have to excuse me."

We rose together.

"I won't keep you," I said.

While I never had a chance to really get to know Ron and Marian Harcourt, my research revealed that their activities extended to more than just travel.

Before I drove back home, I checked my phone. Gallagher Bern. This was his second call and he hadn't left a message. I didn't give it much more thought, until I was at home reviewing my notes. Ah, yes. The Harcourts' lawyer, Aaron Gallagher of Gallagher and Bernson. The caller ID had cut off part of the name. The card Ryan Douglas had given me was still in my shoulder bag. I fished it out and checked it. His direct line matched the number on my caller ID. Why would he want to talk to me? None of the other Harcourt retinue had gone out of their way to do that. This time, I called the number back. After a few rings, a man said, "Yes."

"Aaron Gallagher?" I said.

Before I could even identify myself, he said, "Thank you for calling. I need to speak to you, but I can't right now."

Gallagher's words came out in short, sharp bursts.

"This is Erica Jensen," I said, just to be completely clear. "Would you like to set up a better time?"

"Call you back in an hour or so?"

"Sure."

I wondered which client was being charged for these calls. In the meantime, I updated my flowchart to the extent that I could and tried to connect things. And I wondered if by now, Amy would feel any more inclined to discuss her non-attendance at the memorial service. I also realized I should have shown Minetti the photos I took at the service to see if he recognized anyone in particular. Maybe asked him a bit more about the church. *Damn!* Maybe Gallagher could help with that.

While I waited for the lawyer to call back, I took another look at the Harcourts' social media presence. At this point, their accounts were still active, their images posed or frozen in mid action, expressions ranging from serene to joyful. I had already scanned their accounts for anything obvious, but maybe it was time to take a deeper dive into the data.

Minetti had mentioned ecotourism. As I went through the photos on Instagram, I noted locations and date ranges. Costa Rica, New Zealand, Iceland. They had visited all the obvious touristy places, along with plenty of other places that weren't quite as notable. A few of them were close to home. Day trips.

The Baltimore Aquarium, for instance and numerous places in D.C. Between the government buildings and all the historical and cultural sites, the nation's capital was brimming with well-publicized tourist attractions. And not so well-publicized ones.

I couldn't help but notice that as the dates grew more recent, the number and character of day trips changed. The number of short trips seemed to go up, and the number of long trips that required plane travel or complicated itineraries seemed to drop. But I would have to examine the data more closely to confirm whether my observations panned out.

The Harcourts were definitely into being green. The images of parks, mountain trails, a butterfly exhibit, and petting farms or animal shelters attested to their interest in nature. But what caught my attention was a bright yellow logo on a sign at one petting zoo. I couldn't quite make out the design or the text, so I enlarged the image. The logo was a cute gray-and-white koala. The sign read: Embrace the Wild.

CHAPTER FORTY-SIX

Seeing the koala logo for the second time in as many days set off an alarm. Especially given the place I had last seen it. Okay. It seemed the Harcourts enjoyed working with the church. Maybe they had arranged a church group event at Embrace the Wild, whatever that was. I switched to a search engine and entered "Embrace the Wild" and Maryland. A click on the Enter key and it appeared as the top result.

Based on the photos of visitors posed with presumably tame baby chimps, bear cubs, and other normally wild fauna, I quickly deduced it was a kind of exotic petting zoo. Scrolling down the page, I noticed that the place allowed groups to book events. So maybe it was as simple as that. Maybe the Harcourts had arranged such an event. And maybe Reverend Leland had the card for that reason. But as I continued to scan the page, the word "safari" caught my eye.

At first, I thought they were offering real trips to Africa. But that wasn't the case. They had re-created a kind of African safari experience, complete with a village as depicted by Old Hollywood. Except this one came with Jacuzzis, air conditioning, microwave ovens, and big-screen TVs. And it didn't come cheap.

I was interrupted by my cellphone's ringtone. It was Aaron Gallagher calling back. I started my usual greeting, only to be interrupted. "Ms. Jensen, I need to meet with you."

"What's going on?"

"We need to meet," he repeated. His tone suggested more than the usual amount of lawyerly caution. "I wouldn't ask if I didn't think it was essential."

I thought about it for maybe one nanosecond and then said, "Fine. Where and when?"

"Today. You pick the place."

"How about Kit's Cafe in Kensington?" It's a cool coffee shop not far from where I live.

"Great," he said. "Can you be there in, say, half an hour?" he added, his voice now lilting.

"Um, yeah."

"Meet you there."

"Sure thing." Before I even finished those two words, Gallagher was gone.

I like coffee shops. They are usually safe places to meet people. Certainly safer than The Void. And in this case, I was meeting with a nice safe lawyer, assuming there was such a thing. After hanging up, I drove to Kit's Cafe, and arrived fifteen minutes early to stake out a spot.

Along with my writing pad, I brought a paperback to read while I waited. Tried to read, that is, without great success, as my eyes kept moving from the page to the front door and then around the room. Finally, I put the book down. Now was as good a time as any to people watch, I guess. It's amazing how many people frequent coffee shops and drink Italian-style coffee like they never do in Italy.

During the brief time I was in Italy, I learned a few things about coffee. For one thing, as an American, I needed to make it clear that when I ordered "un cafe," I meant real coffee. In other words, espresso. Not that watered-down Yankee crap. For another, you don't drink cappuccinos at any time other than in the morning. You just don't.

Coffee is not an experience you linger over in Italy. It's gulp-and-go. And if you order a frappuccino, be prepared to be disappointed. Or mocked mercilessly. If you're an American, they will likely mock you in a language you don't understand, even if you think you know Italian. But recalling the perils and joys of Italian coffee brought me no closer to solving my current problems.

I checked my phone for the time. Gallagher was running late. Four minutes, creeping up on five. It was rush hour on a Friday, so maybe he'd underestimated the time it would take for him to get here. Given that his office was in Bethesda, he might be able to make the drive in exactly half an hour—at two in the morning. So I picked up my paperback and settled in to wait.

A half hour later, I questioned the wisdom of indulging in a second cappuccino—on American soil, I enjoy the freedom to be an Italian coffee heathen. Then my phone rang. Detective Gordon. I felt a sensation in the pit of my stomach. This could not be good.

The wait for Gallagher didn't improve my overall temper when I took the call. "Hi, Detective Gordon. Are you calling to arrest me?"

"And a good afternoon to you, Ms. Jensen," Detective Gordon said evenly. "The answer is no. But my partner and I have a few more questions for you."

Weary from the previous night's adventures of Dog the Bounty Hunter, stiff from sitting for an hour, and still in pain, I tried not to snarl as I said, "I can't imagine any way I could possibly help you, since I'm also trying my best to understand who could have killed the Harcourts."

"There's been another murder," he said.

That knot in the pit in my stomach suddenly tightened. "Who?" burst out of me.

"The DL … I'm sorry. His driver's license says his name is Aaron Gallagher. Do you know him?"

I felt slightly nauseated. "We've never met, but we were supposed to. Right now, actually."

"Where were you supposed to meet?"

"Kit's Cafe, a coffee shop in Kensington."

"Wait there." Gordon hung up before I could say anything else. What on earth? How long was I supposed to wait? *This is bullshit.*

I was seated close to the front door with my back to the wall, so I had a clear view of the entrance and the big picture window from which I could view a small section of front parking lot. I considered calling Gordon back for an ETA, when someone knocked on the front window pane. Detective Gordon stood there, looking in at me. I could feel the blood drain from my face.

CHAPTER FORTY-SEVEN

The Lexus was parked in an out-of-the-way corner behind a building in a nearby shopping center. The middle-aged man slumped behind the wheel wore a tailored gray suit, a dress shirt threaded with burgundy-colored pinstripes, and a burgundy tie. A hand and a shirt cuff extended from one arm of the suit jacket. The hand wore a fat gold ring embedded with a ruby red gem and the cuff sported a gold cufflink.

None of these things had protected Aaron Gallagher from the knife that had cut his throat. His body was still limp, head lolling forward. In fact, Gallagher's face resembled that of a fish dying in mid gasp. It also now matched his suit, except for the parts soaked with blood. Fortunately, I didn't have to look at the scene for long. Detectives Gordon and Sully dragged me away to grill me some more.

We returned to the coffee shop so the detectives could grab a decent cup of brew while questioning me. After explaining my presence there, I said, "Gallagher wanted to tell me something, but he wouldn't talk about it over the phone."

Detective Gordon nodded. Detective Sully simply stared at me. "Which explains why your number was in his recent calls," Gordon said. "Found his cell in his hand. Unlocked," he added, as if practicing the justification for the search.

"And why I'm here," I took pains to point out. "My question is, why was his car all the way back there?"

Detective Gordon had a sly look on his face. Detective Sully's eyebrows went up a fraction, which on her was an expression of shock.

"I'm surprised you never thought about joining the police force," Gordon said dryly.

Despite the bad timing of Gallagher's phone call and the fact that he was the Harcourts' attorney, plus the additional fact that it would be pretty stupid or psychotic to slit somebody's throat and hang around afterward reading a paperback, the detectives chose not to arrest me on the spot.

As the detectives approached their car, I asked, "Do you have any prime suspects in the Harcourt case at this point?"

Detective Gordon tossed me a look that said: *Get real.*

I shrugged. "Well, I'm in the clear, right?"

Detective Sully gave me her patented stare. "Yeah. For now."

Predictably, my brief confab with the detectives did not include a spirited discussion of the evidence, but it was clear that they appreciated the oddity of Gallagher's choice of parking places. Since he was supposed to be meeting me, I doubted that he intended to meet anyone else along the way. And he seemed more than a bit rushed when we last spoke, as if his decision to meet me had been last-minute, desperate even.

If I had to guess, I would say someone was with him in the car. Someone who forced him to park in that out-of-the-way spot. A nice quiet place to discreetly slit a man's throat. I wondered if the killer knew where Gallagher was headed and why. And was trying yet again to set me up. *Nice try*, I thought. *Too bad you didn't think to plant bloodstained clothes in my car.*

It was that part of the afternoon when the shadows start to get longer. Rush hour was in full swing. But my next move in the Harcourt matter was best performed at night, long after the commuters had returned to their homes and settled in. So I picked up a wrap to go for dinner and went home to bide my time.

After doing a bit of research on the office space belonging to Gallagher and Bernson, I changed into an old, somewhat snug dark tunic top and leggings and then headed for their building on Old Georgetown Road. My plan was to break into Gallagher's office to look for clues before the cops took them away.

By this time, it was dark. It was close to 2100 hours or 9:00 PM when I pulled into the parking lot. It was hardly full, but it still had a few cars left in it. I expected a few lights to be on in the building, but the pattern looked more like a chessboard. On a Friday night? I shook my head and hoped for society's sake that at least some of those offices were occupied with cleaning crews.

I left the car and approached the building, well aware that the entrance would be locked. Visible through the glass doors, a middle-aged guard sat at a desk. I tapped on the glass. When he looked at me, I motioned a request to enter, pointing at myself, then . . . in. He looked at me quizzically and then turned away. So, I rapped louder on the glass. This time he simply shook his head.

This wasn't what I'd hoped for. But I came prepared. So I tossed all pretense of shame aside and banged on the glass. He looked my way, startled. And I mugged a pleading expression, lips in a pout like a spoiled child, and batted my eyelashes. And almost made myself puke in the process. This managed to rouse the Guard Dog from his chair. He was middle-aged, but relatively fit. His hair was buzz cut, his expression skeptical.

The guard plodded to the door, because (unlike the dorms at Maryland) this place did not have an intercom between the guard desk and the door. Perhaps this was intentional, to keep the guard from dozing off. I didn't wait for him to start the conversation. In the most pathetic voice I could muster, I said, "Oh, please, please, let me in, sir. It really truly is a matter of life and death." I said this looking him in the eye and aiming my small, but perky, boobs right at him.

Either my shameless behavior or the snug shirt was doing its job. His expression softened and he cracked the door open.

"It's unusual for visitors to arrive at this time of night," he mansplained in cool, even tones. "And usually when they do, I'm told about it."

"But, but . . . here's the thing," I sputtered in a husky voice. "It's just that, you know, I'm like a good friend of Aaron Gallagher. I mean, real good friend, you know?" I gave him a suggestive look and struggled to keep smiling.

"And it's just that there's this thing I left in the office," I continued to blather. "It's kind of embarrassing . . . ."

He got one of those knowing smiles on his face, and his eyes lit up in a way that intensified my urge to puke.

"Okay," he said. "I understand."

I'll bet you do, I thought.

Guard Dog leered at me. "I assume you have a key?" He winked.

I forced a grin so hard, I thought I would dislocate my jaw. Nod, nod. The guard held the door for me, and I stepped inside, toward the bank of elevators.

"Ya gotta sign in, honey." Behind me, the guard's voice echoed in the glass-and-tile lobby.

I moved to the guard's station, where I found the sign-in sheet and signed a fake name. I also caught a glimpse of the console behind the guard's desk.

There were monitors, but not quite enough for each floor. But the images rotated. Okay, fine. I got the key. Sure. We're such good friends, he gave me a key. I hoped for the best when it came to gaining entry to the law offices. Whatever happened next couldn't be much worse than what I had already gone through.

CHAPTER FORTY-EIGHT

As the elevator shot up toward the 11th floor, I put on the pair of gloves I had tucked into my pocket—and questioned the wisdom of what I was doing. There were fifteen floors in the building, but only eight or nine monitors at the guard desk. Assuming that the views of different floors rotated proportionately, I guessed that I had a roughly 50-50 chance of getting caught in a lie. With any luck, the office door lock wasn't some kind of bizarre combination of buttons and retinal scan (which seemed excessive, even for a law firm) and would respond to my bump key.

The elevator doors opened onto a wide strip of burgundy carpet that stretched down the hall. The elevator door faced the entrance to the law firm. Through the glass doors, I could just barely make out what seemed to be a smartly decorated waiting area—there was muted light from a hidden source. But there were no clues as to whether anyone else was in the office. The glow of light seemed to come from beyond the receptionist area. Perhaps from a computer or other device someone had left on.

There were no shadows of movement. Hoping the coast was clear, I decided take my chances.

A quick look at the door brought some relief. The lock was not one of those fancy, high-tech ones. Not an easy one, but it was receptive to a set of lock picks, which I just happened to have, along with my bump key.

While I fiddled with picking the lock, my mind wandered back to the guard. I hoped I was right about the security cameras and wondered whether the Guard Dog was sleeping or enjoying my not very subtle attempt to break in.

As each tumbler clicked into place, I was on full alert for any sounds of moving, talking, or other human activity. So far, nothing but silence, apart from the tiny clicks and snaps of my lock-picking efforts. As I cracked the last bit of the lock and pushed the door open, I could hear the elevator start up behind me. I shoved my way through the doors, then bolted past the reception area and down a hall.

It wasn't hard to find which of the offices belonged to Aaron. I spotted an office with an engraved nameplate that identified it as Bernson's. Then I moved down the hall to a corner office. Nailed it. This door was locked, but the mechanism yielded easily to my bump key. I went inside and, without turning on any lights, I quickly scanned the room, its contents reduced to a collection of varying gray shapes in the dim light. A long section of floor-to-ceiling windows allowed the illumination from downtown Bethesda's commercial buildings to wash over the room. I made sure the door was locked before I closed it.

I could easily see a desk large enough to merit its own ZIP code. What money the Harcourts saved on their house clearly went toward legal fees. I used my phone to quickly capture the contents of the various desk drawers. If anything seemed vaguely interesting, I picked it up and inspected it more closely using my phone flashlight under the desk. The picture windows made the office feel a bit exposed. The last thing I needed was to be caught in mid B&E.

Among other things, I found a small appointment book. I flipped through it, scanning for references to anything I recognized. The Harcourts' names appeared. They had been scheduled to meet Gallagher the Monday after I discovered them. Interesting. I took a couple of photos of the calendar entry and thumbed through more of the pages. This revealed that the couple had met with the attorney about two weeks before they died.

Along with snapping photos of all the pages over the two-week period before the final calendar entry, this seemed like a good opportunity to find whatever records there were of Gallagher's last meeting with his late clients.

When I tried to start his computer, I was prompted for a password. I did a quick check for any obvious hiding places for a password list. After trying his initials, I struck out. That was it for me. I needed to focus on what I could get easily.

I moved from Gallagher's office to a small room full of filing cabinets. These guys had been practicing a while. Long enough to digitize to an extent but not give up on paper for good. Each cabinet bore a label that identified its contents in alphabetical order. I checked the labels more closely. In smaller type, each label indicated a hyphenated number prefaced by a single capital letter. The numbers seemed to suggest a date range. I suspected the capital letter stood for the attorney's last name.

A quick scan of the file cabinets confirmed my guess. In no time, I thumbed through the Hs in Gallagher's files. The name "Harcourt" jumped out at me along with the file itself. I took the time to check the previous date range and found only a thin file with their retainer agreement. I grabbed that, too. Each time, I made sure to pull up an adjacent file to make replacing the folder easier. I didn't intend to steal what might be clues for the cops. I just wanted to share the wealth.

Keeping to the shelter of the inner rooms, I found a small, book-lined law library. It was so cute, I went inside to flip through the (temporarily) pilfered files. The contents ranged from dull to yawn-inducing, which made it harder to figure out their import. Rather than agonize, I went for Gallagher's handwritten notes and file memos, figuring they possibly captured his thoughts and concerns better.

I thought I might use a copier to duplicate at least half the paperwork. I found one, but it was off. Damn. And it probably required a password. Damn again. "Times like this, I wish I had a partner," I muttered. I needed to get this done. Fast.

I improvised an assistant in, ironically, a fax machine. People still use these. And this one was on. So I loaded some notes and memos into the fax, hit what I hoped were the right buttons, and managed to make some copies that way. While that was processing, I snapped photos of the remaining documents and took handwritten notes about the other file contents. After collecting the copies, I returned the originals to their files and returned them both to storage.

Then I stole back into Gallagher's office, where I snapped one or two grainy photos. As I took pictures, I heard a *thunk* from down the hall—the sound a glass door makes when opening or closing. Perhaps the cleaning crew was making its rounds. Either that or it was someone I wanted to see even less.

CHAPTER FORTY-NINE

I took one last photo and hurriedly replaced the appointment book where I found it. Then, I retreated into a position under the desk. As I double-checked that my phone was on but silenced and its flash for the camera off, muted footfalls drifted from down the hall to where I crouched. Now and then, they faded out to a brief moment of near perfect silence. When the footsteps started up again, they were very faint.

That is not the cleaning staff or anyone else who has legitimate business here. So . . . it's either a common burglar or someone like me. A person looking for something in particular or something they will know they want when they see it.

Noises were coming from the locked door. Well, not from the door, but from the mysterious visitor. If he or she made it this far, they clearly had the ability to crack that lock.

By this time, my shins were beginning to whine. My back also had a few unkind words for me, but I told them all to shut the hell up. I remained in my crouched position and made myself ready for whatever came in. The lock sprung with a clatter. My head swam with a quick rush of adrenaline. Whoever it was picked the lock as ably as I had. Maybe even faster.

The footsteps came toward me, louder but still low and stealthy. In the gloom, I could just barely see the dark outline of legs. Slim, but well-muscled. Large feet in dark mesh sneakers. The shuffle of papers on the desk. I kept my eye on the outline, considering the angles and waiting. Then, the shushing sounds of drawers, as they were opened and closed. The intruder kicked the desk chair aside. I adjusted my footing.

His body shifted enough for me to know he was bending down to peek into my hiding place. As his midsection became visible, I took aim, launched myself through the leg hole, and hit him square in the solar plexus. My attack seemed to knock the wind out of him.

My trajectory sent us both hurtling against the wall. But while my unexpected partner in crime sprawled almost comically backward against it, his body provided me a cushion and a springboard for pushing myself clear of him. I shoved myself away from the collapsing man, dropped into a roll, and sprang to my feet. My back yipped and my head throbbed, but their complaints were smothered by pure adrenaline.

The man, who'd slid partway down the wall, curled in on himself, stuck a hand out at me, palm forward, while he regained his breath. The gesture seemed like a combined request for me to wait and to back off. After breathing heavily for a few moments, the man stood fully upright and turned my way. The light was dim, but the face was familiar even so.

"Hello, Ms. Jensen." He bared his teeth in a fleeting smile and followed that with the thousand-yard stare.

"Hi, Mr. Adams. Or should I say Parker? And why don't you call me Erica, since we keep running into each other?"

CHAPTER FIFTY

Adams offered another quicksilver grin. "Funny how we keep crossing paths."

"Hilarious," I said. "What are you doing here?

"Good," he said, with a nod. Like I'd passed a test. "That's good coming from you," he added with a smirk on his face.

"Back at ya."

His smile widened. "You're funny."

"And you're a riot. Now, why the fuck are you here?"

Adams crossed his arms. Even in the dark, he looked amused. "I'm sorry. Need to know only."

He gave a quick nod. "Well, I'll leave you to it, then," he said, moving toward the door. "Hope you find what you're looking for."

Adams turned on his heel and started to leave.

"Hold it," I ordered. "You still haven't answered my question."

With a quick shake of his head, Adams swatted away my words and kept moving. Fine. Let's make this fun.

As Adams moved toward the door, I sprang into position and ran at him. By the time Adams realized I was coming at him from behind, it was too late for him to counter me. I slammed into him with full force. We sailed right through the door, hit the opposite wall, and landed on the floor.

Despite my body's continuous reminders about its limitations, I managed to get to my feet, grimacing. When I approached Adams, it was with caution. I turned my camera flash on and aimed it at his face. He was lying sideways on the floor, propped up on one elbow like a harem girl. His expression was still hard to read. He didn't seem to be amused, but he was hardly angry.

"You didn't have to knock me down," Adams said, sounding a touch perplexed.

"You should be more cooperative."

He let out a short, breathy laugh. "Okay, Erica. You got me. What do you want from me?"

"What are you looking for? And why are you looking for it here?"

Adams held up his hand in the palm-forward, "put a pin in it" way he had. He stood with slow, deliberate movements, keeping his eyes on me. "I doubt we're looking for the same thing."

"I don't like to assume anything. Remember?"

We spent a few minutes batting words back and forth in the dimly lit hallway. I wasn't going anywhere until Adams answered my questions. I could keep up the questioning all night, if I had to. Of course, that never works. Direct questions never work. Ideally, one should cozy up to one's source and at least pretend to care about one thing, even if what you really want is something else entirely.

He refused to discuss his client or the nature of his investigation but he did empty his pockets. I asked if he'd taken any photos here. He showed me his recent photos. None were of this office.

"I have not taken anything from this place," Adams said. "So, if you are looking for a particular item, I'm not keeping it from you."

Fine. Problem was I didn't have a particular item in mind. I figured I would know it when I saw it.

"Does your being here have anything to do with Troy Fairchild?"

Adams maintained a mostly expressionless face, but one eyebrow lifted a fraction. *Was it in surprise?*

"No," he said, after a second or two.

"Really? Are you sure?"

"Of course."

Yeah, whatever. Maybe it was a tell. Maybe it was deliberate. I was fast running out of a desire to keep this up. Eventually, Adams turned to leave, and I didn't bother to stop him. But I kept him in view until he actually boarded the elevator. He turned my way, gave me his sneaky grin, and saluted before the doors closed. I watched the floor numbers count down, to make damn sure they reached all the way to L and without stopping. I wondered how he had handled the guard. For all I knew, they could have been drinking buddies.

I returned to Gallagher's office to finish what I'd started. Amid the semi-organized clutter on his desk, I found a photo of him with a grade-school-age kid I assumed was his daughter. A casual photo taken at what looked like a fair or an amusement park. The lawyer and the child sat on a bench, smiling for the camera.

It was the yellow sign that caught my eye. The girl in the photo held a stuffed animal. A plush koala toy. It looked mighty familiar. Then, it came to me. There it was again. The koala logo. *Embrace the Wild.*

CHAPTER FIFTY-ONE

Okay, I thought. The Harcourts' attorney just happened to go to this . . . place that may or may not have anything to do with Troy Fairchild. I brought that train of thought to a screeching halt. *I'm overthinking this.*

But I definitely would take note of the photo. I picked it up and ran into the hallway, where the wall shielded me from view from outside. My phone glowed bright enough to see, but I positioned myself near an emergency exit sign for more light. Hoping to capture the image without disturbing the picture frame, I snapped a few shots of the photo, both with and without the flash. Fortunately, the simple frame had no glass. The results weren't perfect either way, but they were good enough for what I needed.

After returning the photo to its proper place, I performed a last sweep of the office. My investigative train was leaving the station. I could hear the conductor: *Now leaving. Last chance for clues.*

I took the risk of taking a wide shot or two of the general layout, just in case a clue popped out later. The city lights were just bright enough to give me a couple of murky abstracts using the now-ancient phone I purchased five years ago. Perhaps I could sell them as art photos online.

When I left the building, I realized how hungry I was, so I headed for an all-night diner. As I considered my next move over a stack of pancakes, a side of bacon, and some hot coffee, the jukebox sprang to life. There was only one middle-aged couple and one lone elderly man as fellow patrons, so I was surprised when "Yellow Submarine" began to play. The elderly man got up and performed a solo dance routine to it, which was a bit unexpected.

Then I caught a glimpse of what looked like metal tags swinging on a chain around his neck. I could see that they were dog tags. Old dude had probably served in Nam. Maybe he wasn't as old as he looked.

I nursed my coffee while I watched the one-man show. The woman behind the counter didn't seem to notice or care. She went about the business of wiping counters and making clattering noises with hardly a glance at the man. Maybe she had seen that act a hundred times before.

Before I left, I slipped an extra $1 from my billfold, along with what I had to pay plus tip for the counter woman. The old man was back in his seat, with his head down on the counter—his arms crossed underneath for a cushion.

I tucked the bill under one hand. "Hang in there," I muttered. He didn't move. But he was breathing.

Drinking coffee and stuffing my face diverted me for possibly a half hour or so. After leaving the diner, I still felt too wired to just go home. I should have been exhausted, but my encounter with Adams, plus finding that one clue, was like a shot of adrenaline.

It wouldn't be long before the sun came up. The air was still too nippy to lower my car windows completely, but I cracked them before I started my car and took a drive down the nearly empty streets. The chilly air was stimulating. The occasional car zipped past. Someone in a hurry. I wondered why at this hour.

My body was on auto-pilot. Beneath my conscious thoughts, one in particular poked through the surface. Who was the alleged witness to my arrival at the Harcourt house the morning of the murders? As if I had somehow automatically adjusted my course into the requisite route, I found myself turning into the Harcourts' neighborhood and drifting past their house. The crime scene tape was gone.

I doused the lights, drove to a point up the road from the house, backed onto a small side street, and parked at the corner. Then, I sat back and waited, but I wasn't sure for what. I was sure I'd know it when it came along.

Ever since Nick had mentioned that someone had witnessed my arrival last week, I had wondered who it was. I came here with the hope of getting a better sense of the neighborhood. Did anyone make regular pre-dawn visits here on Saturdays? Who would have the best view of the Harcourts' house? I suspected my instinctive attraction to this area was the byproduct of those questions percolating through my mind. I certainly couldn't expect to recognize a frequent visitor after one stakeout, but maybe I could note anyone suspicious or, given the low volume of traffic, just anyone.

I sat for a bit and listened to the car ticking as it cooled. I closed the windows and pulled up Google Earth on my phone. After I had zeroed in as closely as possible on the Harcourts' house, I maneuvered the screen to each house across from them. When I was sure I had reached the front door of each, I zoomed out just enough to see where all the windows were, circling the house and testing each one for the quality of the view. From inside one of the houses, it would have been hard to make out much of the Harcourts' front yard. The shrubbery—

an incredibly tall hedge of arborvitae—blocked visual access enough to make it almost impossible for anyone to have seen me when I arrived that morning.

That left me with one house most likely to have a decent view of the Harcourts' frontage. I did a reverse look-up on the address, and gawked at the result. A listing for "Mabel Forbes." What was *she* doing here?

CHAPTER FIFTY-TWO

Just how many houses did Mabel Forbes own? If she lived in a senior facility, who managed them? Ms. Brooks Brothers? Her boss? I ran a quick check in realtor.com and Zillow. No listing anywhere for either the Columbia house or this one.

I searched on the address for the Columbia house and pulled up a listing on a website. There was the house. A sign in front reading: Sale by Owner. Probably Photoshopped. Ah, Ms. Brooks Brothers. So you're an agent?

I took a screenshot and set that new development aside to be scrutinized later. Then I focused on how best to approach the Forbes house to get a good close look at it without being seen. I reached behind the driver's seat and pawed through the makeshift cargo organizer I had rigged there. It wasn't hard to find my binoculars. I looped the binocular strap around my neck, grabbed my phone and other gear, and got out of the car.

I left the car near the intersection and ducked between two houses to make for the common wooded area behind them. Then I blazed a trail through the tangled underbrush, keeping to the shadowy woods and hoping to stay clear of cameras and motion-triggered security lights. Eventually, I worked my way around to the rear of the Forbes house.

The last time I checked, it was nearly 6:00 AM. About an hour until sunrise. Squatting in the dark, I shivered in the late March air. *What could I learn from watching this house?* It was my back asking that question. Then my brain replied that it wanted to know what might happen here on a typical early Saturday morning—and it told my back to shut up.

Even though I was a distance from the house, I scoped it out for sensors and security lights. My eyes had adjusted to the dark somewhat, but I couldn't see anything in terms of obvious cameras or lights. The interior was a black hole. Not even the smallest sign of light, as if the windows were covered with black-out curtains. I crept toward the Forbes house, keeping an eye out for anything that might become a problem. With my confidence up, I moved toward the nearest window.

Keeping to the side, I paused. I no longer felt cold; in fact, a trickle of sweat ran down my neck. The noise from a distant engine grew louder. A truck or van was coming. I steadied my breath and turned to sneak a look inside the house. And nearly jumped out of my skin when a fierce-looking woman stared back.

"Jesus," I said, then quickly smothered a laugh. The blinds were open, and the interior was impenetrably dark. So dark that when I peeked into the window, all I saw was my own reflection. I knew the blinds were there because I could see the light-colored backing made visible on each side by the faint glow of a street lamp. "Not even a night light?" I muttered. The interior was so dark, it suggested that the house was unoccupied.

The vehicle I had heard earlier had stopped and the engine was shut off. I moved closer to the street. Not far away, a delivery van was parked in front of another house a few doors up from the Harcourts'. Because the engine was turned off, I assumed the driver lived there. The van bore a logo I didn't recognize. Surely he wasn't making a delivery at this hour.

I considered the risks and potential consequences of committing another B&E. Nothing ventured, nothing gained. My feet were already in motion.

This house had a back door that responded politely to my bump key, so I slipped inside and shut the door. I tapped my phone to get the minimal light and moved like a cat as I surveyed the blackness around me. I managed to navigate through the kitchen, through a connecting room, and into what might have been the living room, without stumbling even once. An amazing feat, I thought, until, on closer inspection, I saw that all the rooms were devoid of furniture. When I made my way to one of the windows, I found it covered with a dark film, probably temporary.

"I wonder what the homeowner's association would say?" I inquired of no one. I checked the remaining windows on the ground floor. They all had the same dark film. By this time, I had turned my flashlight on and could see that this part of the house wasn't occupied. Or showed no signs of anyone living in it.

I did the most thorough search possible in less than an hour. If there had been any clues as to when and how the place was last used, they had all been taken away. Not even a dust ball on the floor.

The upstairs windows were also covered in the dark film. *What the fuck?* More than a little bit weird. I stopped at each window and tried to pull the film up enough to get a peek at the view. Impossible to remove. Not without tools I didn't have. So, I unlocked a window and opened it a crack. No alarm, not one that sounded, at any rate. And that's how I found at least two windows with a stellar view of the Harcourts' front walk and front door. It was possible that whoever witnessed my arrival at the Harcourt house last Saturday might have been on the verge of moving out. But somehow, that didn't seem likely.

CHAPTER FIFTY-THREE

What was it with Mabel Forbes and her houses? Perhaps I'd
already met the self-proclaimed real estate maven herself. I took
a few photos of the Harcourts' front yard from different angles.
Not that there was much to see. I just wanted proof of that.

I made my way out the back door and moved around to the
front-left corner where I took a few quick shots of the Harcourt
house from a rather tricky but doable angle. That's when I
noticed a uniformed man leaving the house where the van was
parked. I stopped where I was and watched him as he walked
toward the van. The eastern sky was beginning to lighten into
the murky gray of pre-dawn, but I could make out his features
well enough to see that he was handsome, about my age, a bit
younger maybe. I raised my camera again.

He climbed into the van, fired up the engine, and swung the
van around into a three-point turn. I held down the button on
my phone to make it snap multiple stills without stopping. As
the van rumbled past, the logo on its side came into view. A
clock—the kind with hands—and the name "Round the Clock"

on top of the image. Under the logo were the words (in quotes) "We deliver." I'll bet they did.

It wouldn't be long before the sun cleared the horizon. I made my way back to the car and checked Google Maps for the location of the delivery company. With any luck, the delivery van driver might have seen something.

There was nothing misleading about the company's name. Google informed me that the business was open and they delivered 24/7. I tried to picture the schedule for a typical shift. It didn't square with a driver stopping at home for two hours and then going back to work. Perhaps he was pulling a double shift. Or maybe that wasn't the driver's house. Which raised the question of why he'd entered the house and stayed quite a bit longer than most delivery personnel would. People work at all hours, as I well knew. Nonetheless, I wondered what was being delivered before the sun was up.

I considered the options. Take on the tricky task of questioning a potentially hostile witness or forget about him and potentially miss the clue that could solve the murders? Did I really have a choice? It was now a matter of when, what, who, and how. When was the driver last here? What did he see, if he was here? Who could answer my questions? And how much would it cost?

And then I remembered it was Saturday. Just another Saturday. What was the likelihood I could get this information today? Or tomorrow? Or ever? I sighed. My thoughts were muddled and I felt totally unmotivated. I should have been home in bed.

At that point, I must have drifted off, because from the depths of sleep, a hallucinatory vision of the Helmand Province deserts emerged. I raise my weapon as a car approaches. The resounding bang of an explosion, then muted sounds, as if I'm underwater. My ears ring, as well. The lengthy dissonant medley assaults me. As if the relentless heat and blinding sand aren't enough.

The bloody little boy of my nightmares is running toward me, when I hear an odd tapping sound. And the bloody child turns into a little girl. One clearly not from Afghanistan. I want to ask her a question, but I can't speak. The tapping gets louder. I jerk my head upright and my eyes open. Ow. Now, I had a crick in my neck to go with my bad back. I reached around with one hand and tried to rub it out. Three more raps on the window. I directed my attention toward it, and a cop stared back at me.

As Dirty Harry Callahan would say, "Marvelous."

CHAPTER FIFTY-FOUR

Fortunately, Officer Friendly just happened to be in the neighborhood and noticed me slumped in the front seat. He seemed more concerned than upset with me. In fact, he took pains to make sure I was fit to drive by asking me questions like those doctors use to check for concussions. It was almost a sobriety test.

He took the precaution of asking for my license and running a check on it. The fact that he gave it right back assured me that I had no outstanding warrants. Yet. Finally, he said I was free to go, and I wasted no time leaving.

If they hadn't issued a warrant for my arrest after a week, that was a good sign. Still, I was plagued by the timing of Marian Harcourt's phone call vis-à-vis my arriving to find the butchered bodies. That issue refused to go away. I needed to understand what had happened. Could that delivery man have witnessed my arrival at the house? I tried to recall that morning but couldn't remember if there was a van in the neighborhood or much of anything else, except the horrendous scene in the Harcourts' basement.

But I did not plan to do any more work without at least an attempt at actual sleep. Dozing off in the car not only hurt my neck, but my back was grumbling and small explosions of pain ricocheted inside my skull.

I found my way home and collapsed into bed with all of my clothes still on, including my shoes. Once I settled into the mattress, my brain went into a deep, black inkwell. Darkness and relief for a moment, then a pinpoint of light. The world's tiniest LED expanded slowly into a bright white hole. Which widened and swallowed me into the blinding glare of the desert. And I'm back in Dreamland again. Boots on the ground.

When I awoke, I could see a darkening sky through the window near my bed. I checked my bedside clock. It read 7:45 PM. But what day?

I checked my phone; it was still Saturday. I lay there staring at the ceiling. Then I rolled out of bed and trudged to the window. The streets were empty, except for the usual lines of parked cars. Street lamps threw spotlights onto the vehicles, creating occasional splashes of color on the bluish-gray tableau, like a really old movie, partially colorized. I was still in a half-dozing state when I realized who I needed to talk to— Minetti. But he was probably working. At this hour, the restaurant might be packed, or not. In Maple Lawn? Well . . . .

Before taking off for the restaurant, I called Alex Kingsley. Nick had referred me to Alex, a bona fide private eye, when I needed help with a previous investigation, one lifeline thrown to me by another lifeline.

Since then, I had come to think of her as a kind of mentor. I tried not to impose, but I've learned the hard way that if you need a favor, sometimes the best thing to do is just ask. After we'd exchanged brief pleasantries, I said, "I have an unusual situation and could really use your help with a few things."

"How unusual? And how many things?" Her voice held a playful undertone, but I didn't think she was smiling.

I thought about how to answer. "Unusual because if I don't find out the truth, I could be wrongly arrested for murder."

A short pause. "I see," she said, as if noting the time of someone's death.

"I need a background check," I added. "And some serious digging into an organization called Embrace the Wild."

CHAPTER FIFTY-FIVE

After confirming that Minetti was available, I splashed some
water on my face, brushed my hair, and savored some minty
mouthwash. After sniffing my underarms to make sure I didn't
completely stink, I gave each one a quick just-in-case swipe of
deodorant, finished dressing, and set out for Maple Lawn. The
restaurant had plenty of customers but no wait-list.

Minetti and I met once again in his closet-sized office. My
thoughts drifted to the brief but memorable panic I had felt in
Leland's closet. That place had more elbow room than Minetti's
office. I guess my problem wasn't just because of the tight
space.

"Frank," I said, after he again reminded me to call him that.
"Do you remember any of the people the Harcourts met with?
Did any of them stand out?"

Minetti's brow furrowed. He nodded. "Maybe. I vaguely
recall one or two couples they met with quite often, but I
couldn't tell you who they were. Not offhand."

"Can I show you some pictures?" I went into my photos, found the shots from the church service, and opened the ones of the back and front pews.

I held the phone and swiped through the images, giving Minetti time to scrutinize each one. He scanned the back row photos without comment. When we got to the photos of the front rows, he said, "Hang on. I've seen them before." He pointed to the image of Marge Calhoun and Ryan Douglas.

"You saw these two?" I asked, pointing each one out.

Minetti nodded in the affirmative. "Yeah, them. And the young man on the other side of the woman."

Of course I knew Calhoun and Douglas, but I couldn't identify the young man next to Calhoun.

"And I think I saw those two," he added. He pointed out another man and woman seated farther back. The picture's focus wasn't on them, so their features were tougher to make out. The woman was closer to the camera. She was white. Her worried expression seemed oddly familiar. As for the guy beside her, he was white. That's all I could tell you.

"And you don't know any of them?" I asked, still looking at the worried woman in the background.

Minetti shook his head. Then, he said, "Hang on." He took another look at the photo. Then did a double take. "Well, I'll be. He's grown up."

"Who?"

Minetti pointed to the young man sitting next to Calhoun. "That's Jaden Harcourt. Their son."

And I thought he hadn't shown up for the service. Where did I get that idea?

"But you don't know the name of the woman or the man next to him?"

Minetti looked, shrugged, shook his head.

"Marge Calhoun was the Harcourts' PR woman. The older guy next to her is Ryan Douglas, their business manager."

"Is that so? We were never introduced." Minetti's voice was almost chipper. "Guests don't generally mix with the caterers, and caterers don't very often get introduced to the guests."

"I take it neither of them went to any of the Harcourts' catered events."

Minetti stiffened. "That's not what I said."

I knew that, but I had to confirm. "So, they might have been there, but you weren't introduced to them."

"Exactly." Minetti's smile twisted into a smirk. "And, like I said, they would have no reason to talk to me."

Minetti's mood seemed to darken a bit, but he seemed less angry than amused.

"And you're sure you don't recognize anyone else in any of the photos?"

We took another spin through my photos. He shook his head.

"Nope. I mean, yes, I'm sure."

That left me only a few parties of interest from the service: Ryan Douglas, Marge Calhoun, Jaden Harcourt, and the Mystery Couple. Now, I remembered why I didn't think Jaden was there. Marge told me she had tried to reach him and then acted like she hadn't been able to. But she never outright lied. In fact, she hadn't really told me anything.

It was either really late or really early when I returned home. I felt tired but not quite tired enough to hit the sack. I thought about having some coffee but I poured myself a glass of water instead. I sat at the dining table with my interview notes and research arranged at odd angles around my flowchart, which had become a mish-mash of lines and multifaceted shapes.

It was ironic that, in spite of all the complications social media may have brought to the Harcourts' lives, it seemed likely that their murders might have been the result of a problem close to home.

Then I asked myself a lot of questions. I wondered if talking to Astrid Gunderson, the cool nanny, was worth a trip all the way across the Potomac River and into Virginia. I could always try a FaceTime or Skype session, of course, but it wouldn't be quite the same as a face-to-face meeting. Besides, setting up calls like that deprived me of a favorite tactic: the element of surprise.

And how well did Marge Calhoun and Jaden Harcourt know each other? Why was Jaden at his parents' memorial service but not Amy? And how cozy were Calhoun and Douglas? What were they carefully choosing not to tell me?

On top of all that, I kept wondering what Troy Fairchild was doing camping out at a place owned by the entrepreneurial Mabel Forbes. Was it merely chance that he happened to go to The Void, which Mabel owned, and then stay at a house she owned? And how to explain that Mabel Forbes just happened to own another house across the street from the Harcourts. One furnished like an overpriced storage unit at that.

And then there was Parker Adams, Mr. Yoga Stretch. Come to think of it, I had only his word that someone knocked me unconscious that day at The Void. Maybe Adams was the person who did that. Was he following me in the brown sedan? I really wished I had gotten a good look at the driver.

Since the flowchart had become an unusable mess, I thought I would try to organize the information differently. I made a list of all the people I thought were the most likely sources and then listed all the questions I had for each one. And I wondered how much the now-deceased Aaron Gallagher could have told me.

CHAPTER FIFTY-SIX

I decided to put off calling Amy until a decent hour. I had already imposed enough on her good will by questioning her the day after her parents died. My mind was starting to drift, so I checked the clock. It was too late for anything but sleeping. Eventually, I figured that out and moved like a robot to my bed. And for the first time in ages, I didn't have nightmares. I slept soundly . . . until the banging started.

I jerked upright in bed, my heart slamming against my chest. I had left the blinds open, but even the bright late March sunlight hadn't awakened me. I blinked and rubbed my eyes. The pounding continued.

"Police," a voice called. The voice of Detective Sully. "Open up, ma'am. We have a warrant to search the premises."

Fuck.

I'd be lying if I said I hadn't expected this visit. But I also really and truly wanted to avoid it. I wanted out. And it was becoming painfully clear that the cops weren't going to let me off the hook. I needed to handle this without making the cops' stupidity too obvious. So, not bothering to change out of my PJs, I let them in. They searched. I made coffee.

"Want some coffee?" I asked Sully, with uber-fake cheer. As I moved toward the sugar bowl, I did a brief tango with one cop, who seemed to think he'd find Jimmy Hoffa's body under my sink.

"Mmm?" Sully murmured. A long pause followed. "No, thanks," she added, ten days later.

The smell of coffee held the promise of greater energy than I felt. I inhaled the smell of my freshly made coffee, took a sip, and then took another look at my copy of the search warrant.

"Really nice of you guys not to take my computer," I said. "Keeps me off unemployment."

Sully's mouth tightened. In fact, her whole body seemed to tense. "We are authorized to search the premises only as specified. Possible weapons."

"Not counting my steak knives, I hope." Not to mention the Sig P320 handgun I had produced voluntarily. The one I owned legally.

Two other cops emerged from the sanctum of my bathroom. I half-expected others to pour out, like clowns from a tiny car. In a gloved hand, one of them held my pill bottle aloft.

"Oxy," he announced. "Three whole pills."

"Yeah," I said, lifting my coffee mug. "I'm the East Coast distributor."

Sully shot me a look so hard, it could have punched a hole through me.

"You're on probation, aren't you?" she said.

"No. More like a lengthy stay of prosecution." If Sully knew my record, she would also know that the indefinite postponement was conditioned on my attending therapy. "And not for distribution."

Sully gave me her patented smug look. "I'm aware of your record."

Well, no shit.

She turned to face me. "All of your record. And when I say all of it, I mean *all* of it."

I had no idea what she meant by that, but after a few seconds passed, it dawned on me.

"Oh, you mean my military record."

She nodded. "My mother was a Marine," she added quickly.

For a moment, we said nothing. The two officers glanced at each other, exchanging an unspoken *should-we-even-be-here* look.

I turned to the officers. "You guys find the murder weapon?"

They said nothing. But they went back to their standard cop faces.

Sully inclined her head toward the door. "I think we're done here." The officers wasted no time in leaving. Sully said, "Thanks for your cooperation," and followed them out the door.

"Sure," I said.

What just happened here?

CHAPTER FIFTY-SEVEN

I wondered what Sully's motive was in telling me that her mother was a Marine, and I wondered what they had hoped to find. I also thought about her mention of my previous brush with the legal system, which reminded me of the upcoming group therapy I had to attend. Forty hours, court-ordered. I was almost there, just six hours away from finishing up. Six very long hours. But I'm a Marine. We eat torture for breakfast. This morning, however, I added some scrambled eggs and a second cup of coffee.

Sully had done me the solid of kicking the paper inside when she arrived to serve the search warrant. I spread the pages across the table and ate my breakfast, holding the plate in one hand and managing the fork and pages with the other.

I finished my small-ish breakfast, washed the dishes, and put a few more peanuts out for Rocky. And then my phone rang. It was Alex Kingsley.

"That was quick," I said.

"I thought you might want to know this sooner rather than later," she said, her voice low. Almost comically conspiratorial. "But I can't tell you now. We have to meet."

I would have laughed and said, "Sure. Under a bridge or in a parking garage at midnight?" But her not-at-all-comical tone was chilling.

"Okay. When? Where?"

"As soon as you can. How about Hyattsville? I'm wearing a distinctive orange-and-blue top."

This was an unexpected turn of events. Alex and I had never actually met, always dealing with each other by email, text, or phone. She agreed to meet me in an hour at Busboys and Poets, a local bookstore and cafe. I took my time getting there and still arrived early.

The weather had warmed over the past day or two, and people were out, enjoying the light green buds on the trees and the sun on their faces. The Hyattsville Arts District is another one of those "new urban" mini-cities relatively close to D.C.

As I strolled around the multitude of tidy brick buildings to kill time, the pungent smell of Thai and Mexican restaurant cooking wafted around me. If I closed my eyes, those aromas could easily transport me to a more exotic place. Of course, I had already been to one of those, but my timing was lousy.

As I started my second trip around the block, I noticed an orange-and-blue Mets shirt. The person wearing it was in her late 30s, and she was also wearing jeans and a pair of high-tops. She had shoulder-length brown hair and clear blue eyes. "Are you Erica Jensen?" she asked in a curious and amused voice.

"Alex Kingsley?" I said.

"Yes. It's so nice to meet you."

I revised my previous assessment of Alex. Up closer, I could see the faint wrinkles of a woman in her 40s. She also had streaks of gray in her light brown hair.

We made the usual bit of polite chit-chat as we approached the coffee shop. "I don't usually hang out here," Alex said. "I live in Northwest." Meaning the northwest quadrant of D.C. Residents often describe the city in terms of quadrants, because that's how the place was laid out by that French guy who was clearly obsessed with geometry.

After we had settled in with our coffee, Alex got to the point.

"Embrace the Wild," she said, her voice low. "It's much more than a petting zoo gone wrong."

"Yeah. That whole . . . pseudo-safari thing. Pretty big-time stuff."

Alex leaned toward me. "This is serious."

"Exactly what do you mean?" I did a quick visual scan of the room. No sign of anyone interested in us or any other sign of trouble. Yet.

"It's a front for someone."

"The mob?"

"I don't know. And I'm not sure I want to know."

I squinted. "Why?" When she didn't respond, I added, "Are we talking terrorists? Drug cartels? Sex traffickers? What?"

Alex sighed while shrugging her shoulders, working out frustration or kinks. "Yes," she said.

CHAPTER FIFTY-EIGHT

Not only did Alex uncover a rat's nest of shell companies and so-called nonprofits connected to Embrace the Wild, but her tracks converged with those of various federal agencies. According to her sources, the company was one of the local affiliates in an international operation that potentially violated enough federal laws to get nearly the entire FBI and a few other alphabet agencies involved.

"But that's not why I stopped looking," Alex said.

I nodded, feeling glum about what I figured the reason was.

"The feds have struggled to deal with the illicit use of shell companies for ages," Alex said. "There's nothing unusual about that. But the more I poked around, the tougher it became to find answers."

Alex stabbed a finger on the table. "My search led to highly classified information—references to files I couldn't access. When I turned to trusted sources for help, most of them didn't return my calls. Some did, but then they just clammed up on me, so I had to stop. I felt like I was living inside some movie like *All the President's Men* or *Three Days of the Condor.*"

"Hmm. I've never seen either one of them."

Alex gave me a look that said *poor millennial* and then gave me a capsule description of each.

That substantially renewed my paranoia about the last week or so. "Do you think the Harcourts might have been murdered by criminal conspirators?" As I spoke, I realized my words sounded like they came from a bad movie.

She shrugged. "I couldn't say, but one way or another, they got involved with people who have done more than break the law. Enough to suggest links to terrorists and other bad actors, here and abroad."

"I hate to ask, but—"

She must be a mind reader because she cut in with, "You want me to do a deeper background check on the Harcourts?"

"Yep." If the Harcourts were dirty, they had done a great job of covering their tracks.

Alex agreed to do more digging. Since she had already given me a break on her usual fee, I suspected that she was motivated more by curiosity than by any financial gain. After we parted, more questions came up. Who exactly had the Harcourts gotten involved with? What did they know? And when? Did the brown sedan have any connection to whoever was pulling the strings? Was the ever-so-smooth Parker Adams involved?

Assuming they were innocent, the Harcourts might have been inadvertently drawn into an arrangement with the petting zoo that then made them suspects in a federal investigation— subjects of scrutiny on the national security front. If they weren't involved but suspected that someone was watching them, maybe they thought they should hire a bodyguard. Being watched by the feds? I shook my head. My thoughts were going in circles.

As I drove home, I constantly scanned my surroundings, left-right-rear view, left-right, left-right-rear view, all the way to my apartment. I didn't see the brown car, but I did see a row of sedans in a rainbow of colors. Maybe the owner of the brown sedan had had the car painted. As soon as I went inside, I looked up the delivery service and gave them a call. The man who answered, "Round the Clock. We deliver," spoke so slowly, I wanted to reach through the phone lines to help extract the words.

"Hi, yes," I said, in a more lilting voice than usual. "You provide local delivery?"

"Yes, ma'am." He dragged out the word "ma'am" to almost four syllables. "Round the Clock. Courier and van."

"As you may know, the police are investigating a homicide that took place in one of the neighborhoods you serve," I said, citing the date the police had given the press. "One of your drivers was recently—"

"Ma'am? Can I help you?" The voice had picked up some speed.

"If there was a delivery during the time the killing occurred, it would be a huge help to the police to know if the driver witnessed anything. I'd like to speak with the driver assigned to that neighborhood on the day of the murder from 5:30 to 6:00 AM." Then, I rattled off the hundred block for the Harcourts' house. And all of that without telling a single lie.

The man either coughed or laughed. "Right. And who are you exactly?"

"I'm related to one of the victims." An exaggeration, yes, but it sounded better than, "I found them, and the cops are itching to put me away."

"Hmph." After a long pause, he added, "Okay. I'll check the schedule. What location, day, and time was that again?"

I gave him the details, just as the media had announced them.

"Hang on." The on-hold silence pressed on my eardrum.

I paced the floor, phone to my ear, switched to speaker, did a one-finger dust inspection of my minimalist furnishings, waved at Rocky, who was visible through his usual window, and circled back to where I had started by the time the man came back on.

"This is interesting." He sounded more alert now. "One of our drivers was in that neighborhood on that day, but he arrived at around 5:15 in the morning."

"What time did he leave?"

"It doesn't say. According to our records, that was his final delivery." Anticipating my next question, he added. "He brought the van back at 8:00 AM"

I wondered what the driver was doing during that stretch of time and where he did it. "Did the driver deliver to this address on a regular basis? And for how long?"

The man paused. I had asked too many questions. Shit.

"Ma'am, with all due respect, I would let the police handle this."

"And if your employee was a possible witness, shouldn't he be told?" I threw the suggestion back at him.

"If our employee was a witness," he said, with a bit of a growl, "wouldn't the police know by now?"

I had no idea what the police would know or should know within a week after starting a homicide investigation. Other than something about 48 hours.

"Now, if you'll excuse me . . . ."

"Wait!" I threw up my mental hands and struggled to keep speaking in a calm, completely un-desperate voice. "Please help me. Because, to be honest, I'm not with the police but I need them to solve this. I don't want to be involved, but I am and could really use your help."

A long silence ensued. "Ok-ay," he finally said, drawing the word out slowly. "What do you need to know?"

"Could I get the driver's name and contact info? Maybe a phone number?"

He paused. "I'll talk to him and ask him to call you, OK?"

"Perfect," I said, hoping that I wasn't just doing some wishful thinking.

CHAPTER FIFTY-NINE

Before I finished my call with Round the Clock, the agent said, "I'm glad you called, actually. I had never noticed the weird schedule this guy follows."

"Weird how?" I asked.

"That's why it took me a while to get back on the line. And I have to say, this is embarrassing, because I have people who keep track of this stuff. But when I looked at the raw data, I noticed this driver has been going to that address every week for a while. For at least the last couple of months."

"Always the last delivery?"

"For the last few weeks, anyway. Maybe longer."

"And you're sure it's the same driver?" I asked.

"Yeah, which is also weird. Most guys are willing to trade off on the graveyard shift, but this guy seems to be on it all the time."

Maybe he preferred the relatively traffic-free working conditions. Or maybe he was a vampire. This left me with another question: why that one house every week? I could only imagine. One thing did seem clear, and that was my hunch that I should be looking for clues closer to home.

I gave myself the rest of the day to figure out my next move. Somewhere among all the moving parts, there was a killer or someone trying to set me up as one, but I needed to home in on the motive and opportunity. Why would someone who lives near the Harcourts want to kill them? The usual reasons popped into my mind: jealousy, greed, lust, anger. It always came down to one or more of the Seven Deadly Sins.

But the nature of the murder was so vicious, I had to think it was more than just a killing. It struck me as more like a bloody retribution. A pound of flesh for a grievous injustice, real or perceived. Almost as if the killer was insane with a desire for vengeance. Which is to say it didn't look like a gang slaying. No, a real gangster doesn't care. A cap to the head and on with other business. No, this wasn't business. It was personal.

So along with that aspect, I now had to figure in federal agencies, including ones with euphemistic names and black budgets. Did those things just happen to intersect? Or were they related?

I took a quick look online for my old friend Special Agent Phipps from the FBI. After confirming that he still worked there, I thought about getting in touch, but I had doubts about how much help he could offer. If Embrace the Wild was the target of an enormous government investigation, Phipps might or might not be involved. And even if he knew about it, would he be willing to share?

I grabbed my phone to call Nick. After exchanging the usual greetings, I asked, "Do you have any federal government sources who get involved in money laundering cases or using shell companies to commit crimes?"

The line went quiet for a moment. "I'm not sure. It's not a subject I write on a lot."

I thought about that. "If someone wanted you to write on these subjects, could you do it?"

"Of course," he said, as if it were obvious. "I'm as good a researcher as any other journalist."

"I have an idea, if you wouldn't mind trying it."

The line went quiet again. For much longer. "Yes?" Nick seemed to stretch the word into two syllables.

"It would involve interviewing an FBI agent."

CHAPTER SIXTY

Since Nick seemed to be taking on status as an unofficial operative at the proverbial offices of Erica Jensen Investigations LLC, I gave him a quick recap of what I had unearthed so far.

Nick was willing to try my gambit of digging up more on Embrace the Wild and whatever suspect operations they might engage in. I tried to explain Alex's concerns without spelling them all out.

"Don't worry," he said. "Risk comes with the territory." I detected more than a hint of glee in his voice. "I'll get on this right away."

Since it was Sunday, I assumed he meant the next day. I spent most of the rest of the day doing my best to block out all thoughts of the Harcourts and whatever mess they had stumbled into. And ended up watching the old movie *Full Metal Jacket*. I shake my head over Private Pyle. Then—wham!— Nancy Sinatra sings, "These Boots are Made for Walking".

The movie was ending when my phone rang. Since I didn't recognize the number, I almost ignored it. Then, changed my mind and took the call without saying a word. After a prolonged silence, a tentative voice came through. "I need to speak to someone named Erica."

The caller had a male voice. "Who's calling?" I asked.

"My name's Benny. I drive for Round the Clock."

I was so startled, it took me a few moments to respond. "Benny? Yes, thank you for calling."

I wondered if my phone was tapped. But that would be illegal. Did it matter?

"Did your manager tell you what this is about?"

He swallowed so loudly, I could hear it on my end. "Yeah."

"Oh, good," I added with some extra oomph. Memories of the Gallagher incident floated through my head. "Are you on the graveyard shift tonight?"

"Uh-huh."

"Would it be convenient for you to swing by while you're in that neighborhood?" I emphasized the word "that," hoping he knew which one I meant.

Benny paused. When he spoke, the words came slowly. "You want me to—"

"Come by my house, while you're in that neighborhood." I finished his thought. "I'm at this address." I gave him the number of the empty house across from the Harcourts' residence.

Benny confirmed that he'd be there tomorrow. Really, really early tomorrow.

"Thanks," I said. "I hope that package comes. They say next-day service . . . well . . . shit happens, right?"

"Yeah," Benny said. He sounded lost.

"I'm really looking forward to getting it."

"Uh, yeah. Sure." He added cautiously, "I'll see you." It was a sentence with an invisible question mark.

"Yes, see you then."

After settling on 6:00 AM as the time Benny would, in his words, "most likely be in your neighborhood," I hung up feeling ridiculous. The whole situation seemed over-the-top. I had no idea if Benny could help me. But I was so worried about the way the Harcourts had been butchered and the possible involvement of the CIA or NSA or MI6 or whoever it was, that it was essential to be cautious, especially since the police had actually considered me a suspect—not without some cause.

In any event, the Harcourt matter was doing a number on my circadian rhythms. I had trouble sleeping before, and constantly readjusting my sack time was not helping a bit. And somewhere along the line, I'd lost an hour when the clocks sprang forward.

Before attempting some shut-eye, I squeezed in a couple of chapters from a thriller I'd picked up. Sometimes I wonder why I find this kind of entertainment relaxing.

After managing to catch an hour's worth of light napping between glances at the clock and what seemed like long sessions of staring at the ceiling, I got up, almost fully dressed, put on my shoes, gathered my things, and headed for the door. I figured my ETA in the Harcourts' old neighborhood would allow plenty of time to meet with Benny.

Like all good Marines, I made damn sure to arrive on time by getting there early. I pulled into the Harcourts' neighborhood a couple of hours ahead of Benny's scheduled arrival time. Easing the car past the specified meeting place, I continued to the next intersection and began a three-point turn. Then I drifted back and pulled up to the curb. I positioned my car just close enough to be able to see the delivery van arrive, but far enough away to be discreet and be ready to escape, if necessary.

The time dragged by, but I used it to make some progress on the thriller I had started. It was a paperback that I could read by the light of a small but bright key fob LED. I figured reading wouldn't keep me from seeing a van driving through the area in the wee hours. If I had to pay strict attention, I could listen to a podcast. The book was by some chick named Alex Carr. Not bad at all. *What was it about the name Alex lately?*

By 5:00 AM, I saw lights blinking on in some of the houses. As time passed, the early risers left for work and more lights clicked on. 6:00 AM came and went. I checked my phone. It was 6:02. At least it wasn't a Saturday. By now, several houses had windows blazing with light. A few cars motored past. *Could he be a no-show? Or could this be a setup?* Just as that thought occurred, the familiar van moved into view and stopped across the street from our agreed-upon meeting place.

As the driver came to a stop, I slid out from behind the wheel and approached him, signaling with a couple of quick LED flashes. Benny got out of his van and looked at me as I gave him a quick friendly wave. As the gap between us closed, I could see worry lines across his brow. I smiled, and he flashed me a weak grin. The distinctive *thwack* of a crossbow nearly made my heart stop.

Benny looked around, confused. An arrow protruded at an odd angle from his forehead. He kept looking, even as blood oozed from the entry wound. Circling and looking, until he collapsed.

CHAPTER SIXTY-ONE

Once again, in the wee hours, I had to call 911. In the wrong neighborhood. I thought about running, but what was the point? I had no weapon on me. But had my inquiries led to another killing? Maybe. Maybe not.

This time the police arrived so quickly and in such force, the whole neighborhood turned into a psychedelic circus. They blocked off the street and brought in squadrons of police officers and one serious-looking SWAT crew. Perhaps the National Guard would come next. The normally peaceful facades of suburban ranchers and colonials were splashed with color from the police cars' red and blue disco lights. Radios crackled in the still of early morning.

And neighbors milled about, many on cell phones. I tried to imagine their conversations. *Sorry. Can't come in today. My house is part of a crime scene. Not that I did anything . . . .*

I dutifully spoke to the officer in charge, keeping my statement short, truthful, and not offering more than what was asked of me. Two detectives eventually arrived. Not Gordan and Sully, thank God. Another go-round with Sully would have put me over the edge.

After finishing with the cops, I returned to my apartment and kicked the paper inside, not bothering to look at it. My early edition wouldn't mention what had happened within the past few hours. I tottered toward the bed, dove onto the mattress, and went to sleep, with all my clothes on—again.

When I woke up, midafternoon sun streamed through the cracks around the closed curtains. I considered staying right where I was until it got dark, but eventually I raised myself up on one elbow. After adjusting to the idea that it was still daytime, I swung my legs over the side of the bed and stood up. I had plenty of work to do.

It was possible that Benny's death was not connected to the Harcourts in any way, but I rather doubted it. So why was he killed after I became interested in him? Was my phone tapped? And what, if anything, did the brown sedan and/or Mabel Forbes have to do with any of it?

Could Benny's death be connected with his regular visits to this house? He could have been having an affair or been engaged in some sort of illegal enterprise. Regardless of why, someone had it in for him, but that may or may not necessarily relate to my investigation. I needed to do something while I waited for Nick and Alex to get back to me. This was getting way too serious. I had a powerful need to find out who was following me. And what, if any, connection they had to Embrace the Wild. And why people with answers to my questions were getting killed. For this, I needed some unofficial help. And I knew who I could trust to provide it.

CHAPTER SIXTY-TWO

Two-Bit Terry seemed pleased to be called in to help me. Terry and I went back to high school. Not that we were a couple. Just a couple of oddballs.

I explained the risks to Terry, and he took them in stride. But then, based on what I knew about Two-Bit, risk was never his biggest concern. The real problem was finding the brown Dodge sedan without knowing the tag number or the VIN. Or, more specifically, I wanted to identify the car's driver. I figured this all had some connection to Embrace the Wild. Perhaps it was time to poke the koala, so to speak.

When I suggested we meet, Terry proposed a small coffee shop in Kensington. I warned him about what happened to Gallagher and Benny, but he laughed it off. I put in my order as soon as I walked in, and then took a seat. Terry wasn't there, so I watched the door and breathed a small sigh of relief when he arrived.

It's hard to describe Terry. I don't mean physically. He's tall, but scrawny. Hair: light brown, never combed. Eyes: mud-colored. What's hard is describing him as a person, the one inside the skinny, nerdy package. He's like a mad genius, but also kind of an idiot. Terry knows a little about everything. But he can also be completely wrong about some of those things. On the surface, he comes across almost like a kid. Curious and open. But on the flip side, he was sometimes a little bit too sure of himself. With a practiced smile, Terry could make the unwary believe he had all the answers.

Today, he looked like a gawky teenager from the 1950s, pretending to be a badass in a leather jacket. Made me look like a slacker in my hoodie and jeans. Terry waved in my direction and went over to the counter to order a drink.

When he finally joined me, I said, "When did you become the Wild One?"

"Huh?"

"That jacket. You look like James Dean."

Terry shook his head and grinned. "You're thinking of Marlon Brando. He was in 'The Wild One.' James Dean was in 'Rebel Without a Cause.' "

According to Terry, my life wouldn't be complete until I had seen and appreciated every movie ever made since some French dudes invented motion pictures.

"Now that we've established that essential fact, perhaps we could talk about my problem," I said.

Terry nodded. Like he had a choice. I tried to explain the whole messy situation.

"I don't know for a fact, but I strongly suspect that this bizarre petting zoo has something to do with the Harcourt murders," I said. "Maybe the brown car is involved, maybe not. But it seems like a good idea to poke around Embrace the Wild. Maybe the car will show up, and we'll get a clue."

Terry said nothing. He looked over my shoulder in a contemplative way. Then his eyes focused. He frowned.

"What?" I said.

"That's one way to play it." Terry's voice was laconic.

"You have a better one?"

"Forget the whole thing. Let the police handle it."

I'll admit to being surprised when he said that, but I figured he was playing devil's advocate. I shook my head. "It's not just the Harcourts anymore. Two people have lost their lives trying to help me out. Aside from the bad business of having someone murder my clients and make me a potential suspect, I need to understand why this is happening. For myself, and for the dead people who tried to explain it to me."

"So, will you help me?" I asked, trying hard not to beg.

Terry squinted and thought for a few moments in silence. He finally nodded. "When and where do we start?"

This was more like it. "How about now? At Embrace the Wild."

"Okay. And what is your plan? What do we do, once we get there?" He came down hard on the word "we" both times.

"Just have a look around."

Terry squinted in disbelief, but his smile twisted up to one side, signaling intrigue. "Really?"

I leaned toward him. "I've got to know what's going on there."

CHAPTER SIXTY-THREE

Terry thought it was too late in the day to be visiting a petting zoo. But I found the place using my phone, noted the route, and saw that it was open until 6:00 PM. We had nearly an hour to get there. My friend had also grown more cautious with age. En route, Terry proceeded to question my entire investigative approach.

"Do you even know the layout?" he asked as I drove up New Hampshire Avenue. "Or what you're looking for?"

"Anything that connects my now-deceased clients with any illegal activities. That would be great for starters. As for the layout," I let out a dismissive huff. "You saw how small the place is. Compared to some buildings I've searched . . . ." I let the rest of that thought go.

He snorted. "Yeah, but Google Maps doesn't go inside. And I'm not a Marine."

I placed a hand on his shoulder. "No, but this one has your back."

Given the alarming mortality rate among my recent sources, I needed for this case to end and those words to mean something.

A few minutes before the petting zoo closed, we pulled into a gravel lot in front of a wooden building shaped like a shallow, rectangular box that looked like something out of an old Western movie. The yellow, gray, and white koala graphic on the sign in front stood out. There was no sign of the brown car in the front parking lot.

I did a quick survey of the building's exterior, as much of a survey as possible from a gravel-topped parking lot with families meandering across it, some of whom were heading for their cars.

The gravel lot ended in a thin strip of grassy median that separated the front of the building from the back. Beyond the parking lot, a grassy acreage stretched between the main building and a set of stables linked to it by a footpath. The main building was slightly dilapidated but had managed to stay upright. I did a three-point turn, retraced my route to the front, and parked off to the side of the building beside the median strip. "There must be an office of some kind tucked in there," I said before we left the car. As Terry and I moved toward the front of the building, I continued to check our surroundings.

Business was fairly brisk. Families mostly, or at least people with kids. A small crowd emerged from the building and moved toward the parking lot. There was a similar closing-time exodus from a nearby barn where they sold fresh produce and other country-type products. Terry and I maneuvered our way into the main building, moving against the human tide like salmon swimming upstream.

A hallway nearly half the building's width ran through the structure. The pale light that filtered in from the openings at either end of the hallway provided the only illumination of the interior. Now that the crowd had cleared out, there wasn't much to see. Not far away, I heard the faint rustling sounds of what must have been some of the animals moving around in their pens, but the building was otherwise quiet. The place smelled ever so slightly like shit. We walked slowly into the interior of the building. I wondered where the koalas were. When was the last time you saw a koala on a farm?

"Terry?" I kept my voice low. I put a hand on Terry's arm and he stopped. We stood by a door marked "Ladies." Across the hall, another door led to who-knows-what. I put a finger to my lips and listened.

We could hear a kind of chattery white noise that occasionally rose in volume to the murmur of conversation. I examined the interior of the barn, looking from right to left. Big open entrance, small ticket booth, bench against a wall, door to whatever, then an expanse of uninterrupted wall that created one side of the hallway. In the somewhat shadowy semi-gloom, that was all the detail I could see.

The loud crunching sound of someone walking on the gravel outside overpowered the background noises. "Let's—" I said, then rather than finish the thought, I opened the rest room door, grabbed Terry's arm, and pulled him inside.

Crunch, crunch, crunch. Someone was approaching slowly and steadily. Pause. The whispers of conversation were mixed in with the rattle, rattle, rattle, BANG of the gate being closed.

Terry and I stepped back into the hallway. The roll-down gate blocked the front entrance, but the back entrance was still open. The silence was broken only by a few barnyard sounds and the occasional swell of murmured speech.

"Now what?" Terry asked.

"Did you hear that just now? People talking."

Terry inclined his head, in what could have been agreement or just mulling the question. "I heard something. Want to find out what it is?"

"Yeah," I said, even though I wasn't at all sure. How many people were there? And who were they? Might they be armed? We needed an approach and an exit strategy, and what we really needed was a plan, which I hadn't bothered with. *Was Terry right? Was this a bad idea?*

I tried to think. *This isn't like me.* The memory of the panic attack at the church crossed my mind. But I wasn't panicking. I didn't have time to go through all of that again.

"Let's wait," I suggested, "to see if they come to us." Even as my mind screamed *get out*, my gut said *stay*.

"Sure. OK." He sounded like he was trying to convince himself.

As we stood just outside the ladies' room door listening, I scanned the area out of habit, but there wasn't much to see. However, I could detect the source of the voices. They were raised enough to be heard from behind the door across from us.

Motioning Terry to join me, I crept toward the sounds. The burble of voices rose and fell in volume, enough to hear the occasional word. Just not enough to hear phrases, let alone sentences, before it dropped to the level of humming insects. The hallway was bathed in shadow, but a small amount of light leaked from around the edges of the flimsy, slightly warped door. Along with weak light, the voices emerged—sometimes loud, sometimes just a murmur. We stood in the hallway eavesdropping for several minutes, but I couldn't really make out any of the conversation.

The voices seemed to be moving closer, so I grabbed Terry's arm, and we hustled back across the hall. *Leave,* my conscience shrieked again. *No, I can't.* Once again, I shoved Terry inside the ladies' room. Then we stood at the door, waiting for the owners of those voices to arrive.

CHAPTER SIXTY-FOUR

Terry was breathing hard. My back was giving me the usual grief, but my head had cleared a bit. As we waited, the voices grew louder. One likely belonged to a man, a baritone, and one sounded like a woman, more of an alto. And there might have been a second woman. Hard to be sure when there were two flimsy doors and a hallway between us and the voices.

I checked the rest room door for a lock. Naturally, there wasn't one. Terry maintained his position at the door, as I did a visual reconnoiter of the restroom using my phone for light rather than risk revealing our presence with the glare of the overhead fluorescents.

To call it shabby was being generous. To its credit, it was just big enough to house all of two stalls and a rusty sink. Cheap curtains covered a window wide enough and just low enough to crawl through. The wall may not have been made of brick, but the wood of the exterior wall was solid enough. I shoved the curtains aside and tried to open the window, but the damn thing wouldn't budge. I looked for a lock and came to the conclusion that it was either well-hidden or the window had been painted shut. No wonder the room smelled horrible.

A quick visual survey turned up nothing particularly useful for opening that window. I snatched up a small plastic wastebasket and tried to take out the window with it, but it bounced from my hand. Rearing back, I delivered two swift kicks to the glass. The impact jolted my back but produced a small spiderweb of cracks in the pane.

After a quick pause to listen for any sign that we had been discovered, I took a couple more whacks at it. The cracks in the window now looked like a web-spinning spider had lost its mind. In a pinch, the window would have to do as an escape route. But I couldn't risk further damage to the window without giving us away.

"They're getting closer," Terry informed me in a stage whisper.

I gave the ruined window one last nudge. The glass shifted but wasn't quite ready to give way. Not yet. *Shit.* I joined Terry at the door and took out my phone. *Should I call someone? What would I tell them?*

The murmur of voices became more distinct. I made out two women, definitely. And a third voice, lower register, probably a man, then yet another low-pitched voice. I set my phone to record events.

"Recognize anyone?" Terry asked. He held the door open, a tiny crack, and I listened as the voices filtered through it. Given the growing darkness, my hope was that none of the speakers would notice the tiny opening in the rest room door.

"I think so." One or two of the voices seemed familiar. They weren't in the hall yet, but they'd be there soon.

I nudged Terry. "Shut the door."

Terry eased the door closed.

Just as the ladies' room door shut, the squeak and rustle of the door across the hall came to us. Terry and I froze. I hit *record* on my phone.

"So, we're good then?" I could just make out the voices through the door. The woman sounded confident, but I detected an edge of worry. And a hint of familiarity.

"We're just fine. As long as you all do as I say," said a man whose voice I couldn't match with a face.

"We'd better be fine. Those murders messed up everything." Another man's voice that I recognized immediately, even through the door. It was Reverend Leland's Chamber of Commerce voice. "We really stuck our necks out for you."

From the man I didn't recognize, "Watch what you say. This is bigger than you can imagine." It sounded like a cross between a threat and a plea. *And which murders are we talking about?*

A moment of silence passed. I sensed a shift in the atmosphere, much like the coming of a storm. The back of my neck tensed, as my gut hollowed.

"But killing wasn't part of our deal." Leland soldiered on with his point.

The other man said, "And I thought we'd settled our differences. What a shame."

Then, there was a scuffle. It sounded like a fight. Taking care to remain hidden, I eased the door open a tiny crack and peered through it. My view of the proceedings was minimal, at best, but I could make out the occasional failing arm. The battling duo swung their way further down the hall and the view improved a bit.

One of them held a small object. In the fading light, I caught the familiar gleam of a handgun. The man fighting Leland was vaguely familiar. He was shorter and more rotund than the Reverend. And his clothes suggested that he had been on a safari.

I barely recognized the Reverend without his cleric's collar. Dressed in a polo shirt with wide, contrasting horizontal stripes and a pair of tan slacks, he looked like an aging preppie. Apparently, his skills went beyond the religious. Leland attempted to wrest the gun from the other man's grip.

"Would you two stop it?" one woman yelled. Next thing I knew, the bang of a gunshot pierced the air. I dropped to the floor, taking Terry down with me.

The ladies' room door had drifted shut, but I could hear the woman say clearly, "Don't be such idiots."

That voice I knew. Then Leland spoke in a mocking tone, "Too late for that, isn't it, Marian?" He uttered the name as if spitting out poison.

CHAPTER SIXTY-FIVE

Had I heard that right? What the hell was going on here? I cracked the door open again, beyond curious.

"Don't call me that, you fool. Not even as a joke." The voice wasn't Marian Harcourt's, but it was incredibly similar. The woman moved into view. She faced away from me, but based on height and weight alone, I knew she couldn't be Marian Harcourt's identical twin.

This woman wasn't just tall, she had a warrior's physique. The fading light revealed her muscled arms and slim hips. Amazon Woman probably did a thousand one-handed pushups every day. And popped off a few hundred chin-ups in between the pushups and an endless repetition of tummy crunches. Any resemblance to Marian Harcourt was strictly in the voice.

Leland let the hand holding the gun drop to his side. "Don't call me a fool for defending myself from that fool." He gestured toward his opponent, who was out of view in a state I could only imagine. *Was he dead? Bleeding? Unconscious?*

"I was just trying to scare some sense into you," the man finally spoke up, confirming his very-much-alive status. "Our deal is what it is and there's no denying it now."

Amazon Woman approached the Reverend and reached for the gun. He raised the gun, aimed it at her, and pulled the trigger. *Click.* Leland checked the clip and then his lips curled with thinly veiled self-contempt. "Outta bullets. The Lord really does work in mysterious ways. But let me make myself clear. We're done with you people. Finished."

Amazon Woman cast a withering look at the Reverend. "When did you become so holy?" Her hips swiveled as she turned away from him and I caught sight of a holster on her low-slung utility belt. The butt of what closely resembled a SIG Sauer P320, like my own, stuck out.

"Has he always been this annoying, Hannah?" the woman asked.

Hannah. Oh, right. The pieces of the puzzle were starting to come together in my head, but right now, I needed to figure out our next move. Maybe no move at all would be best, until these people either killed each other or left.

But the voices had fallen silent. My thoughts were interrupted when Two-Bit Terry poked me on the shoulder. He jerked a thumb toward the door. I peeked through the skinny viewing slit.

While Leland, Hannah, and the other man remained where they were, Amazon Woman approached the door to the ladies' room.

CHAPTER SIXTY-SIX

On autopilot, I stood up, tucked the phone into my pocket (still recording), and motioned for Terry to move away, but stay within sight of the door. Then, I drew the hood of my jacket over my head, secured it, and eased my back against the wall. Tucked into the gap between the door and stalls, I watched the door swing open in front of me. I could see the shadows of feet in the gap under the door. Pressed back against the wall, I watched the door close to reveal Amazon Woman, her back toward me. I sent a roundhouse kick into her back, which sent her flying and caused pain to spike up my leg and into my spine. The loud thump of Amazon Woman's landing, followed by the crack of her skull against wood, made me feel a little better. She was now sprawled prone on the floor. She seemed to be stunned, likely due to smacking her head when she fell.

Sidestepping the body, I rounded the stalls and faced the window. By this time, I had pulled my hands as far inside my sleeves as possible. I thought about her gun, but chose not to spend precious time looking for it.

"C'mon," I motioned to Terry, nodding my head toward the window. What happened next was an insane blur.

I tucked deeper into my hoodie and aimed for the window. I ran straight at it, threw all my weight toward the thing, hoping the crumbling glass would give without cutting me to ribbons. My shoulder hit the fractured window and punched through it as the pane's misshapen bits broke apart. I dove head-first through the now-open window.

Extending my hands to cushion the fall, I dropped into a side roll and sprang to my feet. The window was now an open hole that still had some shards of glass clinging to the frame. I picked a sliver of glass from the side of my hand, checked my face and the hoodie, brushing and picking at the few stray bits of glass, then retrieved my phone and stopped recording. Terry climbed through the window frame, while the restroom's overhead lights flickered to life.

My back gave a twinge, but what else is new? I hadn't come here for a fight. Terry and I paused only long enough to make sure we were each still in one piece and then beat a hasty retreat.

We jumped into the car and made ready to leave. But just as I was approaching the exit, a police cruiser swung into the parking lot and pulled up in front of my car. Another cruiser pulled around behind me but did not totally box me in.

A uniformed officer emerged from the car in front of us and looked around. I looked around, too, but I didn't see anyone emerging from the building. *I so do not need this. And let's keep Terry out of it.*

The officer strolled up to my side of the car. He had babyish features and a peach fuzz mustache. He gestured for me to lower my window, even though I was already doing just that. "Excuse me, ma'am. Someone reported that they heard a gunshot. Did you call for the police?"

I tried to look confused. It wasn't that hard. "Who me? Nah." *And don't call me, ma'am, kid.* The kid hesitated.

He looked around. Maybe he wondered why I was there after hours. Or maybe he was just looking. A female officer with whom he might have had home room last year emerged from the other police car. She moved toward us but kept a distance.

"Ma'am," he said again. "Are you okay?"

What the hell? "Of course. I'm fine." *No doubt, I looked a mess. I tried to think. There were trails around here. Somewhere.* "We've been hitting the trails, but went a little deeper into the woods, you know? Off-trail. The branches. They were hitting me in the face."

The officer pointed toward his forehead. "Do you realize you're bleeding?"

Oh, shit. I felt my forehead. Nothing but sweat. I brought my hand away. Red sweat. Great.

"Well, that's why we stopped here. See I know the owner. My second cousin, that is. Once removed. Actually, he was part owner, but he had to sell his share. Which my other cousin's father was totally cool with. Even though the first cousin—I mean, my second cousin—had promised his father not to. I mean, it's a long story. My great-aunt—her name was Gertrude—she was kind of a drinker. So things went to pot after Dad died. So he had to sell. For the taxes, you know?"

The officer had a look on his face that I easily recognized. One that said, "This bitch is crazy."

"It's a long story," I said.

He nodded. "I can imagine."

The officer gave the interior of my vehicle the hairy eyeball, but there was nothing to see.

"Would you please step out of the vehicle?" The young man sounded only semi-authoritative, as if he was not quite sure he had a good reason to make that request. "Keep your hands where I can see them."

I obliged the kid and so did Terry. Each of us planted our hands on the car's roof, legs spread, as each officer searched us for weapons or contraband.

We had nothing on us, fortunately.

Meanwhile, no obvious noises or movements came from the building.

"So, is there anything else?" I asked, while we both got back into the car. "Can we go now?"

The officers glanced at one another. The female officer shrugged.

"No. Yeah. Go." The cop tossed the words out. "We'll take it from here."

With that, I maneuvered around the patrol car and got out of there. As fast as I dared.

CHAPTER SIXTY-SEVEN

"You're bleeding." Terry sounded panicky.

I sighed. "So I've been told," I said. I ran my hand over my cheeks, my chin, my forehead. When I saw how much blood was on my hand, the amount so distracted me, I nearly veered into the wrong lane.

This required a pit stop. I scanned the rural roadside for any sign of a shoulder. After driving a mile or two through the darkness created by the trees, I spied a thin strip of ground between the pavement and the woods. The moon had come up, giving the surrounding woods a silvery hue. I pulled over for a better look at the damage.

My rear-view mirror revealed nothing worse than a scraped chin and some skinny blood trails streaming down my face. It felt like sweat, but I looked like hell.

Terry helped me remove the few stubborn bits and pieces of remaining glass. He pulled a wad of my hard-earned fast-food paper napkins from the glove box and used some of them to help me mop up the mess.

"You realize head wounds always look worse than they are," I informed him. Even so, I had to wonder why I didn't notice that what remained of the window had cut my face. Was I so numb to pain these days that I couldn't even feel it?

"You got any disinfectant?" Terry had just finished rummaging through the glove box.

"Does this look like an ambulance?" I snapped, then paused for a breath. "Sorry."

"Yeah," Terry said. "Me, too."

I dropped Terry off at his car and continued to think about the Harcourt matter as I drove home. My thoughts were beginning to coalesce from random speculations into near theories. The Harcourts had formed relationships through the church. The Reverend appeared to be connected with some shady characters related to Embrace the Wild. If the Harcourts ended up doing business with any of them, they might not have known about any illegal activities until it was too late to back out. Apparently Embrace the Wild had earned the scrutiny of federal agents who keep top-level secrets. But what had the Harcourts done to merit being murdered so brutally? It had to concern more than just their roles as internet influencers.

Back in my apartment, I examined my face carefully and cleaned the cuts, which were already starting to scab over. Not a horrifying sight. More like a dusting of reddish freckles.

I thought about making coffee, rejected the thought, then made it anyway. While sipping it from my mug, I scribbled down a few thoughts for my file.

If the Harcourts worked closely with the church, they may well have gotten sucked into a criminal enterprise hidden within its walls that also included the petting zoo. Alex Kingsley's poking about had overturned a few stones with "scorpions" under them, scorpions of interest to federal agencies. I wondered exactly how many laws the owners of Embrace the

Wild had broken. And how they remained in business. I considered this along with the other evidence I had managed to scrape together.

I reviewed Gallagher's notes of conversations and then shuffled through the documents I had retrieved from his office, organizing them as I went. Checking his calendar, I noticed an entry earlier in the week before the murders. It read: "Meeting re: the Hs." H as in Harcourt? I would have to look through Gallagher's notes for that meeting, which might provide a clue of some sort.

Gallagher had been a rather meticulous if not completely organized notekeeper. All his notes about various meetings were typed and kept separate from correspondence. He seemed to have a paper copy of every email regarding the couple's legal affairs. Apparently, the law is like the military. Kill entire rain forests if you must, but make sure your ass is covered with paper.

Mostly I found things where I expected them. But I didn't see any typed notes memorializing any meeting with the Harcourts during the week before they died. In fact, he apparently kept no meeting notes for anyone during that week.

Then I checked the handwritten notes. A quick comparison revealed duplications with the typed notes, and I almost dismissed them. Until I saw a reference to a meeting about Embrace the Wild. One that was dated two days before the Harcourts were murdered. I checked the calendar. No entry for this meeting.

Rather than knock myself out trying to decipher the late lawyer's handwriting, I opted for some well-earned sack time. I caught a few hours of sleep and returned to the files the next morning with a renewed resolve to find the Harcourts' murderer—and finally figure out why I ended up under police scrutiny. Someone was guilty, and I knew it wasn't me.

I called Detectives Gordon and Sully and got voicemail both times. I told them about an interesting recording I had. One with a voice they might want to compare with Marian Harcourt's voice, which lived on in both audio and video form on the internet. I had also saved the last voice mail from Marian, so one way or the other, I had something for comparison.

The process of deciphering the chicken scratch of Gallagher's handwriting nearly gave me a migraine. Plus, he used an alphabet soup of initials. But I was able to figure out his writing style well enough to determine that the discussion about Embrace the Wild was with MC and RD, most likely Calhoun and Douglas. And mentions of BM and PA. Whoever they were.

I checked back a bit further and found notes with the H's. The scrawl of handwriting became more convoluted and peppered with what looked like code words. They must have been discussing something pretty confidential.

I took a break from the notes and turned my attention to other investigative leads. My research on the three nannies turned up one local address in Reston, Virginia, for Astrid Gunderson. An additional search unearthed the last known locations for Ingrid Swenson and Sasha Krikorian. Ingrid was in the Pittsburgh area. Sasha lived in Bakersfield, California. Bakersfield. Sounded hot.

Reston, Virginia, was within the D.C. metro area, so I started my inquiries with Astrid Gunderson, and since driving to Virginia is always a bitch, I tried to connect first by phone. When she picked up, I introduced myself and briefly explained how I knew the Harcourts before mentioning their murder.

"I know," she murmured. "Such lovely people—"

"They were, weren't they?" I gushed quickly to cut her off. "I keep hearing that. What were their kids like?"

"Oh, they were teenagers." The way she said it suggested that the kids were mischievous. I wondered how mischievous.

"Please tell me about them," I said.

CHAPTER SIXTY-EIGHT

Astrid's feelings about the Harcourt heirs were generally of acceptance and tolerance of their occasional behavior problems.

"Jaden, in particular, acted out a lot," she said. "I tried to talk to him. Tried to talk to his parents. But whatever he did while he was out with whoever, whenever, it never got him arrested or anything so horrible it couldn't be ignored."

"That must have been frustrating," I said. I could hear the memory of it in her voice.

"When I worked for them, he was seventeen. Within a year of legal adulthood. So what was I going to do?" The words poured out of her. "It's not like he joined a cult or committed a shooting or did anything other than hanging out and . . . I don't know. Drinking? Smoking? Ecstasy? Who knows?"

"Acted out in what way?" I asked.

"Oh." That word punched through the line. "For example, I was instructed to monitor his curfew time and I did, for all the good that accomplished. He just ignored me."

"Did the parents know?" That sounded less judgy than, "Did you tell them?"

I heard a sigh from the other end. "I mentioned it. Yeah. What they did about it, I wouldn't know."

She stopped talking. "What about Amy?" I asked.

"Amy had a few problems of her own. But her, I could talk to."

Astrid the Cool One then told me all about Amy and what they used to talk about. While I listened, I wondered how much of the story I was being told, and how much I was not being told.

Before Astrid, there was Ingrid the Quiet One. I called her next. Ingrid was quiet, all right, as in dead. Ingrid Swenson had been killed in an automobile accident two weeks ago. Her partner—soul mate, friend with benefits, whatever—told me this when she took my call. I immediately expressed my regrets at Ingrid's untimely demise and tried to couch my questions in a way that afforded proper respect for the bereaved.

The woman named Lu— "Just L-U," she said. "Short for Lucy"—had been Ingrid's partner for years. She described Ingrid as a reserved and private person. She expressed very few thoughts or feelings about the Harcourts or their kids. However, among those few thoughts, one apparently stood out. Lu claimed that Ingrid was worried at one point about the Harcourts' growing status as internet influencers and the effect that had on the kids' and her own privacy.

"Like I told the police, back then, they were mainly blogging," Lu said. "I think Ingrid was most concerned about their increasing use of social media."

So, the cops had finally reached out to the nanny. I asked Lu if Ingrid had ever talked about the Harcourt kids' behavior. "Did the police ask you about the kids?"

"I'll tell you what I told them. If there were serious problems, she never mentioned them," Lu said. Her voice took on a guarded tone, and I sensed an internal debate on her part. Was she keeping a secret or wondering what more to share?

I hate talking on the phone. If I could just read her face. I needed to do more video calls. Except then, there's no element of surprise. Plus I couldn't make faces while people lied to me.

"There is one thing," Lu said, sounding decisive. "Ingrid kept a journal. I'd be happy to send you a copy, if you think it would help."

Did I think it would be helpful? Does a bear care where the Pope shits? No, but I wanted that journal.

"Do you have a smartphone?" She could send me snaps of the relevant pages.

"No, actually. And I'm beginning to feel like a dinosaur." She chuckled. "But, why should I care?"

I made sure she had my address and asked her to send photocopies as soon as possible. And thanked her profusely before hanging up. I could have told her to send a copy to the cops, but I wanted the first look. It's called competitive intelligence. Besides which, it might reveal nothing. I would be more than willing to share it after I looked it over, if it contained anything of value.

Despite Lu's promise to send me a copy of the journal as soon as she could, I decided not to sit by the door and wait for it. My next call was to Sasha in Bakersfield. The day was far enough along that the three-hour time difference wouldn't be a problem. As the first of the three nannies, I wondered exactly how young the kids were when she came on.

As I listened to Sasha's phone ringing 3,000 miles away, a thought nagged me. When had the Harcourts started making their mark online? They must have just been getting started when Jaden was born. Maybe they were busy at other jobs while they developed their online platform as a side gig.

A woman's voice came on the line, voice mail, actually. Please leave your name and number. Thanks. No cutesy message, no "I can't get to the phone" or "I'm unavailable." Just leave your name and number. No promises on returning your call.

"My name is Erica Jensen," I said. "I'm investigating the murder of Ron and Marian Harcourt. I need to talk to you about when you worked for them and ask you some questions about their children. Please call me when you get this. It's urgent." I gave my number and hung up.

Then I turned to my other work, half hoping I could accomplish a thing or two, when the phone rang. I checked the ID. That didn't take long.

"Hello, Ms. Krikorian?" I answered.

After a pause, Sasha said, "Erica Jensen?" The voice held suspicion and curiosity. "Are you with the police?"

"No, I'm a private . . . researcher, but I have a personal stake in finding out who killed the Harcourts."

Another pause. "You knew them?"

"I worked for them," I said. "Briefly."

"When the police contacted me, I was shocked to hear what had happened. It's been years since I've even thought about them." Her voice sounded dreamy at first but seemed to darken as she spoke.

"Can you tell me what it was like to work for them?"

"You're not with the press, are you?" *Careful.*

"No." I had avoided saying it the first time, but I was tired of dancing around the issue. "I'm not police, not with the press. I'm the person who found them dead, and I'm trying to stay out of prison, because I'm not the one who killed them."

The words poured out of me. At one time, I might have been embarrassed by that and hung up. Instead, I wondered if my group therapist, Susan, would have considered this a breakthrough.

"Then we need to talk," said Sasha the Strict.

CHAPTER SIXTY-NINE

Sasha's information didn't provide much in the way of comfort, but it did provide possible leads to pursue. It also suggested a few potential scenarios. At least ones that weren't wholly implausible. At this point, I could probably tie my brain in knots trying to figure it all out.

According to Sasha, who came on shortly after Amy was born, 4-year-old Jaden reacted angrily to her being hired. It was obvious that he wanted more attention from his parents, and Sasha simply wasn't his Mommy.

"He didn't talk to me, at first," Sasha said. "I'll never forget that. He just shut me out. I'd never experienced anything like that before, especially from a four-year-old."

"But when I tried to talk to his parents, it was pretty clear I wasn't getting through. I mean, they're the parents. Aren't they supposed to do something? Isn't that their job? If it was, they weren't doing it, because no matter what I said, nothing changed."

"How about Amy?" I asked.

Sasha tut-tutted. "She was so cute. So little. But . . . when she got older, she became moody."

"Do you think she . . . ?" I tried to think of a nice way to say "suffered from depression."

"We-e-ll," she drew the word out. "She'd lapse into a funk now and then. But most of the time, I could tell her a story or sing a song, and she would snap out of it.

"Toward the end of my time working for the Harcourts, Amy and I got along fine. Jaden, well . . . actually, both kids struck me as being seriously insecure. It got to the point where I suggested counseling for them, because they seemed to need something like that." She inhaled loudly enough for me to hear and added, "A lot of good that did."

"And the police know this?" I asked.

"Yeah . . . ." Her voice faded. "Thing is, I'm not sure they got the whole picture."

The line went silent. This is why I hate interviewing by phone. What was going on? Was she digging out an old journal? Or making faces at the phone? Or had she hung up?

Finally, a suppressed sob came over the line. "Sometimes I wonder. Should I have told someone? Reported them? For what, taking vacations with their kids? I mean, what's my job here? And what's my obligation? They were the parents. They made the rules. Would the kids have been better off in foster care? No way. What could I do? I had a job, bills to pay, and my own child. So . . . what do you do in a case like that?"

You survive, I thought. *And you live with your decision.*

"The best you can," I said.

"And then, there was Aunt Phyllis."

That stopped me. "What?" I had no recollection of an Aunt Phyllis. "Whose sister was it?"

"She wasn't a blood relative. She was more like a close friend of the family. They called her Aunt Phyllis."

"So what was the problem with Aunt Phyllis?"

"Honestly, she seemed like a bad influence. When it came to the kids, Aunt Phyllis had this way of encouraging bad behavior."

I couldn't tell if this was the truth or if Sasha was just being judgy. But it seemed like an interesting new lead.

"What's Phyllis's last name?"

"Let me think. Akins? Atkins? No. Atkinson. That's it."

Phyllis Atkinson? "Hang on a sec," I said. I flipped back to my copies of Gallagher's handwritten notes. PA. Phyllis Atkinson? Definitely a person of interest.

"Did Aunt Phyllis visit often?"

"For a while, yeah. Until the kids started school. After that, she kind of disappeared. From what I gathered, it was after a big blowup over something. The kids weren't shocked so much as disappointed."

"You don't have a photo, do you?"

"God, no." Sasha laughed. "But I can describe her. About six feet tall and outdoorsy. And, forgive my lack of PC, but I'd say she was mannish."

Holy shit.

"Did the cops ask you about Aunt Phyllis?"

She paused. "I don't think so. In fact, I'd forgotten about how much she affected those kids until just now."

After I finished the call with Sasha, I took another look at my notes. Now my previously scrambled thoughts began coagulating into a vague theory. One that bothered me for reasons I preferred not to think about.

I finished up work with a quick background check for another client. I provide the service through an online marketing platform for freelancers. Yeah, the gig economy at work, folks. Five bucks a pop. Made me wonder why I still wanted that private eye license. Maybe for the same reason I did anything. Seemed like a good idea at the time.

The next day, I checked the local news regarding recent events at the petting zoo. I found an item on page one of the local section. The feds had raided Embrace the Wild.

This was after reports of an after-hours shooting on the premises. Among those arrested were the owners Reverend Arthur Leland and Benjamin Mulligan. Along with the ever-so-helpful Hannah Broomfield. There was a whole lot more to the story at the state and federal level.

So, the BM from Gallagher's notes more than likely stood for Benjamin Mulligan. And whatever Gallagher discussed with Calhoun and Douglas, it probably got him killed. While reading the article, I looked for a reference to Phyllis Atkinson. Or a second unidentified woman. There was none.

"Who are you?" I muttered to myself. "And how many people have you killed lately?"

CHAPTER SEVENTY

My phone rang. When I saw it was Alex Kingsley, I answered right away. " 'Sup, Alex?"

"You should be getting a package today," she said. "That's all I'll say."

This information took more than a few seconds to fully sink in. "Okay. Should I wear protective clothing when I open it?"

"Haha," she said. "No. But remember. Once you see it, it can't be unseen."

"Gotcha. And let me guess. This conversation never happened?"

A longish pause. "I should hang up on you." She laughed. "Not quite that bad. Just had to call in a few favors."

"Well, shit," I grumbled. "Now, I owe you even more."

Alex huffed dismissively. "Don't worry about it. Listen, one of these days, I'll be too old for all this. But I have other options. I can consult for folks and not actually do this anymore." Her voice hinted that she might be kidding. "You're good practice."

I thought about that. It had never occurred to me that my pleas for assistance might actually help her, too.

"Would you teach?"

"Hardly. I would travel. It's getting easier to do things remotely now."

It sure is, I thought. Everything is getting easier. Everything good and bad.

"Well, thank you." The words felt like an inadequate gesture, but the least I could do was thank her before we hung up.

Directing my attention back to the situation at hand, I let my theory stew for a bit, and then saw the pieces of a plan begin to emerge. I grabbed a pencil and paper and scribbled down my ideas as fast as I could. I took one look at the resulting barely readable scrawl and immediately knew what to do next. But before I could get started, Nick called.

"Hey," he greeted me. "Everything okay?"

No. Everything sucks. "Just fine," I said. "You see the article in the *Post?*"

"Yep. And I was able to get the name of an agent who works money laundering cases with the FBI." He paused.

"But," I prompted.

"But, he wouldn't talk to me."

Nick then told me about his repeated efforts to reach the federal agent, only to come up against a stone wall of wary friends and associates, multiple voice mails, and quite a few phone hang-ups.

"I could keep looking," he offered.

"Don't worry about it. For now."

I thanked Nick for his help before we ended the call. Time for Plan B.

I called Terry again. At least I wouldn't have to explain each and every detail, since he'd witnessed so many of them already. I was also pretty sure he wouldn't turn down my proposal.

"Hey," I said after he answered. "Want to help me with some research?"

CHAPTER SEVENTY-ONE

What I proposed to Terry was that he arrange somehow for Marge Calhoun to be away from her office. This could be done any way he saw fit.

I sensed him thinking it over. "Any suggestions on how?" he asked.

"Good question," I sighed.

Terry and I brainstormed the various potential ruses he could use to lure Calhoun out of her home office. Setting fire to her house was probably not one of them.

"Got any handy blackmail material?" he asked.

His voice said he was joking, but his comment prompted a thought.

The photo of Calhoun and Jaden. But there was nothing obviously criminal in it. So they knew each other. Big deal.

But then I said, "Maybe it doesn't matter."

As I explained my idea, Terry caught on fast. Using what little I knew about Calhoun from Gallagher's files, Terry could claim he had "evidence" linking Calhoun to Embrace the Wild, a letter, a memo, or whatever he could come up with. We did our best to concoct a genuine-sounding threat without nailing down too many specifics, but enough to send Calhoun in search of her own spin doctor or lawyer.

"I'll arrange to meet her at a public place," Terry offered. "Hopefully, that way, she won't feel threatened about meeting a stranger."

And hopefully, she wouldn't call our bluff. Maybe even call the cops. My arrangement with Terry would allow me at least an hour or so to perform a quick survey of Marge Calhoun's office. He wouldn't engage her, but watch her from a distant vantage point. As a long-time resident, Terry no doubt could envision the best meeting place while I proposed the setup. The plan was to keep surveillance on Calhoun, who we assumed would wait a bit for Terry to arrive. Then Terry would text me when she showed signs of leaving.

"This should be more fun than last time," he said and then laughed.

My plan was to drive directly to Calhoun's neighborhood but stay out of sight until she left her house for the meeting with Terry. That would maximize the amount of time I had to search for any helpful material or photos. I glanced at the clock. It was only 10:25 AM. I closed my eyes and visualized my first visit to Marge Calhoun's house, recalling the small details. A knock at the door brought that little exercise to a halt.

I got up and moved to the door so I could look through the peephole. It was a college kid dressed like a bike courier with a package. Apparently, I had to sign for the delivery because he also had a clipboard. *Was this the package from Alex? Already?*

I slid the "useless, but why not?" chain lock into place and opened the door a crack. "Hi," I said to the guy. "I take it I need to sign for this?"

"Yes, please," he said. He slid the clipboard, with pen, toward me through the gap.

"You still use clipboards," I observed.

He leaned toward me. "Some people request a signature on paper," he said. One corner of his mouth curled up and he gave me a knowing look. "More than you might think."

Alex clearly wanted to keep the package contents as off-the-record as possible. Human couriers with clipboards and every reason to please the customer was a low-tech privacy option. It occurred to me that the best form of privacy control when it came to any technology was not to use it.

After we had dispensed with the signing formalities, the messenger hurried off and I examined the package. My name was on it, but not my address. The courier either was told where to take it or had my address in writing on a note. Possibly a now-burned note. Alex's P.O. Box was in the return address corner, which made me really curious about its contents. Was I supposed to kill the messenger? I thought about calling Alex back, but I discarded the idea and dove into the package instead.

CHAPTER SEVENTY-TWO

Based on my paperwork, my theories of the case were
solidifying into a truly horrid scenario. Considering the number
of usually sealed records she had sent me, Alex must have called
in more than a few favors. I wondered if any of the items could
be considered evidence. If so, what did they really prove?

The weirdness of the situation struck me. A cursory look at
Alex's research revealed nothing to suggest that the Harcourts
were involved with Embrace the Wild in any way other than
simple visits to the petting zoo. But the way things were shaping
up, the Harcourts' connection to Embrace the Wild was a great
setup for either a modern sit-com or a Greek tragedy; their
murder placed it squarely in the latter category.

The papers showed relationships that had apparently soured.
But it wasn't enough. There might be more than one rotten
apple in the barrel. I needed to identify the one with a motive
for murder and pin him or her down. And a quick check of
Calhoun's office could make all the difference. I would take a
more careful look at the package after I engaged in a harmless
bit of trespassing.

If I could find more solid evidence in there of what I strongly suspected, this would not only clear me but would also show everyone I wasn't . . . what? A crazy vet who killed my own clients for no reason? A worthless wreck? I had survived in a war zone, so I was sure I could manage this.

"Stay frosty," I muttered and got ready to leave.

As we had planned, I left my apartment and timed my arrival at Marge Calhoun's house to ensure that she wouldn't see me. Once in the neighborhood, I backed into a spot near an intersection, far enough away from her house to keep my car out of sight. With my ID and clipboard, I readied myself for another B&E.

Waiting sucks. But after about five minutes, a low-pitched hum snapped me to full alert. The garage door lifted and a late model Mercedes slid out, pausing only long enough for Calhoun to make sure the door closed before she left.

The street was quiet, with only the distant whir of traffic in the background. A lone robin chirped. Hey, it was almost April. The daffodils were blazing yellow, but in a month or so, the tulips would replace their dead asses.

I knocked on the door, then took pains to play with my phone, looking up at the house, and miming text messages. *Yes, I'm here to give an estimate on those cabinets you wanted.* The street was quiet. I doubted anyone was home to care about me, but I kept up the charade, because cleaning ladies could be lurking anywhere. I knocked again, then went for a stroll to the back door. Through its cross-hatched window pane, I saw the kitchen I recalled from my last visit. Using my bump key, I slipped inside.

The silence made the air feel solid. I moved in further. Then, a loud clatter issued from somewhere in the room and my head felt like it was about to explode. On the verge of a flashback, I took a deep breath, and exhaled. When I realized I had jumped at the sound of the ice machine, my face warmed with a blush of embarrassment.

From the kitchen, I turned right and entered the den. First, I checked the photos and found the one I had noticed earlier right away. A photo of the Harcourts at Embrace the Wild. They stood in each other's half-embrace, near the man I now knew was Ben Mulligan. With an actual koala sitting at Marian's feet.

I took a closer look at the cars in the background. One of them was brown, with two people exiting from it. I used my phone to magnify the image so I could examine it more closely. Enlarging the photo brought out the clear dent on the driver's side, which faced the camera. I could see Amazon Woman, aka Phyllis Atkinson, emerge from the car. I also recognized the person who left the car from the passenger side. It was someone I had so hoped not to see.

CHAPTER SEVENTY-THREE

I considered whether to take the photo with me but dismissed that thought in a hurry. Calhoun would almost certainly notice its absence. So, I snapped a pic from an angle I hoped would minimize reflections off the glass. The result was good enough to pass muster.

By the time I received Terry's "clear out" text, I had managed to root through nearly every possible file drawer and cubbyhole. I couldn't get into the computer, but it didn't matter. Despite our reliance on high-tech gadgets for nearly everything, Calhoun had a standard Rolodex full of well-thumbed cards. I snapped photos of what seemed like the most important ones and all the correspondence kept in a dead-tree folder marked "ETW"—Embrace the Wild. Truly high-level encryption.

If I relied entirely on print documents, I would have needed a suitcase to hold all the files on this matter, rather than an undersized accordion folder. Perhaps a rolling suitcase with sturdy wheels.

With my digital plunder stored in my phone, I slid behind the wheel and quickly scanned the images. A movement out of the corner of my eye made me look up. An off-white, two-door sedan appeared at the intersection. The driver gave the horn three quick taps. The car rounded the corner and headed my way. Again, the driver beeped the horn. I set my phone aside, started the car, and pulled out, proceeding with caution.

The car came toward me. The dark windshield obscured my view of the interior. All I saw was a pattern of blackish-gray and grayish-black shapes. The windows appeared too dark to be legal. Just as our cars slid past each other and our side windows lined up, the white car stopped. I had drifted too far forward, so I hit the brakes and eased the car back a few inches. By this time, the driver's side window was down. And it was my good friend, Parker Adams, wearing his usual irritating grin.

I lowered my window. "So, we're playing cops now?"

"We do what we have to do."

"What does that mean?"

Adams' smile instantly vanished. This time, he looked serious as fuck.

"I'm sorry. About everything." His eyes had a look I couldn't read. They hinted at some sort of primal emotion buried beneath his stony facade. "Their murders complicated it all."

"You? You killed the Harcourts?" I didn't believe it. Didn't want to because it would totally mess with my theory of the case.

"No. The Harcourts stumbled across matters that involved a certain investigation."

It seemed like a good idea to choose my words with extra care. "I have been led to believe they weren't involved with Embrace the Wild's criminal activities."

"The details are sketchy." Adams gave me a small grin. "Based on what I know, I suspect the Harcourts were innocents when it came to Embrace the Wild. It seems like they didn't know that their people were engaged in major criminal enterprises. But they might have become suspicious later."

Maybe that's why they hired me to run a background check on a potential bodyguard. They realized, after the fact, how important it was to do that.

"By 'their people,' I assume you mean Marge Calhoun and Ryan Douglas?" I asked.

Adams gave a quick nod and made a grunting noise.

"So that's a yes?" I said.

He said nothing, but I pushed on.

"At least that squares with what I've deduced so far from reading Calhoun's and one dead lawyer's files," I added. *Yes? No? Say something!*

Adams nodded. Not a confirmation so much as a lack of denial. A hand-rolled cigarette seemed to appear out of thin air in his right hand. It was already smoldering. "I doubt the Harcourts even knew about the investigation. It was kept under wraps for reasons of national security."

I released the breath I'd been holding. "What does Mabel Forbes have to do with all this?"

Adams shook his head. "Mabel Forbes? Far as I know, she's someone's gramma."

"Does she ever go by the name Phyllis Atkinson by any chance?" Perhaps the Amazon Woman from the petting zoo had more than one alias.

Adams' head jerked in a motion I took to mean "that's a negative." He waved his cigarette like a baton as he spoke. "Mabel is nearly a hundred years old. Trust me, she's not a criminal mastermind. But someone using her name thinks they are. That's all I can tell you."

I wondered about that. And wondered how much of it was true.

Adams cocked his head and gave me a sideways look. "You ever see the movie *Chinatown*?"

"Uh, yeah, actually. Been a while."

"Like that."

I tried to remember the plot. Something about water and politics. My sister, my daughter. And old people who owned land that they didn't know they owned.

"Was Mabel involved in the Harcourt murders?"

Adams drew back as if startled. "I have no idea."

Getting facts from this man was like trying to catch fog with a butterfly net. "I thought you knew something about how they died."

"I was giving you an opinion based on what I know. The murders intersected with what I do."

Now we were getting closer. "And what exactly is that?"

He shook his head. "Can't tell you."

I fought the urge to get out of my car and strangle him. "Why are you following me?"

He looked even more surprised. "What makes you think I'm following you?"

"Oh, I don't know. Maybe it's that habit you have of just showing up wherever I happen to be. A lot," I said. "I mean, why are you here? What does this place have to do with whatever weird thing you're involved in?"

Adams raised an eyebrow. "In case you hadn't noticed, I'm on your side."

Then he suppressed a grin. "Look. I'm sorry. I just happened to find you after the attack at The Void. Really. My involvement in all of this is very sensitive." The last two words were spoken almost like two separate paragraphs. "But I'm actually quite impressed with you." He inclined his head in a quick bow.

"Thanks," I said. "You still haven't answered my question."

Adams' smirk widened into a grin. "You're good." His eyes gleamed with obvious amusement. "You have potential," he added.

"For what exactly?" *And why was I not thrilled to hear this?*

Adams looked from my face to my shoulder. He fished about for his wallet and produced a card. I already had his card somewhere, but I accepted this one without protest. It read "M. Parker Adams" with an email and a phone number. Plain black print on white paper. Thin white paper.

"Don't worry," he said. "We're done. For now."

I squinted at the sad excuse for a business card. "What do you mean for now? And exactly what are we supposed to be done with?"

He shook his head. "I can see how you ended up in the Marines."

A flash of anger sparked in me, but I took a breath and suppressed a growl. "So, if you had business at The Void, how did Troy Fairchild fit into all this? How did he end up at Mabel's house?"

"I don't know," Adams said. "I assume he knew someone who worked for the people behind the name, and he chose the wrong place at the wrong time."

"Meaning exactly what?" I snapped.

Adams gave me a look one might give to someone who had been suckered into a scheme to make billions overnight.

"He had done business with 'Mabel' and shouldn't have squatted at her house," Adams said.

"So ... it was all just a coincidence." I said, but my voice implied a question along with my skepticism. "What do you know about Phyllis Atkinson?"

Adams' grimace told me I'd struck a nerve. He shook his head. "I know she's bad news."

"Bad news for national security?"

Adams' face darkened. "If I may use a *Star Wars* analogy, you could say she chose the Dark Side."

A *Star Wars* analogy? What next? A discussion of *Lord of the Rings*? "What can you tell me about her? Is she connected to the Harcourt murders?"

He grunted, shook his head, and blew a smoke ring. "I don't know. I wouldn't be surprised if she was. But I gotta go," he said. "See ya 'round, Slinky."

"Wait a minute," I said. "You still haven't told me everything."

"Bingo. You'll make a great private eye someday."

"But—"

"You know your problem?" he said. "You haven't seen enough old movies. You need to see *The Big Sleep*. Right now." He gave me a mock salute. "Catch ya later, kid." He laughed as he rolled up his window.

I watched the dirty white car disappear. I think I'll add Parker Adams to my list of people who need to be investigated.

CHAPTER SEVENTY-FOUR

I spent the rest of the day poring over and processing everything you never wanted to know about the Harcourts. Ingrid Swenson's significant other, Lu, had emailed me digital photos of pages she deemed significant from Ingrid's journal. There were a few mentions of Aunt Phyllis, who I now knew was more than just a friend of the family.

Along with the absence of anything to suggest that the Harcourts knew of any illegal activities at Embrace the Wild, the family connections suggested some very interesting shit was going down here. For one thing, the Harcourts had adopted Amy.

The birth certificate identified Amy's biological mother as Joan Atkinson. The father was listed as "unknown." I checked my notes on the one conversation I'd had with Amy. Back in the beginning, the day after her parents died, she had told me about an Aunt Joan in New York, who she claimed she had never met. Amy said quite a few other things that didn't quite square with what I now knew. I had searched for intel on Phyllis Atkinson. She did not appear anywhere on social media. She might have been one of the few remaining humans on earth with no digital footprint whatsoever.

However, thanks to Alex's ability to dig up sealed records, I had copies of Amy's adoption papers on which the birth mother was identified as Phyllis Joan Atkinson—Phyllis Atkinson, who was more than just an aunt. And according to Adams, she was "bad news." How bad? And why?

Whatever threat she may have posed to national security, it was clear that Phyllis had placed career above motherhood and family, but not so much that she could completely let go of them. I pictured an unplanned pregnancy and an upbringing that frowned on abortion and maybe valued a family caring for its own.

In letting her sister adopt her child, maybe Phyllis saw a way to give her daughter a ready-made perfect childhood with all the right components: a dad, a mom, and a brother. The perfect family. But why the big blow-up? And what had brought Phyllis back? Was it Amy or something else?

Was their falling out the result of the Harcourts' choice of lifestyle as internet influencers? Did the Harcourts' belated concerns represent a threat to something bigger than Embrace the Wild and their particular malfeasances?

Phyllis didn't strike me as one who would work at a desk job. I thought about tapping old sources from my active duty days. Everything about Phyllis suggested military training, as in paramilitary groups, private armies, or government-supported private armies. That kind of work could cause problems with your family life, the kind you can't discuss. Then I wondered how much Amy actually knew about Phyllis. Were they just close as aunt and niece? Or did she know Phyllis was her mother? And who was her father? Could it have been Ron Harcourt? Seemed unlikely, but you never know.

My head became something of an echo chamber as various potential scenarios bounced around inside it. Did Phyllis break off from the Harcourts because of their career or did the Harcourts push her away because of her career? Had Phyllis wanted Amy back? If Ron was really the father, could it be jealousy on Phyllis's part? Or was Marian jealous of Phyllis?

Then it dawned on me. I was fishing for a motive here, when it could have been a simple business transaction. What if Phyllis had been hired to kill them? Surely, there was no assassins' code against killing one's own relatives. Had Phyllis used Amy to get at her parents? Did Amy, God forbid, arrange it? Did they both arrange to set me up? For a moment, I couldn't move. Thinking about this case made me itch. *Deep breath*. The itch calmed down.

I called Amy, only to get voice mail. "Hi, it's Erica Jensen," I said. "We need to talk. Please call me."

It took almost 30 minutes for Amy to call me back. "What is there to talk about?"

"Listen," I said. "Can I meet you?"

"Sure," she said, her voice neutral. "I'm at the house now. How about we meet here?"

I took a breath to steady my voice. "Your parents' house?"

"Yeah."

"I'll be right over."

I hung up and made another call. Time to bring in serious backup.

CHAPTER SEVENTY-FIVE

After making a couple of phone calls, I drove to the Harcourts' house to meet Amy. By the time I reached the area, part of the neighborhood had been thrown into shadow by the patch of woods near the Harcourt house. But the setting sun gave the neighborhood's widely spaced trees a faint glow, and their thin shadows made stripes across the neatly manicured lawns. I parked close to the house but not directly in front of it.

All of my senses were on high alert as I left the car. Clutching an 8.5- by 11-inch envelope of papers, I approached the Harcourts' house. Ever since the episode with Benny, this place creeped me out. God only knew who might be out there watching. Would I get an arrow or a bullet to the head? My concerns about privacy took a back seat to my concerns about survival. Of course, by now, my backup might be in place or nearly there, which provided some reassurance.

With the hope that only the best had been hired to clean up what remained of the former owners, I approached the front door and knocked. Within a minute, Amy opened up. She wore a T-shirt adorned with what could have been the name of a band or maybe a new meme. Along with a pair of distressed jeans that looked outright tortured at the knees.

"C'mon in," she said, turning and leaving me to close the door.

"Have a seat," she called from deeper inside. "Want a drink?"

"No thanks." *Not from you.* I settled onto the beige cushions of a sofa with two Santa Fe–patterned accent pillows and set my envelope on the coffee table. I think the color scheme was supposed to be "relaxing," but it didn't do much for me. The pillows did provide a vivid splash of oranges, yellows, and browns against the neutral backdrop.

Amy returned with a steaming mug of what smelled like coffee. I kept an eye on that cup. She took a seat in a dark-brown accent chair to my left, set down the mug, and folded her hands in her lap. Then, she gazed at me, expectant.

"Amy," I said. "You need to come clean with the police." Her look of disbelief might have convinced me of her innocence at one time, but not anymore.

"What are you talking about?"

I moved the envelope toward her. "You might want to have a look at this."

Amy stared at me for what seemed like a very long time. And then she turned toward the envelope. Moving slowly, as if she were fighting against the current in a wind tunnel, she picked up the envelope, peeked inside, frowned, and slid the papers and photos out onto the table.

"Yeah. So?"

"Take a look at this photo." On my phone, I displayed the one I'd taken of the Harcourts from Calhoun's Wall of Fame. "Who's in it?"

Amy's frown deepened into a scowl. "My Mom and Dad. And some other people."

"Some other people?" I suppressed the urge to laugh. With a two-fingered swipe, I enlarged the photo, keeping the background images in frame. "Who are these two?" I pointed at the two figures emerging from the brown car.

Amy's mouth dropped open, then snapped shut.

"I . . . can't really tell. They're out of focus."

They weren't, but I let that pass and considered my next question as I rooted through the documents. "How much do you know about Aunt Phyllis?"

She pressed her lips into what was almost a hairline crack.

"Were you aware that you were adopted?"

Amy's eyes blazed. "Yes," she snapped.

"And Aunt Phyllis? What do you really know about her?"

She shrugged. "She was a friend of my Mom's from college."

I leaned toward her and gave her a fixed stare. "That's not true." Uncertainty rippled across Amy's previously neutral expression in a series of small twitches in her lips, nose, and eyebrows.

"What do you mean?" she said.

"First, tell me about Aunt Phyllis," I said. "Or is it Aunt Joan?" I added, emphasizing the name.

Amy's eyes narrowed. "What are you talking about?"

"It would seem they're the same person."

Amy blinked a few times but said nothing.

"Tell me about Aunt Phyllis," I prodded her.

She cocked her head slightly, eyes half-hooded. "She hung out with us a lot. Even lived with us for a while. Back when I was a kid, she would tell me the best stories. But around the time I turned eight or nine, she and my parents really got into it. Then she left. Disappeared." Her tone was sour.

"You missed her?" Like I had to ask.

"We kept in touch." Her voice turned wistful. "She traveled a lot, but she wrote to me." She paused, then added with a boastful lilt, "She never put her return address on the envelopes, but I could tell where she was from the postal markings. And you know what's sad?"

"What?"

"My parents never even noticed that we communicated this way." Amy gave me a wide-eyed, can-you-believe-this-shit look. "They were so busy with other things."

"Did you text each other, too?"

"It was hard to text her. She couldn't always do that." Amy's murmur suggested confusion. "She wasn't much for the phone, either. So we wrote to each other."

"When was the last time you saw her?" I asked. "In person." Not FaceTime or Skype or Zoom. IRL.

Amy opened her mouth, but said nothing. "Been a while."

"So that's not you with her in the photo?"

She stiffened. Shook her head as if just waking up.

"Did it ever strike you as strange that this woman who knew your parents in college would continue keeping in touch?"

Amy fell silent. I could feel the wheels turn in her head.

"Well, why not?" Her voice was petulant. "And who could I turn to with my problems? Ingrid, who barely spoke a word, or Sasha, who just put up with me?"

This was interesting, but I needed to get to the point.

"Amy, take a look at this photo again. Isn't that you and Phyllis getting out of the car?"

Amy froze. Then she shook her head. "No. No."

"I know it is. And you know it, too. This raises a few questions. For one thing, why did you lie to me about not being involved with your parents' activities? This picture of you suggests otherwise. For another, why were you and Phyllis there?"

Amy chewed on her lip for a few seconds before she said, "I don't know why, but she wanted to go there."

"She wanted to go there? And forced you to go with her?"

Amy went wide-eyed. "She picked me up to go out for coffee. It wasn't my idea."

I nodded. "Okay. So what were you doing there?"

She shrugged. "She just wanted to look around, I guess. I hung out and just waited."

I shook my head. "I don't think that's going to work."

"What do you mean?" Her voice took on a steely tone.

"Before I get to that, let's talk about Phyllis. How much do you know about her?"

Amy's lower lip ballooned a bit as she pouted. "Enough to like her."

"Did you know that Phyllis is your birth mother?"

Amy drew back. "No." But there was a bit of uncertainty behind the word.

"Did you know that Phyllis is Marian's fraternal twin?"

Amy's eyes widened to the size of small dinner plates. "What?" Her shocked tone was either real or Oscar-worthy.

I let that settle in before adding, "Did you also know that she kills people for a living?"

The room was dead silent except for Amy, who was breathing hard. Then the house shifted and creaked a little. I thought about her non-response to that last question. "Was it her job to kill your parents? How much did you know about that?"

CHAPTER SEVENTY-SIX

Amy laughed with a cackle. "Are you kidding? Are you saying I arranged to murder my parents?"

"You wouldn't be the first kid to kill their parents."

"No!" She almost shouted the word. "You shut up. You don't know what you're talking about."

"Look, maybe I'm wrong. Maybe you didn't arrange anything," I said. "But don't be too sure that Marge Calhoun and Hannah Broomfield will back you up on that."

Amy's face paled. For a few seconds, I thought she might keel over.

"The Reverend and Benjamin Mulligan owned Embrace the Wild. Hannah cozied up to the Reverend and ended up over her head. And Calhoun and Douglas found out and kept it quiet. Since your parents came out clean, I'll assume you knew nothing about that, either," I said. "But someone with a serious grudge against your parents killed them. From what you're telling me, Aunt Phyllis is a most likely suspect. Next to you and Jaden, of course. Heirs are always suspects. So you know, one way or another, the cops will eventually get to you."

"But I didn't do anything," she stated, her voice flat.

"Your denials don't change the facts. Phyllis has made a career of . . . well, killing people. Calhoun and Douglas were desperate to avoid the scandal that would result from associating with Embrace the Wild through the church. Especially after your parents found out and tried to sever ties with them. One or more of them wanted your parents either warned off or eliminated. Your parents weren't dumb, and they knew the risks. That's why they wanted to hire a bodyguard."

And enter me, a burned-out, but recovering vet, trying to be a private eye. All for the sake of a background check.

"Were you aware of any of this?" I asked.

Amy shook her head. Her shoulders slumped.

"Why did Phyllis come back?" I asked.

Amy's lips compressed into an odd grimace. "She said she came back to make amends with Mom."

I considered that. Maybe, maybe not. Based on what I had seen, Phyllis didn't strike me as the type to forgive and forget. She was a person who was not only fully capable of killing, but she possibly had an axe to grind. Amy buried her face in her hands and let out a muted scream. Then, she looked up at me. "No one was supposed to die," she yelled.

Neither of us spoke. From somewhere within the house, I heard a clock tick. "What happened?" I asked.

Amy looked defeated. "We stayed in touch. Aunt Phyllis knew I wasn't happy about living with my parents. She was like my second mom. I could really talk to her. Honestly."

Amy began ticking off a small laundry list of everything right about Aunt Phyllis. For one thing, she could speak directly and without condescension to Amy about her troubles. Like Amy, Phyllis also hated the way her parents spread the gospel of their influencer brands around. She was honest, used cuss words without apologizing, and didn't mind if Amy did the same. She wasn't trying to change Amy. She went on and on. And I let her rant.

"It all makes sense now." Her voice became dreamy again. "After she left, I missed her a lot. But then she wrote to me."

She shivered, although the house was warm. "It wasn't until high school that I saw her again. She arranged to meet me. She had cut her hair and was shredded like a gym trainer, but it was her."

"I never asked what she did, but I knew it was . . . unusual. She was secretive. I accepted that. Now and then, we'd meet for coffee or whatever."

She gestured toward my phone. "Anyway, that photo?" Amy nodded toward it. "This was one of the few times I went anywhere near one of my parents' photo ops. That's when she told me she was trying to reconnect with my parents."

Amy stopped talking. That was it. It might have been true, just not the whole truth.

"Did Phyllis stalk your parents?"

Amy scowled. "How would I know?"

"Was she jealous of them?"

She shook her head hard. "No. She rejected them."

I wasn't so sure.

"Did you tell her about me?"

"No." Amy shook her head back and forth. "I knew nothing about that."

"She found out I was hired somehow," I said. "Because with her voice, she could easily pass for your mother on the phone."

I leaned toward Amy, moving into her space. "Did Hannah or Reverend Leland ask you about Phyllis? Or did Marge Calhoun or Ryan Douglas?"

Amy pouted, eyes glued to the floor. "Sure, I've talked about her. She was important to me, even if my parents didn't like her."

"What did you tell them? Did you know she was a mercenary for hire?"

She clamped her mouth shut, and for a lengthy minute or two, we said nothing.

"I didn't want them to die." She muttered the words at such a low volume, I could barely make them out. As she spoke, all the color drained from Amy's face and her eyes took on a vacant look.

I paused for a moment before I said, "No matter how you got involved with this, if she got too enthusiastic, it's on her. In any case, you won't do yourself any favors by running from the truth or the cops. Or keeping your guilty feelings a secret forever.

"You must have wondered about Aunt Phyllis. How much did she tell you? Did you know she'd killed people before?"

I paused to consider how much more I should say about Amazon Woman. I wasn't sure how much I wanted to know. Maybe her skill set led to her choosing to become a career mercenary. Given the recent overwhelming upsurge of attention on right-wing groups and gun control laws, she might well have joined a cult or a paramilitary group. Did any of that matter? I would leave it to the police to tease that information out of someone more deeply mired in this truly depressing affair. Or at least I could hope for that.

"Someone in this mess must have told Phyllis about me. Did they want to eliminate the Harcourts or just get them to back off? Who set me up?"

I tossed out the questions without having a clue as to whether she had any answers because there was much I could deduce from the circumstances.

"I don't know." Stray locks hung over Amy's face, and she raked them back with one hand. She lifted her face, cheeks now reddened. "Hannah never could stand my parents. She couldn't stand to see them get so much attention. Always so organized. Always just so because of their online presence. People assumed it was all so much fun. Well, Hannah wasn't the only one who found my parents annoyingly perfect." She delivered the last sentence in an accusatory tone.

"So annoyingly perfect they deserved to be beaten and knifed to death?" I asked. "That's excessive, even for me."

Amy seemed to focus on a point somewhere off in space. Then she looked straight at me. My shoulders let go and my back simply relaxed. For once, the pain diminished. But the silence between us was broken when a fist pounded on the front door. "Open up. Police," a voice called. I recognized it as Detective Gordon's.

"Look," I said. "If you really weren't involved in the murder, there are ways to make things go easier."

"Snitching?" Amy gave me a look of disbelief. "Isn't it a bit late for that?"

"I don't know. They say it's never too late." I rose and answered the door.

While officers secured the premises, Detectives Gordon and Sully took charge of Amy. Before they started questioning her, I took Detective Gordon aside.

"Thanks for sharing your voice recordings," he said. "We've issued a BOLO on Phyllis Atkinson and are coordinating with the feds."

"And thanks for backing me up here," I said. "Any chance I could get a peek at Amy's cell phone?"

He suppressed a sigh. "Just a peek. And it doesn't leave my hands."

"Sure," I said. "In fact, this never happened."

I left the house and moved back up the street where my car sat. With only moonlight and what stars could penetrate the smog as illumination, I could make out my Fiesta standing out among the few other cars left on the street. I was almost halfway to my car, when I heard the crunch of footsteps coming from the woods behind the houses.

CHAPTER SEVENTY-SEVEN

I pivoted toward the noise, prepared for anything. From the dark woods, the footsteps continued, growing louder. I doubted it was Phyllis, because I was pretty sure she wasn't stupid enough to go mano-a-mano with me within shouting distance of the cops. If she was going to shoot me, I would already be dead. When Two-Bit Terry emerged, the thought of throttling him crossed my mind just before a wave of relief washed over me at seeing a friend.

"Terry," I said. "Seriously, what the fuck?" I surveyed the streets in search of his car and caught a glimpse of its back end poking out from a distant curve in the road.

"Sorry. I was just waiting for you. My apartment's been trashed."

Slack-jawed, I stared at him. "How'd you know where to find me?"

He grimaced a bit. "After our last encounter, I put a tracking device on your car."

Christ! I should have been sweeping the car for those things. No wonder people were dying around me. But why wouldn't she come after me?

"It's Phyllis," I said. "We're the only witnesses who aren't looking to make a deal with the cops. Or the feds." Now I had to find Phyllis. I figured she wouldn't just quietly go away.

"You got a burner phone I can use?" I asked.

While Terry sat in my car, doing his thing on an old refurbished laptop, I used the burner to call the number I found on Amy's phone for Aunt Phyllis. She had entered the name in a code a kindergartner could crack. SillyHP, Phyllis spelled backward.

I was not surprised by the lack of an answer but was not deterred either. Voice mail kicked in and I said, "Hi, Phyllis. We met the other day at Embrace the Wild. Sorry we didn't have a chance to properly introduce ourselves. I'm Erica Jensen, and we need to talk. Call me."

I was headed toward my car when my phone trilled. I checked the ID that was displaying Phyllis's number and answered. "Yeah"

For a moment, I thought my phone ear had gone deaf. Then, I heard, "What do you want?" She spoke softly, without inflection, as if she was indifferent to my response.

"Where are you?"

Soft laughter drifted from the phone. "You're joking, right?"

"Then why? Why target me?"

A loud snort. "Why not?"

"What was your problem? Why did you kill them?" I asked, wondering if she would answer those questions.

"Look." The pause was so long, I wondered if we had lost our connection. "I get paid to do things. This was a job."

"To make it look like the inside of a slaughterhouse?"

"Okay, I might have gone a bit too far. But I solved the problem."

It was my turn to huff in disbelief. "And you managed to involve your own daughter. Best to keep this kind of dirty work in the family. Way to go, Mom!"

"The cops would never be able to pin a motive on you for killing the Harcourts," she said, as if expecting that excuse to earn my gratitude. "But it was just enough to make them wonder—it provided a slight diversion."

"Hey," I said. "The cops have everything they need. I suggest you keep clear of me and my friend."

I heard a noncommittal "Mmm" from her, and a few seconds later, "Okay."

"How much did Amy know? And what about Jaden?"

"They'll be fine," she said. "Believe me."

Right. "Like I should believe anything you say."

"You should."

And with that, the phone went silent.

CHAPTER SEVENTY-EIGHT

I figured that Phyllis would be long gone by now. It was also a
pretty sure bet that the number I had for her was for a burner
phone. However, given Phyllis's chosen profession, I couldn't
simply forget about her. Not after the way she had set me up.
Or given the murders.

But if Phyllis had broken into Terry's place, she must still be
in the area. Terry said he'd left his place at shortly after 10:15
that morning and returned at 1:00 to find the place in a
shambles. Or in a worse shambles than usual. So Phyllis must
still be around.

Perhaps she was holed up somewhere locally for the time
being. And if Mabel Forbes was somehow connected to all this
crap, Phyllis might have chosen to avoid a paper or digital trail
by staying at one of Mabel's properties. I looked up the real
estate listings for Mabel Forbes. There were only four, and one
of them was The Void. Along with the house in Columbia and
the one near the Harcourts, there was a third house in Towson.
If Phyllis knew people in the underworld, she might very well be
doing business with the mysterious Mabel. Perhaps Troy

Fairchild was not the only person squatting at one of Mabel's houses.

"I've already checked the house in this neighborhood," Terry said. He indicated the one with the blacked-out windows that I had searched a few days ago. "No sign of her."

I shook my head. "You shouldn't have, Terry. She could have killed you."

"True, but luckily she wasn't there."

I placed a hand on his arm. "Let's make sure of that."

On the condition that he help me search, Terry let me borrow a pair of night vision goggles. I drove Terry up the road to his car, where he retrieved the goggles from the trunk. My phone battery thanked him.

My reluctance to include Terry wasn't so much worry about myself as it was for him. Terry's good intentions might have been motivated, in part, by anger at having his apartment ransacked. I didn't need blind vengeance fucking things up even more than they already were.

We returned to the house across from where the Harcourts lived. By then, the police had cleared out and the neighborhood had resumed a more normal appearance. As we entered the pitch black interior, I took point and Terry followed. As a two-person platoon, we did a complete sweep, upstairs and down. If Phyllis came within view, the goggles would reveal her as a glow. But there were no signs of Phyllis herself or anyone else.

From there, we drove separately to the house in Columbia. Terry seemed eager to help instead of being pissed off at Phyllis, which reassured me. And I was glad to have his help. Especially when defending against the likes of Amazon Woman.

We left for Columbia at 9:00 PM. As I navigated the emptying suburban streets, I reviewed the layout of the place from memory. We arrived about twenty minutes later, and we each parked a ways down from the house. Terry and I moved toward the residence together.

"You don't have to do this, Terry," I reminded him.

"No," he blurted out. "I insist."

I didn't doubt Terry's ability to fight. I just didn't want him to get hurt. I also didn't want to be responsible for anyone else's death.

The house was dark and looked well-tended. Early spring flowers bloomed in a row along the front of the house. The odor of fresh mulch tickled my nostrils. Once again, my bump key got us inside. No alarm. I listened for noises. Nothing more than the usual house-shifting creaks. Minuscule sounds.

The air inside was stale, the smell of a house that had been closed up for some time. The place was as I remembered it. This time, I started upstairs.

Enough light came through the windows to make the goggles less of a necessity. Terry and I swept the entire upper floor, including a quick peek into an unfinished attic, where the flashlight on my cell phone revealed bare beams and a carpet of pink insulation.

We followed that up with a quick tour of the first floor. Kitchen, dining room, living room, small bath, and spare room. No sign of habitation.

Finally, the basement. I thought back to the last time I'd been there in search of Troy Fairchild. The almost hallucinogenic memory of a basement threatened to recur. Afghanistan. *Or was it? Was it before that?* I had no time to think. I opened the door and took a deep breath before descending into the shadows.

I planted each foot with care as we descended the basement stairs. Terry moved right behind me, with equal caution.

The dim light from the windows rendered the basement in fuzzy, gray tones. I recalled from my last visit that the space had been empty. But this time, the outlines of several boxes emerged from the gloom.

When I hit the bottom step, I caught my breath when I glimpsed a bedroll tucked into a corner.

CHAPTER SEVENTY-NINE

I snugged the goggles back into place and did a quick survey, but I found no other trace of humans in the basement. Terry stuck with me. I kept my distance from the bedroll. Seemed a bit paranoid to imagine it might be set to explode, but forgive me. After surviving close encounters with an IED or two, one tends to be very cautious.

"Stay back," I murmured to Terry. I approached the bedroll with all the caution I could muster, examining it as I moved. Then I caught a glimpse of some kind of light-colored object on it. Closer examination revealed a folded piece of paper.

I shoved the goggles up on my forehead and unfolded the paper. It was a note. With the light from my phone, I read it. Then I dropped it and swore like a Marine.

"What?" Terry said.

"We brought the goggles but forgot the latex gloves." I looked at Terry, whose face was hard to see in the gloom. "I prefer to keep my DNA as far from this matter as possible, but to hell with it." I picked up the note, letting it dangle from between pinched fingers. "I need to get this to the cops."

Terry glanced at the note. "What does it say?"

"Nothing much," I said. "It's just an address in Towson. You'll recognize it. By the way, we have an invitation to visit."

Phyllis's (or Mabel's?) Towson hideaway was guarded by technology. That was the bad news. The good news was that it was twentieth century technology. The house had a set of motion-sensitive rectangular lights. Apart from the windows, a visual check of the house revealed nothing but a single, battered camera that might have once hung in a convenience store.

I stood across the street from what might be Phyllis Atkinson's last known address and considered the potential scenarios, including who and how many people might be inside. And I checked the time. I hoped to be in and out in 30 minutes or less. Better still, fifteen.

For the occasion, I wore my black hoodie which, along with my dark jeans, would help me blend into the shadows. My gear belt was riding lower on my hips than usual because I had added a few items. And my gun was holstered. The time for subtlety was long past.

This time around, I asked Terry to act as my lookout. He seemed mildly disappointed, but that passed in a heartbeat. We established a lookout spot tucked behind a sign in a small strip mall near the neighborhood's main entrance. From there, he could observe anyone who entered the development and turned my way.

My desire to have Terry play this role wasn't just because it makes sense to have a lookout if you're breaking into someone's home. Nor was I thinking only of the risk to Terry in potentially facing Phyllis if she confronted us. It was that ball of fear that materialized in my belly when I considered that this might be a trap.

The streetlights and a quarter moon provided enough light for me to make out the house's basic features. I examined the angles, picked up a couple of small rocks, and tested the limits of the lighting vis-à-vis the likely camera view. At one point, I deliberately tripped the light on the front of the house. The edges of the front window curtain were outlined with bright light, so either someone was in there or the lights were on a timer. In any case, I saw no sign of an occupant. I did the same routine on the sides of the house. No movement at any side windows. If anyone inside the house noticed my presence, they were being very discreet about it.

Moving toward the house while keeping a distance and angle that wouldn't trigger the front light again wasn't especially hard. I waited for the timed security lights to go out so I could move under cover of darkness, then followed a path with all the right angles and reached the sidewalk without incident. Then, I took a second to scope out the surroundings. The streets were empty, the neighborhood silent as a tomb.

After one last look around, I dropped to the lawn and kept low, worming my way and keeping a distance to avoid tripping the light as I crossed the side yard. After a certain point, the best moves to avoid detection were untested, so mine became instinctive. I belly-crawled a bit more before hitting the inevitable trip point.

When the light came on, I jumped up into a half-crouch and scurried into the shadow of a doorway. I had seen that back door on Google Earth. I counted on my bump key and well-developed lock-picking skills to get me inside.

The half-crawl, half-squirm across the yard seemed to take forever. But I checked my phone for the time. Less than five minutes? Really? My back screamed, *Yes. Really. Now, get the hell inside.*

Using the bump key, I did just that. By now, it was close to 11:00 PM. Phyllis was either miles away or waiting for me here. Or something in between.

CHAPTER EIGHTY

The back of the house was dark enough for me to consider putting on my borrowed goggles. But enough light filtered in for me to see that I had entered the kitchen. Off to my right, perpendicular to the far wall, a doorway led to another room. Before me, a hallway extended straight ahead. About halfway down, there was a door to the right and, at the far end, an opening on the left to a room ablaze in light. I caught a glimpse of an end table and a section of worn futon.

A small foyer separated that room from one on the right, where the muted moonlight gleamed off a wedge of Ethan Allen dining room table. I wondered about the contrasting furniture. Either the owner was in the midst of redecorating or had the same attitude toward decor I had. I was getting nervous as I thought about someone possibly lying in wait for me here. Given the layout, it would be easy for a professional to sneak up behind me. I couldn't drop my guard.

My phone, set on vibrate, chose that moment to shimmy. That had to be Terry. The text read: *Saw a car. But not turning your way*. I nodded and texted back *K*. That was either great or terrible news. So far, I hadn't heard a thing that suggested the presence of another human. Not even a noise from the air handling system. But if Phyllis was here, I had to know.

I finally crept down the hall, checked behind the door, found a closet, gave it look, and moved on. After investigating the room with the futon, I turned toward the dining room. There was just enough light to reveal that no one was there. As I passed the table, I quickly glanced under it, then turned to take in my surroundings and check for signs that anyone besides me was sneaking about.

My phone buzzed again. *Car coming.* Quickly followed by: *Turning.* Then: *Get out.* I texted acknowledgment back but decided to stay. Whatever or whoever was coming, I decided to deal with it.

I moved back into the kitchen and found a closet-like pantry with plenty of shelves but no room to hide. Apart from the kitchen, the only room connected with the dining area was a small one, apparently used only for storage. The roughly 15 × 15 square feet of space held a tasteful arrangement of cardboard boxes. Enough to create a roughly 7 × 5 foot stack along the back wall. Only God knew what sorts of things were hiding in those boxes. The memory of my recent panic attack surfaced. However, despite the room's small size, I didn't panic. Nor did I spend any energy on figuring out why I hadn't done so.

A key rattled in the lock on the front door, and I could hear the door opening. I pressed my back to the wall in the small storage area. I was barely breathing and listening for footsteps. Oddly, I didn't hear any, but I did hear a creaking sound. Then, *snap.* The light switch. The small room brightened a bit. *What is she up to?*

Clearly, I was expected to be here. For all I knew, Phyllis was spying on me via hidden cameras, laughing at my amateurish game of cat and mouse. If she wanted to play, fine. I kept my back to the wall, listening intently for any kind of sound. My spidey sense was on high alert. Every now and then, a muted scuffling noise drifted my way from the kitchen.

My hand moved toward my gun, and my palm rested on the grip. I moved to a position outside the small storage room, eased my way over to the kitchen entrance, and I peered around the corner.

No one was there. Then, Ms. Brooks Brothers entered from the hallway, the not-quite Realtor of the Year I had run across while looking for Troy Fairchild. She wasn't smiling when I stepped into view.

"Hi," I said, trying to keep things light. "Been a while."

She crossed the room toward me and extended a standard business envelope. "I've been asked to give this to you," she said in a manner that hinted that the request was one not to be denied. The envelope had my name printed on it. It was also sealed.

"Go ahead," she said. "Read it."

I tore open the envelope and removed the letter, which was also printed. It read: *Don't worry about me. You stay on your side, I'll stay on mine.*

I let out a sigh. As truces went, this one pretty much sucked. I also wondered which side Phyllis was on and if it mattered. Just as I finished reading, Ms. Brooks Brothers tore the note from my hands.

"If you're done," she said. "Please leave."

"Gladly, after you tell me who the hell you are."

A wry grin crossed her face. "I'm just a messenger."

"So, who's Mabel Forbes?"

She shook her head. "You don't want to know."

CHAPTER EIGHTY-ONE

The next day, I reached out to my old friend Special Agent Phipps. He sounded pleased to hear from me. I brought him up to speed about my recent travails, hoping that empathy might move him to open up to me or at least not shut the proverbial door in my face.

"What can you tell me about the case against Embrace the Wild?" I asked.

"I've heard about it, but I wasn't involved in the investigation," he said. "There are various charges. Endangered Species Act violations, the Lacey Act, that sort of thing."

"Right. I've seen the filing. Do you know if my late clients were implicated at all?"

"No one has mentioned them."

I thought that over and decided to ignore the fact that he hadn't exactly answered my question. "How long has Embrace the Wild been the subject of investigation?"

"I don't know, but I imagine it's taken quite a while to gather all the evidence."

And find willing witnesses? I imagined the Harcourts would have been good ones. "Were the Harcourts important to proving the charges?"

"Look, I'm only privy to so much. It's not my case, and not my subject area. And I only know what I hear."

Continuing to question Phipps seemed like a waste of time. Based on what I'd been told about the Harcourts, they didn't seem like the type to sit idly by if they became aware of an ethical or legal problem with their business. I was fast reaching the conclusion that their decision to hire a bodyguard and to hire me to check his background may have been prompted by threats, overt or otherwise, from people they had come to trust.

"How about Phyllis Atkinson? Or Joan Atkinson?" Or God knew what other name she might use. "Either name mean anything to you?"

"No," he said.

I couldn't come up with any great follow-up questions that would allay any doubts about the Harcourts or my own personal safety. So I thanked Agent Phipps, said goodbye, and hung up.

If Phipps really knew nothing about Phyllis Atkinson, the prospects were dismal for making sure she never bothered me or my friends again. Then again, why would she? Probably only if I got in her way again. I checked my shoulder bag and found Parker Adams' card. I wondered how much I could trust him.

If the Harcourts had offered to or been persuaded to be government witnesses, that would have provided a motive for any business associates of Embrace the Wild to kill them, including Reverend Leland and his handy helper Hannah. It could even include the Harcourts' handlers Marge Calhoun and Ryan Douglas. By not playing along, their attorney Aaron Gallagher had sealed his fate. When you got right down to it, anyone with a vested business interest in Embrace the Wild had a motive to, at the very least, warn the couple off. Perhaps Amy spoke the truth when she said Phyllis wasn't hired to kill them. Even so, the fact that they were dead kept them well out of the matter.

Later, I had a conference call from Detectives Gordon and Sully, which actually went fairly well. Some of what I had discovered might provide a lead on Phyllis's whereabouts, including everything I'd found in the houses. I wasn't at all sure it would help, but Gordon promised to pass all my intel on to the feds, who were also scouring the earth for Amazon Woman. Or so they told the local police.

"So, who actually gets charged for murder here?" I asked.

The line went silent a moment. "This is still an ongoing investigation," Detective Gordon said. "We need to nail down more specifics before deciding exactly who to charge for what."

Gordon then explained that while the church, Reverend Leland, Benjamin Mulligan, and Hannah Broomfield might be subject to all manner of federal prosecution, the matter of proving beyond a reasonable doubt that these people hired a mercenary to kill two witnesses to their malfeasances required evidence of conspiracy.

"We'll know more after we've reviewed all the records," he said, suggesting that he wasn't holding his breath waiting for a huge breakthrough.

"Where does Mabel Forbes fit in?" I tossed out the question not expecting an answer but hoping for a reaction.

A brief silence followed. "Why do you ask?" Gordon said. *Not who is she?*

"Do you know who I'm talking about?" I asked.

When he didn't respond, I explained how her name had come up while I was engaged in another matter. I didn't bother telling them that I was trying to determine the whereabouts of bail-jumper Troy Fairchild at the time.

"I see," he said. "All I can say is that our investigation will follow every viable lead."

"So, who is she?"

After a long sigh, Gordon said, "I have no idea."

Rather than press the issue, I could only conclude that "Mabel" operated a small, but influential, criminal enterprise that offered occasional safe haven to mercenaries, terrorists, and other undesirables. And possibly acted as a confidential informant as well. She might be playing both sides and making out like a bandit. Ms. Brooks Brothers could be either her secretary or her second-in-command.

"But the murders. Was Phyllis hired to kill the Harcourts?"

Another deep sigh from Detective Gordon. "Again, it kind of depends on who you ask. We're still in the process of building the case, and we're still looking for her. Of course, by now, she's probably fled the country."

"Mmm." *She may have left the country but not because she was trying to flee.* She stayed long enough to make an impression on me. One I wouldn't soon forget.

"Were you able to make use of the voice recording?" I asked, referring to what my phone picked up during my brief introduction to Phyllis followed by a quick jump through a broken window.

"Actually, yes we were," Gordon said. "The voices are quite similar, but slightly different, according to one source."

I considered how to phrase the next question. "Are you saying they're not the same? Or was Marian the one who called that day?"

"We can't say for sure," he said. "And, frankly, I can't comment any further on how we're conducting our investigation."

I recalled the sheer intensity of Marian's panicked voice that morning. Did she know what was coming? Or had Phyllis outdone even professional voice actors like Meryl Streep? A throat-clearing sound rumbled from my phone, snapping me back to attention.

"Thanks for digging up that nanny's journal," Gordon said. Ingrid's journal was full of intriguing insights into the Harcourt clan. "We really appreciate your kind assistance," he said, his words coming out slowly, as if he were reluctant to let them go.

It wasn't quite an apology, but I settled for it. "I'm glad I could help." Really, really glad. "So, this isn't an April Fool's joke?" After all, it was the right day for it.

"We never joke about our work," Sully stated in her flat cop voice. "But we don't take ourselves too seriously either," she said in a tiny self-deprecating voice.

"Never a bad idea," I said.

"Listen," Sully added. "You did the right thing." Her voice conveyed a request for forgiveness. I supposed we could do each other that favor.

"Thanks," I said, and on that note, we ended the call.

I wondered how much evidence one needed to charge someone with conspiracy to murder. Ryan Douglas and Marge Calhoun were not listed as defendants in the case against Embrace the Wild. But could they still be implicated in the Harcourts' murders? How much did they know and when? And how to prove it? The legal niceties were beyond me. For all I knew, Amy might get a complete pass. As for Phyllis, I imagined she was the type who always got a pass. Now, for the tough conversation. After ending the call with the detectives, I punched in Nick's number.

"Hey, what's up?" he said.

"Is this the zoo?" I said. "I'm looking for Mr. Lyon."

"Yeah, Happy April Fool's Day to you, too. He's not here. But Mr. Koala is."

"Right. Let's talk about Mr. Koala." I quickly filled him in on the weird events of the last few days.

"Oh, my God. So you're in the clear then."

"Absolutely. But that's not why I'm calling. I wanted to ask . . . . It's kind of a big favor . . . ." My voice gave out on me.

"What is it, Erica? Just ask."

"Will you come with me to my parents' for Easter dinner?" I struggled mightily to get the words out.

I hadn't had Easter dinner or any other dinner at that house since I first returned from Afghanistan. Nick knew about the rift between me and my parents, which hadn't improved one whit since my return to the United States.

Nick didn't respond immediately, so I piped up, "If you have other plans, don't worry about it."

"No, no," Nick offered. "I can arrange it. What brought this on?"

A vision of Amy's stony expression flitted through my mind. Along with Phyllis's extreme solution. "Just seems like a good idea," I said.

ACKNOWLEDGMENTS

There's no way I can include the names of every single person who has helped me navigate the road toward publishing my books, but I need to acknowledge a few key people and organizations. Without them, I might never have undertaken this task.

First, thanks go out to my writers group, always the first to lay eyes on my scrivenings: Shaun Bevins, Mary Ellen Hughes, Becky Hutchison, Sherriel Mattingly, Bonnie Settle, Lauren Silberman, Marcia Talley, and Cathy Wiley. They help me smooth out the worst wrinkles from my plots and keep me motivated. In addition, my deepest thanks go to Sisters in Crime, both the national group and the Chesapeake Chapter, along with the Private Eye Writers of America, and the International Association of Crime Writers. These groups have provided not only comradeship but also great advice and opportunities. I'm also indebted to all the bloggers, reviewers, and readers who have supported my efforts and encouraged me to continue writing, including librarians and bookstore owners who have been kind enough to carry my books.

While writing a book may be a solo effort, getting it published requires help, including editing, copyediting, proofreading, cover art design, and formatting for different media. For what it's worth, I'll always love print books, so count on seeing my novels come out in print, no matter what other formats may come along. My heartfelt thanks to my editor, John Barclay-Morton, publications specialist, along with Laurie Cullen, the best copyeditor in the business, and graphic artist Stewart A. Williams, who created the cover.

Finally, many thanks to my family and my husband, who've been amazingly supportive through it all.

ABOUT THE AUTHOR

Debbi Mack is the New York Times bestselling author of the Sam McRae mystery series. She has also published a young adult novel, *Invisible Me*, and a scientific thriller, *The Planck Factor*. Her first Erica Jensen novel, *Damaged Goods*, was nominated for a Shamus Award in 2021. Her short stories have appeared in various anthologies, and one was nominated for a Derringer Award in 2010.

Debbi, a retired attorney, has also worked as a journalist, reference librarian, and freelance writer/researcher and has had a series of odd jobs too numerous to mention. Along with writing fiction, Debbi has branched into screenwriting and podcasting. Her strongest aspirations are to write her memoirs and travel more.

www.debbimack.com